The Girl Next Door

By

Meg Gray

The Girl Next Door

Copyright 2016 Meg Gray

All rights reserved. No part of this book may be used or reproduced in any manner whatsoever without prior written permission of the author/publisher; except in the case of brief quotations embodied in reviews.

All characters in this book have no existence outside the imagination of the author and have no relation to anyone bearing the same name or names. Any resemblance to individuals known or unknown to the author are purely coincidental.

Cover Design: Gray Digital Ink, LLC

www.meggraybooks.com

This book is dedicated to all my devoted readers. Without you I'm only a writer, but with you I'm an author. ☺

Acknowledgements

First of all, I want to deeply thank my husband Trevor, for being by my side always. And my children for the joy they bring into my life. Thank you to Corrinne for answering all things legal when I had a question. And to my medical expert Sara for her expertise as well.

Also, from the bottom of my heart I want to thank the members of my Launch Team that help and support me to get these books out. So thank you Sheila, Marcia, Nadia, Vicki, Gary, Shaina, Brandy, Christine, Mary, Melanie, Laura, Melanie, Lisa, Linda, Kimberly, Dorothy, Pamela, Yvonne, Caroline, Ann Watts, Sandra, Nancy, Sharon, Pat, Kareb, Sara, Denise, Stephanie, Hilda, Suzanne, Janet, Norma, Andra, Linda, Sharon, Suzann, Fern, Dianna, Marla, Beverly, Teresa, Rebecca, Liz, Linda, Anne, Marsha, Catherine, Shirley, Susan, Terrie, Betty Jo, Anita, Chele, Katie, Kim, Charlene, Laurie, Carol, Andrea, Marylou, Marsha, Susan, Diane, Lisa, VirgieB, Connie, Debbie, Sharon, Lelia, Carmen. Casey, Jane, Julie, Sandy, Pam Susan, Annette, Julie, Melissa, Shelly, Tammy, Sheila, Joyce, Sandra, Lora, Carrie, Cynthia, Patricia, and Lavonne.

One

"Jocelyn Banks opened to the center section of the newspaper, spreading her arms wide inside the cramped interior of her sister's tiny hatchback.

"Would you put that away?" Sophie backhanded the paper. "Can't you see I'm driving here?"

Brake lights lit up in front of them, and Jocelyn lurched forward, pressing her feet against the floorboards as she finished folding the paper in half.

"Looks like we're stopped now." Jocelyn set the paper in her lap, scanning the headlines of page four.

"Not for long," Sophie said as the car began to roll again. "I can't believe this traffic. It's ridiculous."

"I told you we needed to leave earlier." Jocelyn didn't glance up from the national headlines.

"Don't do that," Sophie snapped. "Don't be an I-told-you-so kind of person. Nobody likes them. Besides, we only left ten minutes after six this morning. I don't think those few minutes would've gotten us here before this mess."

"Yes, but if I'd known you were going to need to take four bathroom breaks along the way, I would've suggested we leave even earlier." Jocelyn didn't need to look up to know her sister's green eyes, usually crisp and joyful, were glaring at her.

"You're annoying. Did you know that?"

Jocelyn flipped the newspaper over, continuing to read about the results of a recent population survey. "It's all part of the big sister oath I took before you were born. Thou shalt not knowingly harm or maim thy little sister. Thou shalt love her unconditionally and annoy the crap out of her at every opportunity." Jocelyn grinned. "So, how am I doing?"

"Splendid. A+ for you. Just like always." Sophie looked over her shoulder and changed lanes.

"Hey, listen to this." Jocelyn shook the paper, making it flat so she could read the small print. "A recent look at Portland, Oregon's population growth suggests it may have its largest increase of the century by the next census report. City managers are concerned that the already congested roads and highways will become an even greater problem."

"Ya think?" Sophie said with a snort. "I never would've figured that one out without some special report."

Sophie squeezed her little hatchback between an SUV and a tired-looking pickup truck with rusty patches and chipped paint. A loud unhealthy whirr to the engine made its road worthiness debatable.

"It also says the LGBT population is up two percent, rivaling only San Francisco's growth."

"Fascinating," Sophie said dryly.

She obviously didn't care about the latest news of the city that was about to become Jocelyn's new home.

Sophie looked over at her again. "How do you do that?"

"Do what?"

"Read the paper and have a conversation at the same time."

Jocelyn finished the article, noting the encouragement the city officials felt about the recent uptick in the median income of the working class. It was a good sign that the economy had fully recovered from the recession.

"It's a gift." She folded the paper.

Actually, it was a skill she'd developed in college and then perfected as she fielded every position, from intern, to editor, to receptionist, over her years at her uncle's newspaper. *The Gazette* in River's Edge had suffered through the hard times of the downed economy and struggled to regain its footing. If Jocelyn hadn't been there, her uncle surely would've lost the paper.

Drafting and editing copy while taking phone calls from the community was a normal occurrence when no else was on the payroll except for her and Uncle Larry. But they had survived. With Jocelyn in the role of senior editor for the last two years, she'd been able to hire on a small part-time staff and Uncle Larry had been taking some time off, possibly even flirting with the idea of retirement. Why else would he have insisted she take the position at *The Portland Daily Report*—a newspaper run by his old college buddy Jerry Wilbur?

Jocelyn didn't like being offered a job she'd never applied for. But Uncle Larry assured her that the time she spent filling in at the newspaper, until a permanent replacement was found, would be a great experience.

With two new recently hired freelance writers and Uncle Larry stepping into more of Jocelyn's roles at *The Gazette* she'd acquiesced.

Jocelyn smoothed her hand over the front page of *The Daily Report*. The lead headline read: *Double Murder at Union Station.*

There was a time when she'd imagined her name under a headline like this. Even before she'd enrolled in college, she'd craved chasing the breaking news stories that hit the front pages of every major newspaper across the country. She hadn't cared which city wanted her when she graduated. She was going to make a name for herself as an investigative reporter wherever she went.

But that was all before life intervened and sent her back home during her senior year to care for her dying mother. She'd completed her courses via the web. Her petition for a reassignment to her uncle's newspaper to finish her internship credits was granted so she could remain near her family when they needed her.

With Sophie off at college, her father struggling to find his way living alone, and her uncle's paper careening toward bankruptcy, Jocelyn had stayed in River's Edge. She'd worked hard and was the steadying force that helped see them all through. Leaving her hometown this morning was one of the hardest things she'd ever done. And she wouldn't be here if it didn't mean so much to Uncle Larry.

They veered off the interstate, taking an exit before merging with traffic and immediately taking another off ramp.

Sophie pulled both hands off the wheel for a moment and held them in a v-formation. "City Center, here we come!"

Out Jocelyn's window, the murky water of the Willamette River rolled this way and that, creating foamy peaks. Birds circled over the water. In no time, the car was over the river and swallowed up by the tall buildings of the city. After a few more minutes of stop and go through the traffic lights, they turned onto a semi-quiet street, and the car's pace slowed as Sophie read the address numbers of every building aloud.

"Here it is." Sophie pulled to the curb in front of a sleek, pale-brick building. "Home sweet home." Her sister's green eyes crinkled as she hunched over the steering wheel to admire the multi-level apartment building.

There wasn't much sweet about it if you asked Jocelyn, nothing like the turn-of-the-century house on Main Street where she'd lived since she was three, except for her college years, of course. Thank goodness this was only temporary and that Sophie's yoga mentor, Fiona, who was leaving for a retreat in Bali tomorrow, was sharing her apartment for the duration.

The skies were gray and the air cool as Jocelyn stepped from the car. A steady stream of pedestrians passed in both directions on the sidewalk.

Sophie popped open the hatch and pulled out the suitcases while Jocelyn grabbed two boxes from the backseat. She backed up onto the sidewalk to swing the door closed and stepped right into the path of a jogger, the sound of sneakers on pavement registering with her a moment too late. Hands gripped her shoulders, and she whipped around, expecting to be met with some expletive but instead was greeted by a man's crystal blue eyes and an ear-to-ear grin.

"Sorry about that." The guy let go of her and pulled his earbuds out. "Are you okay?"

Jocelyn nodded, trying to get over her sudden infatuation with the way his hair glistened in the morning light.

Sophie came around from the other side of the car with the third box and stepped next to the suitcases. The jogger promptly lost interest in Jocelyn and went to Sophie. Her sister's blonde hair, green eyes, and to-die-for body, which came from the hours of yoga she performed on a daily basis, had heads turning her way wherever she went. Jocelyn, with her gentle curves and dark brown hair, didn't hold a candle to her sister in the beauty queen department.

"Can I help you with that?" He took the box from Sophie's arms. Wouldn't you know she'd be spared from the light box while Jocelyn struggled with the heavy ones? Why had she thought she needed to bring every one of her college textbooks with her?

"Thanks. That's very kind of you." Sophie grabbed for the suitcase handles, but the guy took one from her.

"You wouldn't happen to be moving all this stuff into my building now, would you?" He nodded toward the apartment building.

"*Your* building?" Sophie giggled, all girly and sweet. A sound that was often endearing, except when she was being hit on by random strangers.

"That's right. Fifth floor." He flirted like it was an Olympic sport. Jocelyn had seen it a thousand times before. Guys like him who knew how to layer the finest sheen of swagger into his words and cock that nice guy grin while oh so subtly measuring up her sister's body. Not that Sophie tried to hide much by constantly wearing skin tight pants and athletic tops that showed off her muscled arms and tight glutes. Yoga—who knew it could make you into a ripped goddess like that?

Jocelyn hefted the heavy boxes about to slip from her fingers and tried to get a better grip.

"That's where we're heading," Sophie said.

"Then please allow me to lead the way."

He led them to the door being held open by a man in a suit. Mr. Jogger held back, letting Jocelyn and Sophie enter first. Gentlemanly was her first thought, and then she feared for the suitcase and box he held. City criminals came in all shapes and sizes, and this good-looking stranger could have been preying on her sister's and her naivety. For all she knew, he was about to bolt down the sidewalk with her box and bag. But then, he walked through the door, and the doorman gave him a curt nod that was just this side of familiar.

"Mornin', Chester," the guy said.

Jocelyn couldn't help but wonder if the doorman's name was really Chester or if he was just too polite to correct the stranger who had no business coming into the building. Never one to ignore her investigative instincts, Jocelyn turned to question the doorman when Chester said, "Good morning, Mr. Lewis."

That put the random stranger theory to rest. Her arms were about to give up their hold on her boxes, so she steered herself toward a table near a wall of mailboxes.

Sophie pushed ahead to the elevator, joining a small group of other people. Her new neighbor made his way to Sophie, who chatted him up like he was an old friend. Sophie's bubbly giggle punctuated the air every so often, and that tiny bead of jealousy Jocelyn had carried toward her sister since childhood came trickling back.

Sophie always captured the attention of anyone in her proximity—their parents, their grandparents, and then boys. All while Jocelyn sat quietly and politely in the corner, waiting to be noticed. Just once, she'd like to think that someone would notice her over her sister.

The elevator dinged, and Jocelyn hoisted her boxes when a painting on the wall caught her attention. The concentric lines of the watercolor ripples and the cool colors pulled her into the image. The work was reminiscent of what her mother used to sell in their family's art gallery. Jocelyn was flooded with the memory of watching her mother work her brush over the paper. She tried to make out the signature, but the long straight lines didn't match the curvy C and B of Carissa Banks.

She let go of the memory and rushed off, boxes in arm, just in time to catch Sophie and Mr. Lewis smiling fondly at each other. Barely a square inch of space remained in the elevator.

"Here, I'll swap you." Her overly friendly soon-to-be neighbor moved to trade places with her outside the elevator.

"No." Jocelyn gently bulldozed him back inside with her boxes. That suitcase and box weren't going anywhere without her or Sophie. Resident or not, he could still be a thief. "You two go ahead." The elevator doors slid closed. "I'll just take the stairs," she muttered and blew a long strand of brown hair out of her eye.

* * *

Sweat moistened Jocelyn's skin in all sorts of unmentionable places as she reached the fifth floor landing and maneuvered through the door. If she ever decided to work out, this would be a great way to start. The five flights of stairs and heavy weights would have her arms and glutes shaped up in no time.

Jocelyn followed the voices echoing through the hall, Sophie's giggles her beacon. She came around the corner and found her sister's new friend seemingly entranced with her every word. Nobody, not even her new roommate who held a striped orange cat, noticed her.

"Can I help you with that?" the man said as she approached, finally peeling his eyes off Sophie.

"Nope. Got it." Jocelyn pushed past the brain-dead women in the doorway. All googly-eyed and purring like revved up kittens. Sophie's voice lowered to a whisper, and the three of them shared a laugh.

"Well, I'll let you get to it," the man said. "Welcome to the neighborhood. Feel free to ask if you need anything—directions, a cup of sugar, whatever." And then he was gone.

The apartment door closed.

Sophie fell against the back of it. "Yum, yum, yum. I'll have some more of that, please."

"Oh, honey." Fiona tossed her tightly spun curls to one side and stroked the back of her orange cat. "He's all look and no touch, if you know what I mean."

Jocelyn knew exactly what she meant.

Fiona put the cat down and greeted Jocelyn with a hug. "Welcome to my home."

Jocelyn glanced over the tidy space decorated in neutral tones. Lavender filled her senses as she took a deep breath. Incense burned on the natural wood coffee table. Potted plants lined the wall with windows, and the soft babble of trickling water, from an unknown source, made the room serenely perfect.

"Thank you for having me," Jocelyn said.

"Oh, Bodhi and I couldn't be happier to have you."

In the corner, Bodhi scratched at the wood floor, then jumped into a potted tree and squatted.

"What's he doing?" Jocelyn asked.

"He thinks it's a litter box." Fiona waved a hand in the air and smiled. "He gets a little confused when he's nervous."

Two

Luke glanced at the clock as he buttoned up his shirt. 8:58 a.m. Looked like he was going to be late again. But hey, he was only good for one major behavioral change at a time. Or at least that's what his questionably educated shrink, Dr. Pike, had told him. The degree from Psychs Online, hanging conspicuously on the man's wall, had him rethinking his choice within the first five minutes of sitting down on the couch. It was a one-time thing, he'd told himself. If therapy had worked for his brother and nephew, then maybe it could help him too.

Luke was doing the best he could to curb his addiction—no, not addiction, overindulgence, according to Dr. Pike—to women and sex. The stodgy man with his round belly and balding head, because meeting with a good-looking female therapist would have been like going to an AA meeting at a tavern, left him with an order to find a new and healthy passion to replace his desire to be with women. He figured it was the shrink's version of take-two-and-call-me-in-the-morning. But Luke didn't call again, and he hadn't returned any of the shrink's phone calls requesting a call back simply to check in on Luke's progress. It was only a matter of time before his mommy/daddy-issues came to the surface. And he preferred not to go there.

Luke's upbringing had been good. Some might even go as far as to call it perfect. More than he could possibly want was provided for him, except his parents. Overly immersed in their careers, Luke's parents often went weeks at a time without showing their faces at the dinner table or before he and his brother drifted off to sleep at night. He didn't like to complain, but he'd missed something in his childhood, and he saw it more and more with every moment he spent with his nephew and Emma—the boy's new step-mother.

The radical decision to visit the shrink came during Luke's third week at the Portland branch of his family's law firm. Bunking in the land of perfection at his brother Marcus's home—a two acre country estate—and witnessing the new shine his brother's not-so-perfect life had taken on, was amazing.

Marcus and Emma were the real deal. True love and all that sappy garbage. It really did exist outside of those Hollywood chick-flicks he'd been known to suffer through on occasion. Luke was fully aware of the good thing his brother had. Hell, he'd even encouraged Marcus to make things happen with Emma—the sweet teacher who'd fallen into Marcus and Brayden's lives when they needed it the most. But he assumed their marriage, like all the others he'd witnessed in his lifetime, would eventually disintegrate into two people living parallel lives under one roof.

But with a highly active second-grader and a baby on the way, the romance and the love were still palpable between the two of them. Not just in public and for show like his parents pulled off time and again but in private moments too. Luke had overheard them speaking all lovey-dovey to each other while staying with them, and when no one was looking, they still gazed at each other with adoring eyes.

If Luke didn't love his brother and his family so much, he'd have to hate them.

He fled their fairytale existence for the solitary life of his own apartment where he could let companionship come and go as he pleased.

Only once he'd arrived and started to unpack the boxes he'd had sent from Seattle, he came across a package of newspaper secured with tape. A legal disclaimer attached to it stated that the contents had been broken before packing.

Needing to see the damage for himself, Luke had undone the paper, and broken bits of the vase that had been thrown at his head by a scorned woman, tumbled to the floor. It had been a stark reminder of the stupid path his life was taking, and that's when he'd looked up the ridiculous shrink.

He slipped the strap of his leather messenger bag over his head as he walked out the door. He was still a good fifteen minutes from the office. At the corner he stopped at a food cart to grab a copy of the latest tabloid magazine, a cup of coffee, and an apple. Now he was going to be at least twenty minutes late. But hey, being late was his thing and he was going to make sure to do it right.

What was the worst that could happen? His brother wasn't going to fire him from the family firm. Maybe Marcus would pile on another pro-bono case, but with the way Luke had been settling every sexual harassment and child custody case in record time, Marcus couldn't keep him on the bench much longer. Even though he was enjoying the challenge of the lower profile cases much more than he'd imagined.

Marcus had assigned him the cases as a way to let him know he had to earn his place in the firm—that it wouldn't just be handed over to him. Marcus was a hard-ass, but compared to their father in Seattle, Uncle Bill in L.A., and that prick Johnson in Denver, his brother was an angel to work for. If staying in Portland meant being the firm's chief pro-bono associate, he'd stay here until he died before ever leaving to work under another managing partner.

The magazine was tucked under his arm as he walked into the office building and boarded the elevator. Doors closed and he bit into the apple. At the eighteenth floor, he tossed the core into the receptacle outside the Lewis and Son's Law Firm office. As he wiped his hands, a slim, elegant woman in a white silk jumpsuit strode from the door. Her wrinkled face belied the youthful look of her body. Had he first seen her from the back, he would have taken her for a twenty-something. Even though it was obvious her skin had been well taken care of, the brackets around her mouth and the creases branching from the corners of her eyes told Luke she was much closer to his mother's age than his own. A black scarf with large round polka dots was tied around her neck, and a belt in a matching pattern hung loosely over her hips.

"Well, well, well," she said, punching the button for the elevator. "What an unexpected treat running in to you out here." She batted her eyelashes at him from over her shoulder.

"I'm sorry," Luke said, infusing his famous charm into the apology. "Have we met before?"

"Not exactly," she said coyly as the elevator opened. She stepped in and turned around. "But we're about to become very good friends." She waved her fingers, letting them fall one at a time, her red lips parted.

The doors closed, and he shook off the interaction. Something about her seemed familiar, probably a client he'd passed before. But there was no friendship about to bloom between them, not only because of the age difference—older women had never been his thing—but because of the promise he'd made to his brother when he came to work here. No office affairs. And that included clients. So whatever the woman had in mind, it wasn't going to happen.

Luke walked through the doors of the law firm, and Gretta, his brother's personal secretary, peered over her glasses at him.

"Good morning, beautiful." He set the coffee and magazine—a guilty pleasure of hers that only he knew about—on her desk. It kept her from delivering the chastising words he knew he deserved for being late.

She stashed the magazine in a bottom drawer, picked up the cup, and pointed at the conference room.

"Would they really miss me if I sat this one out?" It was just another meeting where everyone would get assignments but him, and later Marcus would call him into his office and drop another pro-bono file in his lap.

"They most certainly would." She gave him a stern motherly look.

"All right. But if I get in trouble for falling asleep in there while everyone talks around me, I'm going to blame you."

The phone next to Gretta rang, and she answered it as he dragged his feet toward the conference room. Inside, the long table was filled with partners and associates, like himself, who were granted the privilege of sitting in on these weekly meetings. Only his privilege was given to him because of his last name, whereas the others were asked to attend based on their outstanding contributions to the firm. As usual, the only seat available was in the front, right next to his brother.

Luke slipped his satchel strap over his head and snuck toward the front as Marcus talked about a client's account that was transferring to them from the L.A. office. Everyone in the room, including his brother, was ignoring his late arrival. Not that it mattered much. These meetings were never about him anyway. He was simply here for the sake of appearance.

Marcus slapped the blue folder he'd been holding down in front of Luke. "And Luke will be handling the deal."

The deal? What deal?

Silence lingered in the air. Not the usual banter that accompanied assignments as the partners kidded each other about needing one another's help and passing along good luck wishes with the difficult clients they were pleased to see passed off to someone else. The senior partners at the other end of the table were mute. Warren Poindexter steepled his fingers and leveled a cold stare at Luke while Tippy—officially W. Tipton, but Luke didn't know what the W stood for—sat with his sparse eyebrows arching in surprise. The other two seemed disinterested.

"Let's move on to the merger of..." But the rest of Marcus's words were lost on Luke as he opened the file and read the name Lottie Jones.

Lottie Jones, the empress of La-Ti-Dots, a world leader in women's fashion. Her corporation was relocating to her hometown of Portland. And Luke was running point.

How in the world did this just happen?

* * *

Luke cleared the conference room with everyone else and went to his office. He sat and stewed for exactly ten minutes before Tippy walked, or rather waddled, into his office. The short, round man transferred his briefcase to his left hand and held up a fist.

"Congratulations on the big deal," Tippy said like he was talking to a child.

"Thanks."

They exchanged an awkward fist-bump, because the only person he could ever remember fist-bumping before was his nephew, and having a senior partner in his office doing that was, well…awkward.

"Have you ever worked with Lottie before?" Luke asked.

"No, not me." Tippy pulled a handkerchief from his breast pocket and dabbed at his forehead. "She's not exactly my kind of client."

"Really? But she's looking to acquire some real estate on this one. I'd think you or Poindexter would be better suited for this."

A flicker of curiosity crossed the man's face for a moment before disappearing. "Well, I guess you *are* suited for it. Your brother wouldn't put you in charge if he didn't think so, now would he? Do you mind if I take a look?"

"Not at all." Luke pushed him the file. He'd take any help he could get. Why had Marcus done this? What was he trying to prove?

"Ahh, this'll be a cake walk. There's some prime real estate on the east-side of the city. Should be perfect for Miss Jones."

"Thanks."

"Anytime." Tippy handed back the file and blotted his forehead again. "Now if you'll excuse me, I'm off to meet my niece for coffee. Lovely girl. You should meet her sometime."

"I'd like that," Luke said as Tippy turned away. Not that he had any interest in meeting a woman that could have possibly inherited her uncle's baldness, but Tippy seemed to have a good heart. "How's Maude?"

Tippy's back stiffened, and he slowly turned around. His eyes were desolate and lost. "Fine," he said with an absent nod. "She's just fine. Spending a bit of time at her sister's in Omaha right now."

"That's good to hear." Luke smiled. "Will you be taking some time off to join her?"

According to Marcus, when Tippy's wife had been diagnosed with kidney failure a year ago, the absentminded attorney had gone even more absentminded. Hopefully this trip was a sign that the dialysis treatments were effective.

"No." Tippy kneaded the handkerchief in his hand. "This is their time together."

"When will she be back?"

Tippy's eyes brightened with his smile. "Soon. Very soon." And with that, he turned and left.

Not wanting to waste another minute asking himself questions he didn't have the answers for, Luke walked down the hall to his brother's office. He dropped the file onto Marcus's desk. "Do you mind telling me what this is all about?" He sat and braced his elbows on his knees.

"Ahh, the Jones file." Marcus leaned back in his chair and smiled. "I would think you'd be thanking me for this one."

"I would thank you if it was a mid-level client. But someone as high-profile as Lottie Jones? That's just putting a target on my back. I'm not even a partner yet." Tippy may not have had a problem with the assignment, but surely some of the other partners would. They always did.

"Which is something that can be remedied based on the outcome of this deal. That's why I agreed to you taking the lead on it."

"You agreed to it. Meaning Dad put you up to it."

Marcus's face fell. "No. He didn't. He has no idea about this, and I don't like the implication that he influences my decisions here."

"Sorry." Luke squirmed in his chair. "Then who did you agree with to put me in charge?"

"Lottie herself."

"Of course. I believe I met her this morning at the elevators. She promised we were about to become very good friends." He cocked his head at his brother. "And you know as much as I do what that implies."

Marcus chuckled. "I don't believe that's exactly what she meant. Unfortunately, Uncle Bill and his team of idiots let her down. Right now, she needs a gentle and attentive hand to assist in this relocation process, which is something I believe you're very equipped to handle."

"You didn't see the way she came on to me at the elevators. I'm telling you, she's got plans of her own."

Marcus repressed a smile. "If that's the case, then I'm sure you, of all people, can handle her. Am I right?"

"Look, I'm not going to roll over and be a boy-toy for some cougar just for the good of the firm." A bead of sweat broke out on his upper lip. "I have principles, you know."

"I know you do. But you also have a way with women that the other partners lack. Lottie is going to be a handful, and with me off to the conference in Florida in a few weeks, I don't want to leave just anyone to handle her case. I want you to do it. And so does she."

A handful? Lottie Jones was going to be more than a handful, and he was going to have to apply every ounce of his strength to let her treat him like the toy she thought he was in order to get to the objective of the deal.

Luke fell back in his chair, letting the air escape his lungs.

Do you have anyone in your life to support your decision? Dr. Pike had asked him. His answer had been yes, thinking to himself that it was a lie, but maybe he was wrong. His brother had been to hell and back, bucking the belief of everyone in the Lewis family that therapy was for crazy people. Marcus and Brayden had been seeing a therapist every week for almost two years now. And the results spoke for themselves. If anyone could handle his truth, it was his brother.

"I'm trying to change."

Marcus leaned forward and rested his elbows on his desk. "I know. Don't think I haven't noticed all the Friday nights you've spent playing Xbox with Brayden instead of going out like you used to. I see you taking your life more seriously, and that's why this is the perfect time for you to take on a client like Lottie. There'll be a corner office opening up by the end of the year, and I can already see your name on it."

"Shit." Luke tossed his head to the side, looking away from his brother. His gaze landed on the swollen gray cloud lazily skirting across the sky. He returned his focus to his brother, facing him eye-to-eye. "Now you do sound like Dad."

"Perhaps." Marcus shrugged one shoulder. "But the difference between him and me is that he *wants* you to become a partner, whereas I *know* you can become a partner. You're a damn good lawyer Luke, and if you want this opportunity for yourself, you'll do it. I'll be here to support you, but it's time for you to take control of what you want."

"Don't use that psychological mumbo-jumbo with me." It was practically the same thing Dr. Pike had said to him. *Take control of what you want.* "Just because you see a therapist once a week doesn't mean you get to play one with me."

Marcus grinned. "I'm not trying to pull a therapy session over on you, just trying to be your big brother. Honestly, I don't care if you make partner or not. You're your own man. But, I have to wonder why you've stuck with lawyering for this long, doing just enough to keep yourself from getting fired, but never pushing harder than you have to. Except with those pro-bono cases. I've never seen anyone more focused and persistent, pulling off amazing verdicts like you've been bringing in. You have a passion for the law. Otherwise you wouldn't be here."

Who needed therapy when you had a big brother telling you how it was better than you could tell yourself?

Luke reached for the file. "I'll do my best. But let's not go talking corner offices just yet, okay?"

"Okay," Marcus said as his intercom buzzed.

"Stacy from Portland City Real Estate is here," Gretta said.

"Right on time. Now that's a surprise. See her to Luke's office. He'll be there in a moment."

"Why's she going to my office?"

"Because you'll need an agent to help with the purchase." There was an elongated pause as a tinge of pink hit Marcus's cheeks. "And because I promised Emma I'd have Stacy help the next time we were working on a commercial deal."

"Oh, you are a sad excuse for a man? A real sucker. Your wife's got you tied around that little finger of hers, doesn't she?" Luke stood and gathered his file. "She says 'jump,' and you say 'how high?'. I can't believe I have to call you blood."

He left his brother smiling behind him. The good fun they had together was a perk to this job. He didn't know what he'd been thinking sticking around Seattle for so long in the founding office under the keen eye of his father. He shuddered as he thought about how close he'd come to driving through the city on his way to California where he'd planned to ask Uncle Bill for a job. That would have been a huge mistake. No, Portland had been the right choice, and Marcus was correct. Luke did love the law. But, did he love it enough to want to commit to being a partner and marrying himself to the firm?

Marriage. The word had never blended well with Luke's name. Not when it came to the firm and certainly not to a woman. But the scary thing was, since he'd come to live in the picture-perfect land of Marcus and Emma, the thought had crossed his mind more than once. On quiet lonely nights in his apartment, with a Scotch in his hand, he'd admit to himself that he wanted the picture-perfect life too. But he wouldn't settle for just anyone. That much he knew for sure.

"What do we have here?" he said with the practiced charm he'd used since grade school to get himself out of countless scrapes. "Isn't this the perfect way to start the day? Finding a beautiful woman waiting for me in my office."

"Oh stop." Stacy swung the ponytail she almost always wore to the side, the long strands settling over her shoulder. "I'm here because you need me."

There was a playful purr behind her words. She was his equal in so many ways—just as flirtatious and one-minded as he used to be. When he'd first met her, the possibility of the two of them hooking up had crossed his mind, but since she was his new sister-in-law's best friend, he'd permanently deleted all thoughts on the matter. He'd had principles even back then, just not as strong as they were now.

"So," he sat behind his desk. The Lottie Jones file was thick, and he scanned it, reviewing the details as quickly as he could. "Okay, so I'm looking for a large building. Six thousand square foot minimum. Somewhere on the east side should be good. Room for offices, a gymnasium, and child care. Possible warehouse space." He looked up. "Aren't you going to write this down?"

Stacy dropped her elbow over the back of the chair and crossed her legs. Her short skirt rode higher, shooting off the come hither vibe. One long manicured nail seemed to have captured her attention, a tactic to make him work at getting her attention. He'd seen it done a thousand times. "No, I've got this. Six thousand square feet. East side. Offices. Gym and child care. I can think of seven buildings off the top of my head right now."

"Good." Luke closed the file. "Then, you won't have a problem getting them on my desk by the end of the day."

"I'll have them for you by the end of lunch." Stacy uncrossed her legs, very catlike, and moved to the edge of her chair. She laid her arms one over the other at the edge of his desk and leaned forward, a valley of cleavage tugging at his gaze. "But first, I have a proposition for you?"

"You do?" He kept his eyes on hers.

"Yes, I have a wedding to go to this weekend, and my date just cancelled. So, will you take me? Please. Pretty, pretty please?" Her lips turned to a pout. "Emma said you would."

It was his turn to play the role of sucker, since the mention of his sister-in-law had him acquiescing without batting an eye. "Sure, I can take you."

"Yay." Stacy clapped her hands. "It's at two on Saturday at The Willamette Hotel. I'll meet you at your place since we can walk from there."

"Okay, but just so you know, I'm not putting out."

She stood and leaned over his desk, letting her shirt fall open in front of his eyes. Black lace hugged olive skin. "Oh, you'll be begging me to *let* you put out by the end of the night," she said before she turned and walked away.

It was exactly the kind of line he would have delivered. And if it had been anyone other than Stacy trying to entice him, he'd probably be lacing up his sneakers for another jog around the waterfront right now.

Three

Sophie fell backward against the mattress on Jocelyn's floor. A contented sigh slipped from her sister's lips. "I think I've died and gone to heaven."

Jocelyn put more books on the shelf which emptied her second box. She flipped it over and cut through the tape, squishing it flat to store it in the back of her closet until the next moving day. "Why do you say that?"

Sophie moved her arms and legs over the bedding that had, just a few moments ago, been perfectly smooth.

"Because this bed is divine. Feel it. You'll sleep like a baby here."

Jocelyn ignored her sister as she dragged the final box across the bamboo floor and started to unpack it. She pulled out the jewelry box her grandmother had given her, a few framed pictures, and the small stack of books she'd acquired over the years to read for pleasure. Maybe now she'd finally have the time to read one of them.

"It'll be like sleeping on a cloud," Sophie said dreamily.

"More like sleeping on a mattress on the floor. Now get up and help me finish unpacking." Jocelyn threw an old faded bunny slipper at her sister.

"Eeeew. Gross. Get that thing away from me." She tossed the slipper back to Jocelyn.

Jocelyn turned her back, and the slipper bounced off her shoulder, falling to the floor with a quiet plop. Not willing to let the assault end there, she returned fire with both slippers. Sophie rolled to one side, avoiding the ambush. The room filled with laughter, and the "Ommm…" from the living room grew louder.

Once Fiona had given Jocelyn a quick tour of the apartment, she'd rolled out her yoga mat and assumed the meditation position—legs crossed, palms up, and fingers pinched.

"Shhh," Sophie put a finger to her lips. "You're disturbing her meditation."

"Me?" Jocelyn hissed as she pulled a stack of clothes from the suitcase and set them on the bed next to Sophie. "You're the one screaming like a little girl back here. Now put those clothes on hangers and hand them to me."

Sophie sat up, scooted to the edge of the mattress, and picked up a pair of pants. "You're so bossy sometimes."

"It comes with being the oldest child."

"Yeah, well, you're good at it."

A quiet moment passed between them.

"You're so lucky," Sophie said, all the playfulness swooshing out of her voice. "Getting to move here and live in the city. It's so exciting."

"It's not that exciting." Jocelyn looked around the bare-bones room, having an instant urge to be transported back to the safe and familiar confines of the only home she'd ever known. She took the shirt Sophie handed her. "Besides, this is just temporary."

"I know, but even if it's just for a little while. You get to be *here* and not stuck in River's Edge."

"You say that like it's a bad place to be."

"It's not bad." Sophie tucked another hanger inside a shirt. "It's just small. And boring. And completely uninspiring."

"How can you say that? Plenty of interesting things happen back home. The harvest celebration. The governor's visit last year. The new school project. And who can forget the scandal on the city council? Judge Godfrey sleeping with his intern. Those kinds of things happen in small towns just like they do in big cities."

"I'm not talking about newsworthy events. Those things don't interest me." Sophie grimaced. "A place like this offers so many more opportunities—new places to visit and new people to meet."

"But River's Edge is where you grew up. It's where people know you and care about you."

Sophie shrugged. "I just find it so confining. There's hardly anything to do in town, and I want to start my own yoga studio, not work for Madame Christine teaching a one-hour class three times a week for the rest of my life. There's not enough clientele back home."

Jocelyn stiffened. Sophie wanted to leave? This was news to her. "But what about your job at Ramirez Vines? I thought you liked working in the tasting room."

"It helps pay the bills, but I don't love it. I want to be somewhere that has a vibe like the city."

Jocelyn bit her tongue. She wanted to remind Sophie she'd been off trying out different cities and different vibes since she left college. Each one too this or too that. It was probably only a matter of time before Portland was no longer shiny and new for her sister either.

"You never know what the future holds." She tried to sound supportive. "But you can't leave Dad right now."

"Why not? He's a grown up."

Jocelyn's heart raced. "You promised you'd be there while I'm here. You can't go back on your promise now."

Sophie's green eyes went serious. "He really is fine on his own. I wish you could see that."

Jocelyn didn't see it, and neither would her sister if she'd paid any attention these last few years. But Jocelyn only had herself to blame for that. Having shouldered all the burdens after their mother was gone so her sister didn't have to, meant Sophie didn't see what life was like for their father. Maybe now she would.

But maybe she wouldn't…and for the one hundred and fiftieth time since she'd accepted her temporary job, she wondered if she'd been wrong to leave River's Edge. There was still so much her father and her uncle relied on her for. What if something went wrong while she was away?

She let out a deep sigh. "He's never lived on his own. The yardwork, the housework, the cooking…it's all too much for him to handle on his own along with the running the gallery. I wish you'd reconsider moving back into the house. That way you could help him more."

"No." Sophie shook her head and handed Jocelyn the last hanger. "I don't need to go back to my lace-curtained room. Dad's got no feng shui going on in there." Sophie shuddered. "I like my apartment above Madame Christine's. It might be small, but it suits me much better."

"Fine." Jocelyn dropped to the mattress next to Sophie. "Just promise me you'll check in on him every day."

"Yeah, sure." Sophie crossed her arms over her knees. "I talked to Mom the other day."

Jocelyn turned away. "Stop. I don't want to hear it."

"She said this move is going to be good for you."

"I said I don't want to hear it." Jocelyn couldn't stomach the idea of Sophie sitting down with Madame Christine for a psychic reading. Communing with the dead? It wasn't real, and she didn't know how Sophie fell for it so easily.

"She also said to be careful."

Jocelyn snapped her head back in Sophie's direction. "What's that supposed to mean?" *Wait.* She didn't mean to ask that.

"I don't make the news. I just report it." Sophie nudged her with an elbow and smiled as she threw one of Jocelyn's famous lines right back at her.

"Ha. Ha. You're very funny, but please don't go telling Dad about your little chats. I don't think it'd be good for him."

Sophie gave a non-committal shrug, and Jocelyn was about to make her pinky swear when a scratching sound pulled her attention to the open suitcase on the floor. Bodhi was inside, mistaking the corner for his litter box.

* * *

"So Fiona's pretty much awesome, isn't she?" Sophie pulled open the door to the vegan deli not ten steps from the front door of the apartment building.

Besides the way she'd scooped up and babied Bodhi after Jocelyn had shrieked at him to get out of her bag, she seemed nice enough. "Yeah, she's great, but I don't think her cat cares for me very much."

"Oh, you heard what she said. He's just sensitive. Give it time."

Time? Sure, how many more times was she going to have to scrub out her suitcase before the old cat adjusted? Fiona had even suggested Jocelyn keep her shoes out of sight because he'd been known to mistake those as well.

Sophie ordered them each a rice bowl, and they found a table for two in the corner.

"This is such a great place," Sophie said. "Did you see how many restaurants there are on this block alone? You'll never have to cook."

"Yeah, it's great." Jocelyn pushed her tofu bits to the side.

"Maybe you can get your new neighbor to bring you here sometime."

"And why would I want to do that?"

"Because he seems nice."

"He seemed nice because he couldn't take his eyes off you."

"That's not true."

"Of course it is. Guys like that aren't interested in girls like me. You're way more his type than I am."

"What type am I?"

"Fun. Flirty. Hot."

"You're all those things too, you know. I mean, we *are* sisters, aren't we? It's got to be in our blood or something."

"Or something." She dropped her gaze to the table.

Jocelyn had tried the fun and flirty routine in college. At the first opportunity to shed her A+, serious-student reputation that had followed her since middle school, she'd embraced partying and staying out all night. The freshman classes were simple and didn't require her to spend hours studying, so she'd joined her roommate and friends at all the parties. It was where she met Paulo, the starving art student who read her poetry and sketched her picture. It took less than two weeks for her to be swept away and lose her virginity to a man that said and did all the right things. Her principles took a vacation until the day he decided to try out his time-tested moves on some other unsuspecting freshman. He dropped Jocelyn like a bag of dirt and her principles hopped the first plane back to reality, shaking a finger at her that bruised her already broken heart.

They were the most sensual weeks of Jocelyn's life, but she refused to revisit them. The sting of being nothing more than a good time to someone far outweighed the electrifying memories. From that time on, she'd sworn off every smooth-talking, fine-looking man she'd met.

"Hey, let's start digging out that fun and flirty side of you with a trip to the mall." Sophie pulled out a pre-paid cash card.

"Where'd that come from?"

"Dad and Uncle Larry pooled some money together so I could take you shopping."

"Really?"

"Yep. Uncle Larry kept talking about how you'll be running with the big dogs now and need to look the part."

Ah. The big dog analogy again. Jocelyn hadn't had the heart to correct his comparison. From her experience, big dogs were nothing to be intimidated by. In fact, the Saint Bernard and Great Dane were two of the animal kingdom's most gentle giants, slobbery kisses their only weapon. And nothing compared to their loyalty and laid back dispositions. She could only hope *The Daily Report* was run by such loving people. Little dogs on the other hand scared the daylights out of Jocelyn. The high-pitched yapping of those little ankle biters was equal parts annoying and frightening.

"Well, what are we waiting for?" Jocelyn asked. "Let's go find somewhere to spend it."

* * *

After dinner at a restaurant that served meat, so Jocelyn could get something more substantial than rice, she and Sophie returned to the apartment with their arms bogged down by heavy shopping bags. Inside, the aroma of lavender instantly set Jocelyn's frayed nerves at ease.

At first, the shopping trip had been fun, picking out a few new outfits. But Sophie insisted on another store and then another, claiming the last of the funds had to be exhausted before she'd let them return to the apartment. It was only after adding dinner to the tab that they finally drained the last penny.

Jocelyn had no idea how her father or uncle were affording all their generosity. She took the clothes to her room and hung them in the closet, pushing aside her overwhelming guilt and pledging that she'd pay them back.

Back in the living room, she met Sophie, who'd come in from the patio where Fiona was sitting.

Bodhi rubbed against Jocelyn's leg.

"Hey, look at that," Sophie said. "He's warming up to you already."

Jocelyn didn't move, afraid the cat may mistake her shoes as a place to potty, but he just flipped his tail up and walked away.

Sophie dug her keys out of her purse. "I think I'm going to go."

"Okay." Jocelyn was sad to see her sister—her last tie to home—leave so soon. But if Sophie left now, she'd get home at a reasonable hour. "Drive safely. Call me when you get home."

"Actually, I'm not going home just yet." A touch of pink rose in Sophie's cheeks. "And if Dad asks, I'm staying with you, okay?"

"Do I get to ask where you'll be?"

Another blush washed over her sister's cheeks. "Not yet. But I'll be in touch. Love you."

After a quick hug, Sophie left, and Jocelyn's mind started to race. How was she going to get to the bottom of her sister's secret?

Bodhi's soft fur rubbed against her leg again. Jocelyn knelt and stroked the cat's head, happy to see they were finally on their way to becoming friends. Warm air breezed through the patio door, and Jocelyn wandered out to find Fiona on the balcony, lounging in a chair that overlooked a lush courtyard. The gardens were protected on all four sides by the tall walls of the building. Apartments directly across the way also boasted wrought iron balconies while the apartments lining the sides only had windows that opened up to the beautiful outdoor space. Fiona's corner apartment was tucked nicely in the shade of the building.

"Can I join you?" Jocelyn asked.

"Uh-huh." Fiona flipped a page in her magazine, head tilted down but eyes flickering up.

"You have a lovely view from up here." Jocelyn settled into the chair next to Fiona.

"Uh-huh," Fiona said again.

"What are you doing?"

When Fiona didn't answer, Jocelyn followed her gaze through the courtyard to the adjacent apartment, where one slightly sweaty and shirtless neighbor of theirs was performing a set of pull ups from a bar braced in his doorway.

For the love of mercy. Leaving the curtains open so he can show off every rippling muscle—and what a fine set of ripples it was—to the neighborhood was beyond vain. Jocelyn slumped down and swiveled the chair so her back was to the window.

"Is there anything else I need to know before you leave tomorrow?" Jocelyn asked.

Fiona turned a page, her eyes still on the neighbor's window. "Shhh," she said. "Give me ten more minutes. He's about to start the chin ups, and that's my favorite part. Mm-mmm. Then we'll talk."

Four

Luke leaned against the counter in his kitchen as Stacy sat on the couch, holding her compact mirror and generously reapplying another coat of lipstick. Her hair was pulled tighter than usual, drawing even more attention to her dark eyes. Her dress was tight too, not that Luke would have expected anything different. It was short—also not unexpected—and the lacy hemline barely covered her backside. Although it was exactly the look he knew she was trying to achieve, it made him incredibly uncomfortable.

Luke adjusted his tie and cleared his throat. "Are you all set?"

With one more glance in her mirror and a final smack of her lips, Stacy dropped the tube of lipstick in her purse and snapped it shut. "I'm ready."

"Great, then let's get this thing over with." He held out a hand, offering for her to lead the way to the door.

"Geez, Luke." She rolled her eyes in passing. "Can't you at least pretend this might be fun?"

"I won't pretend until I have to. Don't you want a jacket? It might be cold by the time we walk back."

"No, I don't. I make it a point to never bring a jacket. If I did, then I wouldn't need to borrow one later, would I?" She walked her fingers up his tie as he slipped into his suit jacket.

"Well, you're not getting mine." He ushered her through the door.

Stacy linked her arm in his. "Oh, you just wait. I've got moves that are going to make you want to give me the shirt off your back. Don't go thinking I've never seduced a noble man like you before."

"I'm so not a noble man."

"Sure you are." Stacy chuckled and tapped him on the stomach with her purse. A flirty move that—if he were interested—would be a clear sign they were going to end up back at his place tonight.

At the corner, they nearly collided with a woman carrying a shopping bag. Stacy leaned in to him to keep from toppling over, and the other woman dropped her keys.

"Here, let me," Luke said, righting Stacy and reaching for the keys. When he came up, he was eye-to-eye with his new neighbor—the one who'd just moved in with the cat lady. Her gaze was trained on Stacy. Whose wouldn't be with that scanty getup she was wearing? "Can I help you to your door?"

"What? No." His neighbor blinked at him like she was coming out of a coma. "Thanks, I can get this."

She tried to swipe the keys out of his hand while Stacy examined a fingernail, but he pulled back.

"It's no problem. You're hands seem full."

"No, really. I can handle it." Curt impatience boiled in her voice.

"Okay." He handed the keys over. "Your sister mentioned you were the insanely independent type. I'll have to remember that."

Shock fired from behind her blue eyes, her keys still hanging from her fingers.

He graced her with his most charming smile before taking Stacy by the elbow. "See ya later, neighbor."

As he waited for the elevator, he did everything he could not to glance back and check if those eyes—blue-gray like the evening clouds lit by a full moon—were still watching him. How had he missed the depth of her eyes before?

Stacy said something cheeky about his striped tie, and he laughed appropriately, but his mind was still stuck on those amazing eyes. The elevator arrived, and before he stepped on, he chanced a glance back down the hall, but his neighbor was gone.

* * *

Weddings were barely tolerable when a person knew the bride and groom. And when he didn't, they were even worse. With an uninterested date—Stacy had been doing her own bit of scouting since the moment they entered the marble-accented ballroom—he rarely spent a moment alone. If he wasn't such a devoted brother-in-law, he'd have left Stacy to end the night on her own, but then he'd have to explain himself to Emma. So, he was making the most of the open bar, and by the time he was on his third vodka and tonic, the dancing was underway.

Some time ago, Stacy had latched onto a man not much taller than she. A spider tattoo spread across the back of his neck and halfway up his bald head. The two of them were swaying to the music out on the dance floor.

A perky blonde sidled up to Luke. "You wanna dance?"

"Sure," he said, as a round of squeals broke out behind him.

One look over his shoulder told him he'd been the subject of a plot. He didn't mind, though, it was fun to fulfill the whims of young ladies. And she was young. Possibly still in college. He grabbed her by the hand and led her to the dance floor, determined to show her and her friends how a real man could dance.

The young coed's name was Taylor, and she was in her third year at Portland State. After two dances, he was bored with their conversation. It was a new phenomenon he was still getting used to, this need for conversation. There was a time not so long ago when talking didn't matter.

He asked for her number, knowing it would signal the end of their time together. Plus, it would likely make the night a success in her book. More squeals came from the crowd in the corner when she'd rushed away from him. Luke smiled to himself, pleased he'd played his role just right.

Women—sometimes they were too easy to figure out. And sometimes they weren't.

He found Stacy at the bar, doing a shot. Spider-tattoo slammed his glass down and asked for another round for the both of them. Stacy threw it back, and Luke did a quick calculation of what he'd seen her drink so far. There was no way, with her tiny stature, the two glasses of wine, the two shots, and the champagne were going to be tempered by the half a lobster tail she ate at dinner. And chances were that the drinks he witnessed her consuming weren't the only ones she'd had. Her precarious perch on the edge of her stool looked a good deal like a woman who was in no shape to make judgments for herself.

Instantly Luke questioned the integrity of her new companion. What sort of man continued to serve a woman in her state? The kind with no good intentions, that who.

"Hey there, Stace. Having fun?" Luke grabbed an olive from the bowl on the bar and popped it in his mouth. Spider-guy gave him the once-over from the corner of his eye.

"Yeah." Stacy pawed his arm. "Isn't this the best wedding ever?"

"Sure is," Luke said, all smiles. "I see you made a new friend. Luke Lewis." He held his hand out.

"Mickey," the guy said, not taking his hand.

"Yesssss. 'Is name's Mic-key." Stacy's head bobbed forward and back as she laughed. "It's so cute."

The girl was so obviously soused. Luke signaled the bartender. "Can I get a water here, please?"

Mickey turned his attention to the dance floor. Perhaps in an effort to find another guest to prey upon, but Luke wasn't going to let him run away so easily.

"So Mickey." Luke popped another olive. "How do you know the bride and groom?"

Muscles tensed beneath Mickey's pressed shirt. "How do *you* know the bride and groom?"

Ahhh, deflection. A definite sign that something didn't add up about Mickey. "I don't," Luke said. "So, what about you? What's your story with them?"

Mickey studied him, as if trying to assess how to answer. "Yeah, well I work with the bride."

Luke turned up his friendly smile. "You do? At the real estate office?"

"Yeah, yeah. At the office. She's a real go-getter there. Everyone loves…" He glanced around the room. "Marie."

A fast song with a heavy beat played, the dance floor thinning slightly.

"Yeah, that's what I hear." Luke nodded. "So what side of real estate are you in, residential or commercial?"

"Commercial." Mickey leaned back against the bar, loosening up.

"That's incredible. I've just started looking at some properties for a client. Big places with lots of room for offices. That kind of thing. Do you have any good rec's I should look into?"

Stacy bobbed her head to the music.

Mickey blew out a breath and shook his head, like he was racking his brain. "There's a place downtown by the river for sale. Big white building. Used to be a bank, I think."

"Oh yeah. I know the one you're talking about. I'm going to check it out Monday morning."

"Yeah, right on." Mickey picked up his shot glass.

"You know what, Stace?" Luke gently elbowed her. "Mickey here might be a good addition to our team. Why didn't you tell me about him before? We could always use more hard-working agents on our deals."

Mickey's eyes grew big as he gulped down his shot.

"That's how you two know each other, right? The office. Because Stacy works there too. With *Marnie*."

"What? I don't work with him," Stacy said, pointing.

"I know you don't." Luke didn't take his eyes off Mickey, who seemed to have nothing to say for himself. "So tell me again, Mickey. How do you know the newlyweds?"

The bald man's dark eyes sunk beneath his brows.

"Wise choice," Luke said. "Keep your lies to yourself. It's one thing to crash a wedding for the free food and drinks, but to liquor up a guest with the intentions of doing God-knows-what next isn't cool. Now get your coat and see yourself out before I call my friends at the Portland PD and run your profile by them."

Stacy gasped, and when Mickey didn't protest, Luke's stomach turned. The wretched man went for his coat and left.

"If he comes back," Luke said to the bartender, sliding him his card, "Call me, and I'll make certain he gets an escort out."

The bartender nodded and slipped the card in his pocket.

Stacy shivered. "Is he… Did…"

Luke pulled his jacket off and wrapped it around Stacy. "Here you go. You look cold." He braced his hands on her shoulders. "What do you say we get out of here?"

* * *

Weak morning light filtered in around the edges of the curtains in Luke's apartment. He padded over and pulled on the string, letting daylight flood the space. Stacy groaned, and he took a seat across from her, watching her eyes blink awake.

"How'd you sleep?" he asked as he slipped on his sneakers.

She groaned again and pulled the blanket up over her head.

It took less than five minutes for her to sit down and pass out right here on his couch last night. He hadn't bothered to move her somewhere more comfortable. Instead, he threw a blanket over the top of her and switched off the light. It was for the best. The smell of a woman on his sheets would have been bad medicine for the ailment he was trying to cure.

He folded his hands together as he waited for her to sit up. Her palm immediately went to her head as she assumed the classic hangover position.

"Did what I think happened last night, really happen?"

"I don't know." Luke leaned back. "What do you think happened?"

"Did I almost go home with a criminal?"

Luke called the police as soon as he'd retreated to his bedroom last night to file a report on Mickey. Since no actual crime was committed, the desk clerk he spoke to simply wrote down his complaint, took his name and number, and said she'd have someone call him back if they needed more information. He didn't even know if this guy had been reported for previous offenses or not. "I don't know. Mickey never admitted to having any ulterior motive, but he sure didn't stick around to defend himself last night."

"God, that would've been awful." Stacy rocked her head back and forth in her palm. "See why I don't go to weddings by myself?"

Luke got up and went to the kitchen. He didn't want to hear Stacy cry about her pitifulness. It was going to get her in trouble one of these days. From the fridge, he pulled out a water bottle and brought it to her.

"Drink up," he said.

She complied, and he sat down in the chair across from her again.

"Thanks." Her hair fell across her face, and she pushed it back. Makeup streaked her usually perfect porcelain skin.

"You're a decent person." Luke leaned forward and rested his elbows on his knees. "And you deserve to be treated as such. Don't sell yourself short, Stacy. You don't have to settle for these paper-thin hook ups if you don't want to."

"I know." She nodded, then smiled. "It's fun most of the time, except for when it's not. I just wish I could find somebody great like you." Stacy's lips quivered like she might want to smile, but Luke felt the vulnerability in her words. He knew exactly what it felt like to fill the void of wanting someone special to love you by hooking up with the first person who looked willing. It was fun, until it wasn't.

"Yes, but we'd never last, and then what would Emma say?"

"Ahh, but we'd have some bang up kinky sex along the way." Stacy took another swig.

Luke shook his head. "You're a rare one, aren't you?"

"You bet I am." She stood on unsteady legs and made her way to the bathroom.

Five minutes later, she was out with her hair pulled back into its traditional ponytail and a fresh mask of make-up in place. Her eyes were bright, and her steps confident.

"You know, since I *am* here and did stay the night, we could, you know…" she looked back at his bedroom door, "…complete the evening."

"Yeah, I don't think so." Luke couldn't believe her bounce back. Hadn't they just talked about how the two of them would never work out?

"Awww." She closed the distance between them and straddled him in the chair. "You're going to ruin my reputation."

Luke bit the inside of his cheek, maintaining his willpower. Her fingers slipped into his hair, and he wanted to go thoughtless right then and there, to fall back into his old pattern, but the aftermath would never replace the five minutes of pleasure.

He grabbed her arms and eased her off. "I'm sure you'll rebound. Now, I'll walk you out. I have a pickup game at the gym with Marcus."

He brushed past her and went to the door. The distinct prick of high heels against his wood floor followed him.

* * *

The gym was never crowded on Sunday mornings. That's why Luke met his brother there right after Marcus went to church with his family—quite the family guy his brother had become.

"You're not late," Marcus said in mock-surprise when Luke found him on the basketball court.

"Of course I'm not late. We've got some ass to kick this morning. And you need to work on your jump shot."

"I don't need to work on my jump shot. And I wish you'd show up at the office like this more often."

"We've all got to have something to hold out for, don't we? Now, pass me that ball."

Marcus bounced the ball to him, and Luke clapped his hands around it, palms stinging. He dribbled toward the center, the hollow echo of the ball hitting the floor bounced off the walls of the empty court.

"Hey, how was the wedding yesterday?" Marcus asked as he put up a block in front of Luke's half-court attempt at the basket.

It missed terribly, and Marcus jogged after the wayward ball.

"It was about as you'd expect a wedding would be where you don't know anyone except your date." He put a hand on his brother's back and moved in on him, backing toward the basket.

Marcus laughed, spinning around and jumping for the shot. "How was Stacy as a date?"

The ball saw nothing but net, and Luke grabbed the rebound. "I've had better."

Marcus put his hands on his hips, his eyes hard.

Luke set himself up for the two point shot and peered over the ball. "She slept over."

Swoosh. The ball slipped through the net. No backboard needed.

"Luke!"

Marcus missed the rebound, and Luke trotted off to retrieve the ball from beneath a bench.

"Calm down." Luke set the ball on his hip, cradling it with his arm. "She drank too much and was about to go home with a very unsavory character. But, I stopped her and brought her back to my place where she slept on the couch."

"Is she all right?"

"Yeah." Luke shook his head. "We had a talk about it this morning. She seemed upset, but five minutes later, she was trying to get me into bed. Like nothing tragic almost happened last night."

Marcus rubbed his temples. "I don't know what happened in her life to make her think this is how she needs to live. Emma worries about her. A lot. Thanks for taking care of her last night."

"Yeah, sure." Luke dribbled again.

Marcus uprooted his feet and tried to block Luke's shot this time. The ball hit the rim and fell back to the floor. Marcus caught it, and Luke waited for him near the free throw line.

"Hey, before I forget." Marcus held the ball with both hands. "Can you watch Brayden for us on Friday night? There's a play at the theater I want to take Emma to."

"Does this mean I don't get a home cooked meal from my favorite sister-in-law?"

Marcus nodded. "I thought I'd take her out, someplace nice downtown, and give her a night off."

Luke threw up his hands like his life had been ruined. "I don't know if I'll survive this. I need Emma's home cooking."

"Why don't you learn to boil a pot of water for yourself one of these days, little bro?"

"Right. Like you've ever boiled water."

"When it was just Bray and me, I did okay."

"I beg to differ."

Their childhood nanny had stuck with Marcus and Brayden even after they moved from Seattle to Portland. Luke was pretty sure all his brother's meals were taken care of before Emma came along.

"Differ all you want, but you still couldn't scramble an egg if your life depended on it."

"Let's just see about that." Luke stepped closer to Marcus. "Why don't I watch Brayden at my place on Friday? I'll cook for all of you before the play. And then you can tell me what you have to say about my cooking."

"Really? You're going to cook?"

"And you're going to love it." Luke nodded toward the men that had just walked onto the court. "Now, let's take on those two and show them what the Lewis brothers are made of."

Five

Jocelyn watched the tear drop blip on her phone's screen. It still hadn't moved. For two days, she'd watched the tracking app—all a part of the family plan she'd set up years ago—on her phone. It showed Sophie in Albany, a suburban town south of the city. And it hadn't moved. Her big sister concern fused with her investigative instincts led her to researching her sister's whereabouts. She doubted Sophie and her flighty brain remembered consenting to the app back when the plan was set up, but she had, though Jocelyn had never felt the need to use it until now.

She tried calling Sophie again, but her sister didn't answer. Bodhi stretched out and turned belly up on the couch cushion next to Jocelyn. She scratched it, despite the dissension that had happened between the two of them last night. Waking at two a.m. with the cat squatting between her feet sent her flying from beneath the covers. She tore off the blankets, not wanting the puddle to seep to the mattress. The rest of the night she'd spent on the couch, huddled under a thin blanket while the washer and dryer cleaned her bedding.

"Let's not have another night like that, okay?"

Bodhi simply widened his jaw, prompting a yawn from Jocelyn as well. Her head rested against the back of the couch, and the next thing she knew, she was blinking her eyes awake. It must have only been for a moment, because Bodhi was still beside her in his upside down position. The phone rang, and Jocelyn jumped for it. Sophie's cutesy picture showed on screen.

"Hello," she said, rubbing her eyes.

"Hey, it's me. I see I missed your calls this weekend."

"Yeah. I tried you a dozen times. Where are you?"

"I'm home."

Home? Jocelyn checked the clock. Her little nap had ended up stealing away her entire afternoon. She shook her head, clearing the sleepy cobwebs from her brain. "What were you doing in Albany?"

"You didn't just ask me that, did you?"

"What? Like I don't have the right to know where you were? You're my sister, and I was worried."

"Did you follow me? Is that how you know where I was?"

"No." Although, the thought of jumping into a cab and tracking her down had crossed Jocelyn's mind. If the town wasn't over an hour away, she may have done just that. "I'm an investigative reporter, remember? It's what I do."

A long calculated pause followed before Sophie spoke. "It scares me that you did that."

"What scares you?" Jocelyn snapped.

"That you couldn't leave it alone. Not knowing where I was."

"I'm your sister. I was worried about you. Is that so wrong?"

"No. But not respecting my wishes is."

"So, why didn't you just tell me where you were going?"

"Looks like I didn't have to. You took care of that all on your own."

"Well, it's not like it was very hard."

Sophie huffed. "This is un-be-lieve-able."

"Believe it. Now spill. What were you doing there?"

"It's none of your business. And I'm going to hang up now, before I say something that will put us at risk of hating each other."

"What are you talking about? What's wrong with me checking on you? You're my little sister."

"Who's all grown up now and doesn't need a babysitter. So, whatever you did to find me, don't do it again. Find yourself a hobby, because tracking my every move is no longer an option. Goodbye."

Jocelyn held the phone to her ear a moment longer, until she was certain the dead air signaled that her sister was gone. Well, it looked like her nomination for sister-of-year was out the window. She couldn't understand Sophie's hostility. All Jocelyn had done was look into her sister's whereabouts, and Sophie was treating it like she'd committed a capital crime.

And who was she to tell Jocelyn to get a hobby? Starting tomorrow, she'd have time for nothing more than keeping up with the city's news. Reporters didn't have spare time.

Tomorrow, she'd be running with the big dogs.

* * *

Like all first days, Jocelyn's was rife with jitters. The fact that she was about to make her debut at *The Portland Daily Report* as a Dalmatian was only causing her more anxiety. How had she not seen it before? The black splotches on the white silk blouse were one-hundred percent fire dog inspired.

She twisted at the waist, examining the blouse and black pant combo. *Ugh.* She smoothed her hands over the soft silk. *Why did I buy this again?*

Then she remembered Sophie's gushing words when she'd stepped from the dressing room. "Look at the way it hugs your curves. It's so slimming."

And that's all it had taken—just a few complimentary words from her muscle-toned sister—to convince her to buy the outfit.

The thought of Sophie had her checking her phone again. The blip on her app had disappeared sometime in the night—guess Sophie had remembered the tracking app—and the message of *I'm sorry*, that she'd sent first thing this morning still hadn't been returned.

Jocelyn set the phone down with a sigh and pulled on her suit jacket, the black overlay toning down the spots.

"What do you think?" Jocelyn looked down at Bodhi.

He licked his lips, having just downed his breakfast with a dose of anxiety-reducing meds sprinkled on top.

"Do I look like a dog?"

Golden-green eyes stared back at her before the cat turned away, flipping his tail straight into the air.

"You're no help." She turned back to the mirror. "Hello," she said to her reflection, rehearsing the introduction she had planned for herself today. As the hours moved closer to the start of her new job her confidence had started to sag. What if she was getting in over her head? What if nobody respected her? She didn't like thinking that she'd gotten this job simply because her uncle had asked an old friend for a favor. If anyone questioned her credentials she wanted to be ready to show everyone she deserved to be there. "I'm Jocelyn Banks, three time People's Choice Award winner in the tri-county area for my reports on community issues. During my time at *The Gazette*, we were recognized as the fastest growing paper five years in a row—before *The Tri-County Post* boosted their social media department and left the rest of us in the dust," she added under her breath. Pushing aside the sense of defeat she felt when their circulation numbers started making another decline, she lifted her chin. "But that's going to change. *The Gazette* will be fine."

In the living room, Jocelyn checked the hands of the clock on the wall. They seemed to be moving exceptionally slow this morning. She prided herself on getting to work early every day, but now that she was working for someone else, she had to adhere to their schedule. And Mr. Wilbur had asked her to arrive at nine. She paced behind the couch before deciding a slow walk to the office might be a better use of her time.

In the lobby of her building, Jocelyn lingered over the beverage station, running her credentials through her mind again and again. She pumped hot water into a cup and added a tea bag. Tacked to a bulletin board on the wall were several notices. Jocelyn looked them over and stopped when her eyes landed on one that read:

*HELP needed at Miss Annie's soup kitchen.
Located in the historic Hitchcock Building
Dinners at 6 p.m. every day of the week.
Breakfast at 8 a.m. on Saturdays.
Come one, come all.*

That might be a nice hobby, if she needed one.

After another few minutes passed, Jocelyn tossed her tea bag and headed for the door. Chester held it open, and just as she was about to pass through, her sweat-drenched neighbor came jogging up, nearly colliding with her in the doorway. A drop of tea sloshed out, singeing her hand, and she gasped.

"I'm so sorry." Mr.—oh, what was his name again—backed up to let her pass.

She fixed him with a downright dirty glare as she passed, which he must have mistaken for *please, won't you walk with me.* Because much to her frustration, he appeared by her side.

"Hey neighbor," he said.

She nodded and picked up her pace, trying to stay unruffled. *Hello. I'm Jocelyn Banks—*

"Beautiful morning, don't you think?" he asked.

"Mmhm." She tested the temperature of her tea with her lips, attempting to stay focused on making a good first impression at her new job. *Three-time People's Choice Award winner—*

"Where are you off to this morning?"

"Work." She kept her gaze forward, refusing to grant the ear-to-ear grin he was shining upon her any credit for the warmth she felt creeping around inside her.

Was he making a pass at her? She shook the distracting notion from her mind. *—for my pieces on community issues.*

Her neighbor kept pace with her. What could he possibly be after? Nothing about her compared to his hot date from the weekend. She'd seen the two of them walk out of the building together Sunday morning. Her in the same clothes as the night before. Jocelyn had learned to add two and two together a long time ago.

"Okay, well…" He put his hands on his hips when they stopped at the corner crosswalk. "It's been great talking to you this morning. We should do this again real soon."

She turned as he jogged back to the apartment building, completely taken aback by his unaffectedness. *Would he ever get the message?*

* * *

The Portland Daily Report office was all brick and beams on the inside. A very calm energy buzzed beneath the tall ceilings. Where were all the people? Where was all the action? Jocelyn approached a curved reception desk and cleared her throat.

The woman behind the desk didn't look up. "Welcome to *The Portland Daily Report*. I'm Dena. How can I help you?"

"I'm new here. My name is Jocelyn Banks and…"

The woman's head jerked up. Her small eyes peered over black cat glasses as she looked Jocelyn up and down. "So, you're the new girl. Huh? Not what I expected." Dena pulled a pink sticky note from her computer screen and walked out from behind her desk. "Right this way."

Concrete steps led them to the second floor. Dena's lace-up ankle boots scuffed each stair, while Jocelyn followed carefully, her black heels barely making a sound.

"This is the news floor." Dena kept walking but pointed along the way. "Editor's office. Break room. Conference room. And this is where you'll be."

The cubicle they stopped next to was across from the glass-walled conference room and couldn't have been more than a five-foot by five-foot square. So much smaller than her private office in River's Edge. No one in the surrounding cubicles looked up. Each was busy clacking away at a keyboard or talking into a phone.

"I'll be at the front desk if you need me. But I don't refill coffee cups. I don't order your lunch, and I don't pick up dry cleaning. I only take messages for you when you're out of the office. So answer your phone and return your messages in a timely manner. HR needs your paperwork by the end of the day. It's in your email. Username and password are right here." She handed over the sticky note she'd been carrying. "Jerry said to see him when you're settled, so he'll be expecting you any minute. His office is beyond the stairs where we came out. Only door over there. You can't miss it."

Jocelyn blinked, her mind still processing the rapid list Dena had just run through. Finally, she nodded, and Dena turned to walk away. But then Jocelyn noticed her temporary nameplate—a folded piece of paper stapled to the side of her cubicle. *Jocelyn Banks, City Beat.*

"Wait," she called after Dena. "I thought I was doing investigative reporting."

Dena flipped her hands up. "Not my department. You'll have to take that up with Jerry."

Jocelyn dropped into her seat and ran her hands along the smooth surface of the desktop. This was hers. Her own desk in her own cubicle in the city. She stowed her bag and set out the one picture she'd brought, the one of her family—her whole family. They never took enough pictures. Something that couldn't be remedied now.

This particular snapshot was from Jocelyn's high school graduation.

"Well, here goes nothing," she said to the faces she missed more than anything as she stood and tugged at her jacket.

She found Jerry Wilbur's office and knocked.

His voice came across loud and clear. "I don't care what they're charging you for advertising. We've had a contract for eighteen years, and if that doesn't mean something to you, then I don't care where you take your business." Without taking a breath or changing his tune, Mr. Wilbur called to her. "Come in."

Jocelyn pasted on a smile and walked in with her hand extended. "Hello, Mr. Wilbur. I'm Jocelyn Banks. You knew my uncle." She wasn't supposed to lead with that. *Accolades, remember? You deserve to be here.*

Mr. Wilbur, with his round face and slack jowls, pulled his lips back, revealing a line of fine white teeth. "Aww, Larry Banks. That takes me back to the good old days." He half-stood, engulfing Jocelyn's hand with his giant one as he shook it. A Saint Bernard came racing to mind as he motioned for her to take a seat, cocking his head to one side. So maybe

Uncle Larry's analogy hadn't been that far off after all. "Tell me. How is your uncle these days?"

"He's good. Busy running *The River's Edge Gazette*."

"Which I understand you've been an integral part of these last few years."

Jocelyn's cheeks heated. "Yes. I received the People's Choice Award three times running for my community issues reports."

"Yes. I saw that. Your portfolio showed what excellent work you've produced. I was particularly moved by the human-element you so craftily wove into all your stories. Your uncle couldn't stop telling me what an asset you've been to the paper."

"Well, I was lucky for the opportunity."

"And we're lucky to have you here now." He pitched forward in his chair and slapped the desk open-palmed. "I'm guessing Dena's given you the grand tour and all the specifics."

Jocelyn nodded.

"Great." Mr. Wilbur smacked his palm again. "Robert Kaminsky is our senior editor and your immediate supervisor. He'll help you out with anything you need. Now go out there and get me a story. And make it interesting. I'm getting tired of sending out the same news stories every other paper in the world is printing. Get something fresh. Something new. Something insightful."

Jocelyn stood, feeling inspired. Fresh and insightful—that was her. "I'll get right on it."

"Good to hear, Miss Banks. I can tell you're going to be a great addition to this place." Mr. Wilbur gave her a wink and a nod as he dismissed her.

As Jocelyn returned to her cubicle, she passed Robert's office. The door was open, but no one was inside. It was just as well. She'd get her paperwork into HR and then track down her boss for her first assignment.

An hour later, as Jocelyn was signing the last of the new-hire paperwork, a short, thin man pulled up to her cubicle opening, pushing a silver wired cart. He didn't smile, and his small pinched face instantly reminded her of a tiny rat terrier. Whoever he was, she hoped she didn't have to work with him much.

"Hello." She smiled.

He returned the gesture, although Jocelyn would have called it more of a sneer than a smile. "Hello. Are you settling in?"

"Yes, thank you," she replied.

That sneer grew wider. "Good. Good." He pushed the wire cart through the opening. "I'm Robert Kaminsky."

"Oh." She immediately regretted the shock that must have registered in her eyes, because the sneer just turned to a full baring of his teeth. She tried to recover. "Nice to meet you."

"Since this is your first day," he said, not returning the pleasantry, "You can start by sorting the mail. We're running a little behind on it. Anything addressed to Mr. Wilbur comes through me first, so just add it to my stack, and then deliver it to each person's desk by the end of the day."

Jocelyn eyed the shopping cart full of envelopes and packages. Really, she was being given mailroom duties?

"But—" She snapped her jaw shut when Robert fixed her with a scowl as if he'd been waiting for her to challenge him.

"Great," he said, that sneer returning to his lips. "I'm also having Dena forward all the press releases we've received over the last month to your inbox. So look over those as well. And remember, we're only looking for big city news, not cutesy little stories like you did at that small paper of yours. Got it?"

"Got it."

"I can't tell you how great it is to finally have a little extra help around here."

His fakery was undeniable, but Jocelyn just smiled, refusing to let her new boss bait her. She'd play nice…for now.

Six

Luke waltzed into the office carrying a rose at a quarter till noon. He planned to stick around to get a few pats on the back for a job well done before taking lunch. A nice walk to the food carts sounded like a good idea on this glorious spring day, where the birds chirped louder and the sky was bluer than usual. Today, he'd become a hero in the eyes of thirteen women—probably even all of womankind—but he was trying not to let his ego get too big. It was just one win, but a very big win.

Maybe he'd see if Marcus wanted to forgo the healthy brown bag lunch he brought every day for a greasy burger, stacked with lettuce, tomato, and a mountain of onions.

Speaking of his brother, there he was leaning over Gretta's desk. Marcus straightened the moment Luke breezed in. "Where have you been?"

"I've been out celebrating with thirteen gracious women." Luke beamed. He'd done well today, and he wasn't afraid to flaunt it. He turned to Gretta and laid the long stem rose on her desk. "This is for you. For all your help."

The woman blushed and smiled as she picked up the flower, probably fighting to maintain the appearance she was on Marcus's disgruntled side. Luke had ingratiated himself to Gretta more than enough to have won a bit of loyalty. The last few weeks, with his paralegal still out on maternity leave, he'd charmed Gretta into donating some time to his cause. She'd spent several lunch hours researching names, addresses, phone numbers, and employment histories for his case.

He spun around to face Marcus again. "I just got not one, not two, but thirteen women to come forward in that sexual harassment case against the CEO at Prestige Bank, which supplied more than enough evidence for my client's case."

Dennis, Marcus's long-time associate, popped into their conversation. "How did you do that?" he asked, pushing up his glasses. "I mean get so many women to come forward."

Luke threw an arm around Dennis's shoulders. "Because women love me. They trust me. They talk to me."

At least most women did. His uptight neighbor who had spared barely a word for him this morning seemed immune to his charms. For the life of him, Luke couldn't figure her out. He'd feared he was losing his touch until he sat down to a celebratory brunch after the trial with the women who'd treated him like a god for speaking up against the injustices they'd suffered.

"If you'll excuse us," Marcus said with a nod to Dennis and Gretta. "It's time for my brother to earn the love and trust of another woman right now."

Luke was ushered to his office. Before he could sit down at his desk and settle in, Marcus threw a file on the desktop.

"Lottie Jones is none too pleased with the options you presented her this morning."

"What do you mean?" Luke slid into his chair and opened the file containing the list of properties he and Stacy had compiled for Lottie to consider. "She didn't like any of these choices?"

"Not a one. And when you couldn't be reached this morning, she was dialing *my* number, wondering why her lawyer didn't have the time of day for her."

Luke closed the file. "I was in court. Winning a big case. Do you know how long these women have waiting for this to go to trial? How emotionally taxing it has been for them? The difficulties they've experienced in finding other employment? This was important."

"You're right." Marcus's jaw clenched above the white collar of his lilac-colored shirt—an obvious selection from one of Emma's latest shopping trips. But the soft color was a big contrast to the deep red of his brother's face right now. Marcus took a deep breath, his voice calming. "You did a great job and I don't mean to minimize your efforts. But I need to know you're fully on board with your commitment to this deal with Lottie. From now on, I want it to be your only focus."

"But I have a child custody hearing next month and a meeting with a client about a possible housing discrimination case that need my attention."

"Pass them off to Dennis or Blair or Abigail."

"Yeah." Luke scoffed. "Abs will love that."

Marcus's face went hard again. "I don't care, and neither should you. This deal is to be your only concern right now, got it?"

"Do I ever." Luke wondered where his brother's changed disposition was coming from. It sounded like he was concerned about Luke's competency, just like everyone in his life.

"You claim women love you and are willing to talk to you. So why don't you call Lottie and find out exactly what she wants before you present another list. And get it right this time."

Marcus stormed out the door, ending a scene straight from the pages of Alfred Lewis's how-to-intimidate-the-staff playbook.

Luke shook his head, hoping this wasn't a permanent relapse into the unhappy man his brother used to be. These performances were a rarity, but every now and again—especially when his brother suffered sleep deprivation—the beast would come out. Luke wondered if Emma's pregnancy hormones were keeping her up at night. Knowing Marcus, he'd stay up with her and feed her ice cream or whatever new craving she'd been having and save the cantankerousness for the office.

Before Luke could open the file, Tippy came into his office, his limp more exaggerated than usual. A stack of papers fanned out of the side of his briefcase. Luke was about to mention them when Tippy blurted, "Talk of what you did is spreading like wildfire around the office."

"What I did?" Luke couldn't believe Marcus had let it slip that Lottie was already disappointed in his performance. He'd thought his brother had more discretion than that.

"With Prestige Bank." Tippy's eyes twinkled. "Your name will not soon be forgotten over there. You're making a real name for yourself. Good for you." Tippy tilted his chin before limping out the door.

Luke leaned back in his chair. *A real name for myself, huh?*

Lacing his fingers together, he pressed them to the back of his head. He was making a name for himself all on his own and didn't need the Jones deal to help him with that. Maybe a corner office with a view and the status of being a partner wasn't what he needed right now. *One change at a time, remember?*

Luke picked up the file. Marcus could have his precious deal back. He'd let his brother find someone else to play puppet for Lottie because he wasn't interested, and he was about to make that very clear. He was almost to Marcus's office when his brother's voice met him in the hall, and he stopped short.

"He hasn't screwed anything up yet."

"But you know he will." It was Xavier Poindexter. The man had remained as executive partner when Marcus was named managing partner last year, the decision leaving him bitter and disgruntled toward the Lewis brothers. "Now, let me in on this deal. You can't just let some associate sink it for the firm."

"Nothing is sinking, and I'm assisting as needed. There's nothing for you to worry about." Marcus's tone was even.

"Oh, I'm plenty worried, all right. Playing favorites with your little brother. It doesn't sit well with the other partners."

"Then he or she is welcome to come to me and express them personally." Luke didn't need eyes on his brother to see the intimidation radiating through his posture. He'd grown up with it, and every Lewis man had it in spades. Except him. Luke never was much of the intimidating type.

But Xavier didn't sound like he was backing down. "Well, I'm here, and I'm telling you now. I don't like it. Not one bit. You're putting a rookie into a game he doesn't know how to play, and he will strike out. Now, put me on as lead counsel. He can follow me around and actually learn a thing or two."

"Luke is more than capable of handling this assignment. He just got thirteen mistreated women to take a huge risk in speaking out against a man who made sexual advances at them in the workplace. That's something you or any other partner or associate in this office could have done. He's a damn good lawyer, and I have full confidence that he'll knock this deal out of the park. Now back off my brother and this deal. If I catch one whiff of your name coming anywhere close to Lot-Ti-Dots Enterprises, there'll be a very unfortunate case of reassignments going on in this office."

"Don't you dare try to threaten me." Intimidation punctuated Xavier's words.

"I don't make threats. I make promises. And I promise you, you have nothing to worry about."

Luke turned back to his office and glanced at the file in his hands. No one in his family had expressed that kind of confidence in him before. He'd stick with the deal. For his brother. And he would make sure Marcus never had to stand up for him again.

He sat in his chair, dialed the phone, and waited for an answer. "May I speak to Ms. Jones, please? This is Luke Lewis calling. Her attorney."

Seven

The office was quiet this morning. The tap-tap-tap of fingers flying over keyboards was the only sound floating above the cubicle walls. Most likely it was the sports editors, probably hurrying to meet another deadline. Sports coverage kept the small team of writers busy around the clock, unlike Jocelyn, who'd just completed another round of mail sorting. It had only been a few days, but Robert still kept her busy with menial tasks while he dished out the breaking news stories to every other junior editor on staff.

He'd humored her by stopping by her cubicle yesterday and asking her to research the current state of gas prices, saying there might be something worth reporting there. The day before, she'd practically begged him to let her out to interview the director of a youth organization that was planning a community service project. He'd reluctantly agreed, and both features were due tomorrow. She was determined to make them her very best work, hoping the stories would pop off the page.

The local youth organization was an incredible group that partnered some of the community's most at-risk teens with some of the city's most high-achieving students. This weekend they were organizing a park cleanup, and Jocelyn hoped her article would drum up some support from the community to join the young men and women. It was exactly the kind of story she wanted to write. The human element of the teens trying to turn their lives around shined through her words.

She read over the opening paragraph again. It still needed work, but she'd come back to it. The rest of the story flowed, and her quote from the director, Frank, was encouraging. The program was still young, but he boasted about how two-thirds of last year's graduating seniors had gone on to college. Jocelyn smiled to herself, remembering the pride she'd seen on his face.

Suddenly, the air in the room changed as Robert charged through, circling the cubicles. The clicking of keyboards stopped. The thunder in his steps was muted by the gray carpet underfoot, but his beady eyes were focused and intent.

"Where's Pearson?" he yelled from the other end of the room as he spun around. "Where's Knox?"

No one said a word, the answer obvious.

"I have a breaking news story and no one here to cover it! This is…"

Jocelyn stood. "I can cover it."

Robert blinked like he was seeing her for the first time in his life. "You, but…" He glanced around the office again. "Fine."

He darted over to her desk as the tapping of keys started up again.

"It's a protest." He slapped a piece of paper down on her desk. "Here's the address. Homeowner wants to cut down a hundred-year-old oak tree. Make sure you get the story, the whole story, and keep me informed as it unfolds."

Jocelyn gathered her things and picked up the address. "Okay," she said as she brushed past Robert.

Adrenaline pumped through her veins. A protest? She'd never covered a protest before. In River's Edge, nobody ever protested. There was the threat of a teacher strike a few years back, but that had ended before it started.

Jocelyn jogged down the stairs, at the same time struggling with her jacket. The morning rain had left it damp, and judging by the gray covered sky, she'd need it again. Once outside the door, she flipped up her collar and hailed a cab. Dropping into the backseat, she rattled off the address and sat back. Her first big story was about to break.

The cab pulled behind a news van, KNZZ 33 painted across the back doors. Lights flashed up ahead as a police cruiser turned onto the residential street. A small group of people spilled onto the roadway. As Jocelyn threaded her way through the thin crowd, she kept a lookout for the picketers, assuming they must be gathered on the other side. She pulled out her cell phone and readied the camera so she'd be sure to get a picture of the signs.

By the time she'd reached the center of the onlookers, where the other reporters were stationed, she still hadn't seen any picketers, nor had she heard any chanting. Everywhere she looked, people were just standing around. She followed their gaze—up to the branches of a tree. A gorgeous oak, full of green leaves, filled the sky. Its upper branches tapped the rooftop of the white cottage-style home boxed in by a white picket fence.

"What's the latest?" she asked a cameraman standing near her.

The man pulled away from the eyepiece for only a moment. "City showed up to cut this tree down and found a person up there."

"Any idea who it is?"

"Not yet." He repositioned his camera as a woman in a red pant suit came up to him.

"Just talked to the police. They're going to make a statement. Make sure you get in close." She glanced at Jocelyn.

"Jocelyn Banks, *The Portland Daily Report*," she said, holding out her hand.

The woman gave her a smirk before pushing her cameraman to the front of the crowd.

A police officer with a thin, dark mustache stepped away from the picket fence and positioned his hands on his utility belt. Jocelyn squinted through the drizzling rain and tried to get a good look at his name, but she was still too far away. She did her best to elbow her way to the front but was pushed back again and again. The officer was talking, but she couldn't make out his words. Finally, she ended up on the far side of the crowd. A woman in a bathrobe and slippers made room for her.

"Please clear the streets and return to your normal activities. This is a non-emergency, and we need to get our officers back to work."

"Officer Reyes," the red pant suit woman said. "Can you tell us this protester's name?" She thrust her microphone forward.

Officer Reyes looked up into the branches and then down at the sidewalk. "I have no comment on the identity of this person, and seeing as how no laws have been broken, we do not intend to further our investigation."

The woman next to Jocelyn let out a heavy breath as the reporter tipped her microphone back to her mouth. "So, what you're saying—"

Officer Reyes held up his hands as he stepped off the curb and started ushering people away from the scene. Other officers joined him, and Jocelyn took the opportunity to step in and snap a picture. She couldn't see much and hoped the camera had had better luck with capturing the image of the person in the tree. But the view screen showed her nothing more than a dark dot among the leaves.

"It's time to move along," an officer said, grasping her elbow.

"I'm going." Jocelyn shook her arm free as she tripped over the buckled sidewalk.

The officer caught her from taking a full tumble. "You have to watch where you're going," he said, none too compassionately.

She turned, about to give him a retort, when she saw Officer Reyes talking with the woman in the robe. Jocelyn's investigative radar perked up. "Thanks, I will," she said absently and dropped her phone in her pocket.

Stepping lightly over the broken pieces of sidewalk, she glanced up at the person in the tree. Nothing. She didn't pick up anything more than a glimpse of black pants and a black sweatshirt. Once she reached the other side of the property, she turned back. Officer Reyes was getting into his car, and the woman in the robe was being led away by another woman in a jogging suit. Together, they turned up the sidewalk of the neighboring house and went inside.

Jocelyn looked up at the tree again. The person's body was turned away from her, and it was smaller than she'd first noticed. Her phone buzzed inside her pocket, and she pulled it out. A text from Robert, asking for an update.

She replied, letting him know she was heading back to the office. The police had left and asked for the area to be cleared.

His reply returned quickly, telling her to stay put.

She was about to text back, asking why, when her phone rang.

"Hello?"

"Are there still protesters on the scene?" Robert barked at her.

"It's not really a protest." Jocelyn looked up at the tree's branches. "Just one person sitting in a tree."

"Is that person still in the tree?"

"Yes."

"Then, the story is not over. Don't come back here until you have something, got it?"

"Got it." Jocelyn dropped her phone in her pocket again.

She found a spot under the branches to shield herself from the rain.

The woman in the red pant suit paced along the sidewalk next to the news van. She was covered in a clear plastic poncho and talking into a cell phone. Probably trying to make the same case to her producer that Jocelyn had tried to make to Robert.

"Let's go. Pack it up," the woman shouted the moment she was off the phone. Her crew scrambled, quickly stowing their equipment in the news van. "The mayor just called a press conference to discuss the recent outbreak of gun violence in the city and his position on gun control. We've got to be across town in fifteen minutes."

Her excitement had gotten the attention of half the reporters on the block. Soon, only a handful of journalists remained on the street. By noon, it was down to Jocelyn and one other reporter—the man in black jeans and a leather jacket with a camera slung over his arm hadn't moved from his seat on the curb since she'd gotten there.

A delivery truck pulled up, and a man carried a box to the house. He rang the bell before returning to his truck. Jocelyn joined the other reporter. His position across from the house would give her a good vantage point to see if anyone retrieved the package.

She came out from under the cover of the trees and put her collar down, thankful the rains were finally taking a break. The man on the curb lit up a cigarette as she sat down beside him.

"Looks like we both got stuck on this story, doesn't it?" she said.

The guy puffed out a cloud of smoke.

"Jocelyn Banks, *The Daily Report*." She held out her hand, hoping he'd receive the friendly gesture.

Instead she got a face full of smoke as he turned in her direction. "Bob, *Portland Storm*."

She stifled the cough rising in her chest and held her breath until the smoke had cleared enough to let her breathe again. *The Storm*. She remembered scanning through the pages of that publication. She'd likened it to the local version of the tabloid magazines. Gossip, hearsay, and unflattering pictures that no other publication would print filled their pages.

"Bet you got some good shots with that camera." She pointed at the telephoto lens.

Bob grunted before he took another drag on his cigarette.

Not very talkative.

The women Jocelyn had seen go into the neighboring house came out now. The original jogging suit lady got in her car and pulled out of the driveway while robe and slipper lady—who'd traded her outfit in for a jogging suit, several sizes too big—waved goodbye. When the car was out of sight, the woman walked along to the picket fence and glanced up at the tree.

"Do you think she's a neighbor?" Jocelyn asked.

Bob gave an I-don't-know sounding grunt and blew out more smoke.

"Well," she said, tired of Bob from *The Storm* and his smoke puffing. "I've got to pee. Maybe she can help me out."

Jocelyn stood up and crossed the street. "Jocelyn Banks, *The Daily Report*." She held out her hand to the woman only to have it ignored for the third time that day. "I was hoping there was a restroom nearby that I could use."

The woman pulled her eyes off the tree. "Sorry, but no." She scowled at Jocelyn. "Why don't you go back to where you came from?"

"Trust me, I would, but my editor insists there's a story here, and I need to stay put until I get it."

"Of course. The media is nothing but a bunch of salivating dogs, looking for a story. Well, I'm sorry, but we're not going to be your story."

We? "Is this your tree?"

No answer.

"We all have a story. Take me, for instance. I was born in the back of a van in San Francisco. Think about how many different ways that story could be painted."

The woman gave her a wary look.

"I bet you're picturing a couple of long-haired irresponsible hippies, aren't you?"

The woman's face remained unreadable.

"Well, that's not who my parents are…were," she corrected. "But that's what most people first envision. I bet that's how this feels. Like people don't understand what's happening. So, how would you like your story painted?"

The woman dropped her head. "With truth."

"And what *is* the truth?"

The woman covered her mouth with her hand as a swell of tears lined the edges of her eyes.

"Do you know the person in your tree?" Jocelyn refrained from bringing out her notepad and voice recorder. She needed to get the woman talking.

"She's my daughter."

"Do you have any idea why she climbed up there?"

The woman nodded and then shook her head. "I might have an idea, but I can't say for sure. We don't exactly talk much anymore."

"How old is she?"

"Sixteen, last month." The woman's eyes traveled to the branches.

"I remember being sixteen." That got a tug from the woman's lips.

"Me too," she said wistfully. "But it's been different for Makenzie."

"How so?"

"We lost her father last year."

Jocelyn's heart ached. "I'm so sorry."

"And then her best friend committed suicide a few months back. And with each loss, the media coverage made it worse. Writing about how my husband had alcohol in his system at the time of the car accident that took his life, insinuating he was a drunkard driving his family home from dinner when he'd only had one glass of wine. And then the reporters came circling after her friend died because they'd been seen at school having an argument. Can you imagine how horrible that was for her to read about how she may have pushed Cassidy to end her life when that's not how it happened at all?"

Jocelyn refrained from agreeing. "What really happened?"

"They were arguing because her friend wanted to go see a movie after school, and we had a counseling session that same day. Makenzie was embarrassed and didn't want to tell Cassidy the reason." She wiped away a tear. "She won't go back to counseling now, and I hate to see how much she's hurting. I wish I knew what to do."

Jocelyn reached out. One person offering comfort to another. She wasn't supposed to let her emotions invade the story, but this hit a little too close to home. "I don't know if anyone else is going to write this incident up or not. Chances are they won't since nothing much happened. But, I'd still like to tell your story and Makenzie's if you'll let me. I'm not even sure if my editor would print it, but I'd like to make sure that someone hears the real story."

The woman's eyes glistened with more unshed tears. She glanced across the street at Bob, then back at Jocelyn. "Do you still need a restroom, or was that just a line?"

"Actually, I do."

"Then, please come inside. By the way, my name is Marilyn."

"It's nice to meet you." Jocelyn followed Marilyn into the house without a backward glance at Bob. She didn't want to give him the impression she was getting anything more than a trip to the restroom.

Marilyn directed her to a small guest bath on the main floor. When Jocelyn emerged, Marilyn was setting two cups on the table.

"Tea?" Marilyn asked.

"Yes, please." Jocelyn took a seat as Marilyn poured hot water over an English tea bag. The woman walked out of the room and returned shortly with a newspaper clipping, a crashed car pictured beneath the headline.

Jocelyn read the article. It sounded exactly as Marilyn had said, like her husband had been irresponsibly drinking before driving his family home. It was the power of the press, with or without intention readers could be led down a speculative path, and sometimes that path was't always filled with truth.

"It's my fault," Marilyn said as Jocelyn finished reading.

"What do you mean?"

"Today. Turning this into a bigger deal than it is."

Jocelyn pulled her phone out. "Do you mind if I record this?"

Marilyn shook her head.

"Go on."

"Makenzie knew the tree was scheduled to be cut down today. The city's been after me to take care of it. It's too close to the house now, and the roots are making a mess of the sidewalk and street. They finally said I had to have it taken care of, or they would fine me. So, we set a date. I didn't know it would bother her. When I woke up this morning, I couldn't find her. She wasn't in her room. That's when I called Officer Reyes. He was a friend of my husband's for years, and he's been helping out with Makenzie as much as he can. He showed up right after the city workers, and that's when I found out Makenzie was in the tree. And then, I don't know what happened. News vehicles and more officers started showing up."

"Have you been able to talk to her at all?"

Marilyn shook her head. "I didn't want to draw any attention to her with all the media around."

Jocelyn thought for a moment. "There's a window on the back corner of the house. Do you think she could talk to us through there?"

"I don't know. Maybe." Marilyn led the way up the narrow staircase, her hand running along the worn wooden railing. She pushed through a door to a room strewn with clothing and a Justin Bieber poster on the wall. On a shelf was a picture of a little girl—Makenzie when she was small—dolled up in a dance outfit and tap shoes. Another frame was next to it. Makenzie was older and dressed in a sparkly red gown. She was on the arm of a man who Jocelyn assumed was her father. *Daddy Daughter Dance*, was on a banner behind them.

After an hour of talking through the window with Makenzie and her mother, Jocelyn had the story of a young woman's need to say goodbye before losing one more piece of her childhood. The tree had housed a swing her father used to push her on, and she and her friend Cassidy had spent many afternoons picnicking beneath the shade of its branches when they were younger. All she'd wanted was a little time to say goodbye before the city had to chop it down.

"Will you come down now?" Jocelyn asked.

"Not until all the reporters are gone," Makenzie said.

Jocelyn looked across the street to where Bob still sat, puffing away on another cigarette.

"Okay, I'll call for a cab and leave. Maybe you can call Officer Reyes and have him remove Bob over there or at least distract him, so you can climb down."

Makenzie nodded, her brown eyes glistening. "I'm real sorry Mom. The city will fine us now, won't they? I didn't mean for all this to happen."

"I know you didn't," her mother said. "And it's okay. I don't care about the city fining us. I care about you."

Tears were in all their eyes as Jocelyn said goodbye and watched for her cab to arrive. When it did, she threw a look in Bob's direction, but he didn't return it.

As soon as the cab pulled away, she sent a message to Robert, informing him she was on her way back and she'd gotten the facts. Then she let her mind start to piece together the words she would use to tell Makenzie's story.

Back at the office, everyone was busy with the mayor's press conference and the five car pileup on the interstate that happened less than an hour ago. No one noticed Jocelyn as she sat at her desk, typing out the story of Makenzie—the girl in the tree.

Jocelyn packed up her things, ready to sneak home. She'd almost finished her stories on the recent increase in gas prices and the community organization—something she could easily complete from the comfort of her couch this evening—when Robert popped his head into her cubicle.

"I thought you said you got the story on the tree." He yelled so loud, it silenced the rest of the newsroom.

"I did. I just submitted it—"

"Then why is there a picture circulating right now of the person falling from the tree. *The Storm* is the only one that got that photo. You didn't get it." Robert's whole face turned a fiery red. "Pearson," he yelled across the room. "Get to the hospital, and get me a full report on this protester." Robert turned back to Jocelyn, his lip curling. "You better hope this person doesn't die, because it will be on you for not getting the story."

He turned away, stomping back to his office when she stepped out of her cubicle. "I hope she doesn't die," she called to his back, "because she's a person. Someone's daughter. Someone's child. And you would know all of that if you read the story I submitted."

Robert stopped in his tracks and slowly turned back to face Jocelyn, fixing her with a glare. The silence that had fallen over the newsroom grew infinitely louder. His mouth moved like he was chewing on his next words when he glanced around the room. He must have realized all eyes were on them. "Get back to work," he shouted before stalking back to his office.

Jocelyn left, stopping by the hospital on her way home. Reporters swarmed the front conference room. Pearson, with his shiny bald head downcast, sat at a table, tapping on his phone.

"They're not letting anyone in," he said as she walked by, but she ignored him.

Officer Reyes was stationed at the door. He held up his hands when Jocelyn approached.

"Hello, Officer. I'm Jocelyn Banks from *The Daily Report*."

"I'm sorry, ma'am. The family asks for privacy right now."

"I understand." Jocelyn lowered her voice. "I was with Makenzie and her mother this afternoon. I know what a huge support you've been to them. All I want to know is if Makenzie is okay. Off the record."

The officer's eyes softened. "She is. No life-threatening injuries."

Jocelyn let out a sigh of relief. "Thank goodness. When you see them next, please tell them I'm thinking of them."

"Will do." The officer nodded gruffly before raising his voice. "Now get out of here, and take a few of your friends with you."

* * *

Jocelyn quietly slipped into the office the next morning. What a week. She was almost grateful for her low-status position on Robert's list. It meant she wouldn't be spending the weekend chasing after the stories he thought the readership craved.

Last night, she'd refused to listen to the news or look at the headlines. The media surely would have had a heyday with Makenzie's story, and she couldn't bear to hear it.

Today, she was determined to keep a low profile. Robert's door was closed, and she scurried by it quickly, afraid he might catch a whiff of her as she passed and open the door to sink his teeth into her pride again. Keeping her head down, she sat at her desk and hurried to appear busy with email. Her mind had been too occupied with Marilyn and Makenzie last night to finish her features. They only needed one more read through, but still, she couldn't focus.

"Impromptu staff meeting," Dena's high pitched voice yipped as she walked through the aisles of cubicles. "In the conference room. Jerry's on his way. Let's go, people."

Jocelyn hung back and followed the last of the staff into the room. Robert sat near the front, twisting a pen between his fingers. She didn't need to look at him to know he was still scowling at her. As everyone got seated, Jerry came into the room, a stack of newspapers in his arms.

"Good morning," he boomed, dropping papers in front of everyone on the opposite side of the table from Jocelyn. "Here," he said when he got to the front, handing over the rest of the stack to Dena. "Finish passing these out. One for everyone. This is a great news day."

Jocelyn looked down at the front-page headline as Dena handed her a paper. *Girl in the Tree*. It was her headline but not her picture. Makenzie was free falling from the branches.

Jerry held up the pages. "*The Storm* may have gotten the picture, but *The Daily Report* got the story. No one else had these words. And now the whole rest of the city is reporting our news."

Jocelyn slowly started to read the lines. These were her words. This was her story. Her eyes quickly plowed through the rest of the article.

"This is the kind of groundbreaking stuff people want to see. Heartfelt, real stories."

Jocelyn beamed.

"Great job, Pearson. I don't know how you did it. Covering this and the mayor's press conference all in one day, but this is the kind of story we want more of."

Pearson?

That's when she noticed the name in bold lettering under her headline read Abe Pearson, not Jocelyn Banks.

Her face must have registered the shock, because Robert was smirking at her.

Jerry clapped his hands together. "That's it folks. Just wanted to say great work and keep it up." Jerry left the room, and so did the rest of the staff, Pearson avoiding eye contact with her as he passed by.

"Why is Abe's name on my story?" she asked Robert, blocking his exit.

The little man reattached his flimsy smirk. "Because he finished the story when you didn't. So, I gave him the credit."

Jocelyn found the two inches of print Pearson had added right above her closing paragraph about how Makenzie fell from the tree and escaped with nothing more than a sprained ankle and a bruised rib. Robert pushed past her and left without another word.

All day, Jocelyn tried to let go of her anger. If this was how the big dogs played, then she wanted to be let out of the yard. Taking credit for someone else's work was malicious and unethical. She rubbed her temples and tried to refocus on her articles.

"Let's go, Banks. I needed that story yesterday." Robert snapped his fingers as he stopped in front of her cubicle.

Perfect, like him staring down his pointy little nose at her was going to help her focus. She didn't like this passive aggressive type of authority he seemed to think he had over her. What had she ever done to him? He'd ripped her story right out from under her, and she wasn't about to forget it. She reread the closing paragraph of her story on the recent hike in gas prices. It was completely uninspiring jargon, but it was news. And so she hit submit.

At least the piece she'd carefully prepared about the youth organization and their community clean-up was stronger.

The piece would be buried on page five, but Jocelyn hoped enough people made their way that far into the paper to learn about the work of the organization that also spent time volunteering at the Senior Center. It was a far more moving story about the good things that go on around the city than all the dreadful accounts of murder and mayhem.

"Get that article submitted, or neither of your stories will make it to print for tomorrow. Got it?" he shouted loud enough for every person in the newsroom to hear. "Pearson, there's a house fire on the northeast side. Get there, and get the story. We may need it to fill Banks's columns."

The extreme effort everyone was making to avoid eye contact with her made it obvious how much no one envied her at the moment.

Tears bubbled to the surface as she reread the last line, hit submit, and closed down her computer. The work week was finally over.

Jocelyn walked home beneath a gray and drizzly sky, the perfect combination to match her melancholy. This new job wasn't shaping up to be anything like what she'd expected. Turning into her building, she tried to leave her work behind as she caught the elevator. The moment the doors opened, garlic and butter filled her senses. And it smelled so darn good.

Letting her nose guide her, she ended up at her neighbor's door. So the good-looking workout maniac had a taste for fine Italian cuisine, did he? Jocelyn thought about the block of tofu and bean sprouts in her refrigerator. The small bag of provisions she'd purchased for the week were gone now, leaving only Fiona's leftovers in the kitchen. Whatever was behind this door would taste so much better. If only she'd made friends with him when she'd had the chance, then she wouldn't be standing here fantasizing about butter and garlic and noodles. There definitely had to be noodles. And bread! Surely there was bread with melted butter settling into the crevices of the white fluffy bread…

A woman's moan lanced through the door, cutting her out of her daydream.

"Oh Luke, you outdid yourself tonight. The fettuccine was amazing."

"If you thought that was good," the unmistakable smooth tone of her neighbor replied. "Just wait until you see what I have in store for dessert."

Jocelyn was jolted back to reality, the image of her neighbor entertaining a gorgeous woman with his interpretation of dessert squelching her appetite.

Eight

Luke watched Emma lean back and rub her belly. It was hard to believe that in less than three months' time, he'd be an uncle again. Marcus watched his wife too, every ounce of love he had for her evidenced in that one simple gaze.

"So what *is* for desert?" his nephew, Brayden, asked.

"Well, it just so happens that I have a chocolate cream pie in the fridge."

"Oh, Luke." Emma moaned, still rubbing her belly. "Fettuccine Alfredo and now chocolate cream pie. You sure know how to worm your way into this girl's good graces."

"You've always been easy," he said with a wink. "If you weren't, you'd have held out for someone better than this old man for a husband." He nudged Marcus with his elbow.

Marcus reached for his wife's hand. "I'm not that old."

Emma giggled as Marcus kissed her fingers.

Luke pushed back the pang of jealousy that always seemed to surface when he saw his brother and sister-in-law so in love. "How can you live with this?" he asked Brayden. "All this smooching. All the time."

His nephew shrugged as he folded his hands on the table.

Emma tore her eyes away from her husband. "How about some of that pie?"

Luke stacked their plates and went to the kitchen. As he passed the window, his eyes were involuntarily drawn to the window across the way. It was the same window he'd been glancing at all week. A thin line of light traced the outer edge of his neighbor's curtains, and he yearned for a glimpse of her. All week, he'd tried to intercept her, hoping to cross paths again, but it hadn't happened. And he couldn't explain it to anyone—not even to Dr. Pike when he'd finally returned the doctor's calls for a quick check in—why his mysterious neighbor had him so captivated.

"Let me help you." Marcus followed with the serving bowl and bread basket.

"Make him give you the recipe," Emma called, clasping her hands on the underside of her belly. "I have to know how he made that sauce."

Just then, a cell phone rang, a high tinkling sound.

"That's Audrey." Emma moved from the table to catch her sister's call. "Do you mind if I take it? We've been playing phone tag all day."

"Of course not."

She hurried to her purse on the couch, the very beginnings of a pregnant waddle in her steps. Emma put the phone to her ear and found some privacy in the corner of the living room to talk to her sister.

"So this is your big secret to tonight's meal."

Luke turned around to find Marcus staring into the garbage can, the inside lined with to-go boxes.

His brother looked up. "And here I'd thought you said you could cook."

"Yeah, well, I tried." Luke pointed to a pot in the sink, and Marcus lifted the lid. A mass of thick mushy noodles sat in less than an inch of water.

Marcus pulled one out, pinching it between his fingers. It disintegrated, falling back into the pot. "What was this supposed to be?"

He knew his brother was trying to contain his laughter.

Luke pulled the pie out of the refrigerator and set it on the counter. "They were supposed to be homemade fettuccini noodles."

"For who? A giant? These are huge."

"Yeah, I know." Luke flipped the pot over, dumping all the noodles into the garbage disposal.

Marcus cleared his throat. "Hey, I'm sorry. I wasn't trying to make fun. You made a solid effort, and I appreciate that." His brother cleared his throat again but couldn't contain the laughter that boiled over this time. "I'm just sorry it went so terribly wrong."

"Yeah, laugh all you want. But your wife loved my takeout. So it looks like I know how to do at least one thing right."

"You're right. She did love it. And it's not our fault we don't contain a genetic predisposition for sound culinary skills." Marcus tossed the used napkins into the garbage and let the lid close. "Although, I am pleased to announce that I'm perfecting the peanut butter and pickle sandwich Emma's been craving at half past midnight every day this week."

Brayden joined them, climbing up on a bar stool. "That's so disgusting."

"I'm with you, little man." Luke pulled a takeout menu from a drawer. "Here's my secret recipe. It may come in handy after the baby is born, when she's not craving peanut butter and pickles."

"Thanks." Marcus folded the paper and shoved it in his pocket as Emma's voice went quiet. She crossed the apartment and joined them, sitting next to Brayden.

"I have bad news," she said.

"What is it?" Concern weighed heavily on Marcus's words.

"Audrey's in-laws are coming over from Ireland to surprise them with a visit next week."

"Doesn't sound like much of a surprise anymore," Luke said.

Emma smiled. "It was a surprise to Audrey to learn this today. And…" She looked to Marcus. "They're staying for a month."

"Oh." Marcus's eyebrows arched like something had just registered. "Oh!"

"Yeah." Emma nodded. "So, I don't think I'll be going to Florida with you for the conference."

"Why not?" Luke asked.

"Because Brayden was going to stay with Audrey while we were gone. Now, with her in-laws—and I'm not talking about just Finn's mom and dad, but his extended family too, which means there'll be thirteen additional guests in her home—it's too much to ask her to watch Brayden too."

Marcus reached across the countertop and grasped his wife's hand. "It'll be okay. We'll figure something out. Maybe he can come with us."

Emma shook her head and ran a hand over Brayden's hair. "No. I don't want him to miss that much school."

"I'll call Mother. Perhaps, she'd be able to stay with him."

Twin pairs of horror-struck eyes landed on Marcus. Alfred and Margret Lewis were not the doting type of grandparents. Leaving Brayden alone with them for a full week would likely be torture for the little boy. Nor could Luke imagine Emma being comfortable leaving Margaret alone in her house.

Mother had never graciously received Emma, not even after she and Marcus were married. And things between them became worse when Emma encouraged Mother's live-in housekeeper, Maricella, to branch out and start her own bakery. An endeavor that had become so successful, her husband Guillermo, who'd been the gardener and Father's driver, left to work for his wife. Now, Alfred had to use a car service, and the new hire, Hettie, who cooked for his parents, wouldn't touch the housecleaning outside of the kitchen. When Margaret Lewis told the story, it was that Emma had ruined their existence the day she met Marcus and Brayden. Personally, Luke had his own version of the story.

"Um, yeah, no…that…" Emma, who never uttered an unkind word about anyone, struggled to finish her statement.

But Brayden's rapid head shaking seemed to do the talking for her.

"What about *your* parents?" Marcus asked.

Emma shook her head again. "Dad's still recovering from shoulder surgery, and neither one of them likes to drive in the city. I'm afraid Brayden would never make it to school."

"That'd be okay with me." Brayden smiled.

"If only you knew someone who lived close by." Luke slid another piece of pie onto a plate and passed it to Brayden. "Someone who's unattached, so Brayden would get all of their attention."

Marcus's eyes twinkled. "Yes, if only. But really, I don't think Stacy would be up for it."

"No," Brayden wailed. "Not Aunt Stacy. She still doesn't even know my name. She calls me B."

"No, you're right," Luke agreed, slicing another piece of pie. "Stacy wouldn't do at all. It would have to be someone who's incredibly responsible."

"That would be a must." Marcus dipped his fork into the piece of pie Luke served him.

Luke continued. "And smart. And fun."

Marcus chuckled. "Yes, if only someone that perfect did exist."

"And witty. And charming. And good looking."

Marcus looked across at his wife, eyes hopeful, before turning back to Luke. "What do your good looks have to do with you being a qualified babysitter?"

Luke broke into a giant grim. "So you *do* think I'm good looking. I was just checking."

Emma folded her hands. "That's very thoughtful of you, but we couldn't ask—"

"Then don't ask. Let me offer. I'd love to hang with my nephew for a week. It'd be fun. Right, Bray?"

"Yeah!" Brayden bounced in his chair.

Luke cut into the pie, pulling out the fourth and final piece. "I've already shown you I can pull off a well-balanced family meal, haven't I?"

"Yes, but he'll also have homework every night," Emma said.

"Smart." Luke pointed to himself. "Remember? I've got it covered." He feigned a worried look. "Unless they've got you working the quadratic equation?" he asked Brayden. "I never did figure that out."

His nephew looked up, completely puzzled.

"Of course not." Emma laughed. "They've just started learning their multiplication facts."

"Then we're good."

"The commute to his school can get pretty long if you don't leave our house early enough." The trepidation in Emma's voice was palpable.

"What if Brayden stayed here?" Marcus offered. "That way the school is a lot closer."

Emma's mouth dropped open, but she didn't have a quick rebuttal.

Marcus turned his attention to Luke. "Emma can make arrangements for him stay at the after-school program that week, but you'd have to make sure to leave work by twenty to six to give yourself plenty of time to pick him up. Would that be a problem for you?"

"Not at all." Luke took a bite of pie.

Marcus smiled. "I didn't think so. By the way, what time did you clock out this afternoon?"

Luke licked a smear of chocolate off his hand. "When did we start clocking in and out? I must've missed that memo."

"It's an expression. And you know what I mean. Don't get too wrapped up in other things and forget about him, okay?" Marcus lowered his voice. "He needs consistency."

Luke sobered. "I promise. Brayden will be my top priority."

"Where will he sleep?" Emma asked, glancing around the apartment.

"Let me worry about that, okay?" He winked at her. "Brayden, you like camping, don't you?"

Brayden lifted a shoulder.

For the next few moments, it was quiet as they finished eating.

"That was delicious." Emma pushed her plate away. "Now, if you'll excuse me. I need to walk."

Emma circled the couch before making her way to the bathroom.

"Thank you," Marcus said.

"For what?"

"For offering to watch Brayden for us." He ruffled his son's hair as Brayden hopped out of his seat. "I know she's been looking forward to getting away and relaxing before the baby comes."

"I think you're the one who's been looking forward to it." Luke teased.

"You're right. I have. Life as we know it is about to change in a big way very soon, and I won't deny wanting to spend a little time alone with my wife before it does."

Luke clapped his brother on the arm. "And I can understand why."

He glanced at the digits on his clock when Emma came back into the living room. "You two better go. They don't hold the curtain for anyone." He held open Emma's jacket, and she slipped her arms inside. "Not even beautiful mothers-to-be."

"You're a good, kind man, Luke Lewis," Emma said, laying a hand on his chest. "We're lucky to have you in our lives."

But he was the lucky one.

Brayden ran over to kiss his parents goodbye and then, before the door had closed, he dragged Luke back to the table where he'd been setting up a board game.

"What are we playing?"

"Monopoly." Brayden sorted his money and tucked the edges of the color coordinated piles under the board.

"I hope you're not as good at this game as your dad was when we were kids. He always beat me."

"I'm better," Brayden said with a twinkle in his eye.

Nine

Jocelyn passed by many beggars with open hands and bodies sleeping in doorways as she headed for the historic Old Town district. She hustled across the street against the red light, more interested in reaching her destination than obeying street crossing laws. The sidewalk population had quickly changed, and she didn't like the discomfort that walked alongside her.

A group of men across the street in an open parking lot stopped their basketball game. Jocelyn felt every one of their eyes on her as she passed, uneasiness gripping her. This was nothing like River's Edge. She was used to recognizing every face she passed on the streets, not shrinking away from the lingering gazes of strangers. Turning the corner, she reached the four-story brick building she'd set out for.

Each step she climbed was occupied by a person covered in layers of clothing. The winter may have been over, but the mornings still served up chilly temperatures. Most of the people waiting were men, a few women, and many of them puffed out clouds of smoke, creating a haze for her to walk through. A sweet smoky aroma—definitely not from normal, everyday cigarettes—mixed with a foul stench beneath the covered entrance.

A man stepped out of the shadows as she neared the door. The hood of his sweatshirt was pulled low, obscuring his eyes. "Where do you think you're going?" he asked, standing in her path. "Line's that way."

"I'm here to serve." She was thankful her voice didn't sound as terrified as she felt, being confronted like this.

"Oh, I think there's only one good way for you to serve me this morning." He yanked on his pants as if he were adjusting his belt, but he was clearly insinuating something else.

Low-toned voices chuckled around her, and she realized she was surrounded by men. The door was within her reach, but when she grabbed for it and pulled, it didn't move. Her face must have gone panic struck, which only incited more non-comical laughs from the men around her.

"Like I said." The man sauntered toward her. "There's only one kind of service I need you to provide me."

The unhealthy swell to the man's gums and the rancid smell of his breath caused her to step back. She bumped into something solid or rather someone.

"Leave the girl alone." The voice was hoarse and gravelly.

"Oh yeah?" The man with the hoodie jerked up his chin. "What's it to you, Sarge? I bet you could use a little time with a lady too. How long's it been?"

A giant, bear-paw sized hand reached around her and stopped the other man's advance. The man she'd backed into quickly stepped between her and the other man. "I said stand down, soldier."

"I ain't your soldier, old man."

Sarge seemed to grow five inches right before her eyes. "You will obey an order from your commanding officer, or people will die."

"Ain't nobody gonna die. Jus' havin'—"

The giant hand moved to the man's throat, his hoodie falling back. Terror filled his eyes.

"What's going on up here?" Another man hustled up the steps, a basketball tucked under his arm. The backpack he wore fell to the ground as he intervened. "Sarge! It's okay, Sarge. Let go."

As if a trance had been broken, Sarge released his hold and shrank back to a hunched shell. Sarge shuffled behind her and slid to the ground, pulling his army green jacket around him.

The other man gulped air back into his lungs.

"You okay, Vic?" the guy with the basketball asked, but Vic just swatted him away and went back to his place in line.

"And what about you?" The guy turned to Jocelyn. "You okay?"

She looked back at Sarge, hunkered against the brick building, and nodded.

"I'm Eric." He offered a hand. "You must be new around here."

"I am." She took his hand. "I came to help serve, but the door's locked."

"All the volunteers enter through the back door. Come on. I'll show you." He hoisted his backpack to his shoulder and walked down the stairs.

Jocelyn was glad to follow Eric away from the line of men watching her. Down the side of the building, Eric banged on a brown metal door with KITCHEN stenciled on it in black paint.

*Brown door on the alley side of the building...*those words quickly came to her from the last email she'd received. Jocelyn had assumed she'd find the door inside, not outside. If only...

"Who's that knocking on my door?" a woman's voice called from inside.

"That's Miss Annie." Eric smiled.

Miss Annie. Jocelyn relaxed at the mention of the woman she'd corresponded with via email.

The door flew open, revealing a plump woman with a face that lit up like the sun as she smiled. "Oh, it's you."

"I brought you a new volunteer," Eric said.

"You must be Jocelyn." Miss Annie motioned them inside.

"Yes. I'm sorry I'm late. I guess I got a little confused about where the door was."

"Uh, oh. What happened?" Miss Annie's sunny features turned dark.

Heat rose in Jocelyn's cheeks, her embarrassment stoking the fire.

Eric filled in the details, saving Jocelyn from having to recount her run in. "Looks like Vic was trying to give her an unwelcomed greeting. But Sarge stepped in before I got there."

Miss Annie folded her arms and raised her brows. "Sarge stepped in, you say?"

"Caught him with a vice grip around Vic's throat."

"Oh dear." Miss Annie tsked. "Is everyone okay?"

Eric nodded. "I think so. I'll head back and check on them now, but I wanted to make sure your new help got back here without any more trouble."

"Well, thank you kindly." Miss Annie ushered Jocelyn into the kitchen. "We'll see you soon," she called over her shoulder as Eric stepped back outside.

Sausage sizzled from a pan, bringing Jocelyn back to her childhood and the Sunday morning breakfasts her mother used to serve. A handful of people bustled around the counter space.

"Here, you'll need one of these." Miss Annie pulled an apron from a hook.

Jocelyn traded her coat for the white cover up, tying it at her waist.

"Sorry to hear you had some trouble this morning. Next time, have your cab driver drop you right here at the back door."

"Thanks, I'll do that." Jocelyn kept it to herself that she'd walked the whole way. But she would certainly enlist a taxi for her next trip to the kitchen.

"All right. Well, this is everybody. Everybody, this is Jocelyn. Introduce yourselves when you can, but we're scheduled to serve in ten minutes and don't have one single pancake on the heat." Miss Annie turned to Jocelyn. "You ever flipped a flapjack?"

"Yes, I have."

"Perfect, then that's your job for today." Miss Annie handed her a pancake turner. "Your griddle is over there next to Isaiah. He'll show you how to turn it on. I'm going to go finish setting up the tables."

By the time Jocelyn pulled her first batch of pancakes off the griddle, Miss Annie had returned with a long line of people following behind her.

"It's service time. Let's show these good people what we've got for them this morning."

As Jocelyn started pouring the second batch, she heard Miss Annie's tone go angular. "I hear you were messing with my help this morning, Vic."

"I's jus' playin' wit her." Vic's wicked tone sent prickles up Jocelyn's spine.

"You ever do that again to my help or any other guest and you'll be getting your meals somewhere else, you got me?"

Jocelyn kept her hands busy at her station, trying her best to ignore the chilly stare boring into the back of her head. She didn't want to cause trouble, but she also didn't want to stand in fear of the people she served.

"Yeah, I gotchu," Vic said, and Jocelyn let out the breath she'd been holding.

The line seemed to start moving again, and Jocelyn flipped and poured more pancakes. When the last plate was served, and Jocelyn's batter bowl was empty, Miss Annie sent her to circulate the tables, offering seconds.

Miss Annie leaned in as she handed Jocelyn a tray. "Be sure to smile and take the time to say, 'how you doing?' okay?"

Jocelyn nodded and started on one side of the big room. Her first stop was a table with a woman and four kids, their ages ranging from infant to preteen.

"Did everyone get enough to eat?" she asked as she balanced her tray on the edge of the table.

"Yes, we did," the woman answered for all of them.

"Can I get anyone a second helping?"

All the eyes turned to the woman, who, upon second inspection, looked easily a decade younger than Jocelyn herself.

"No. We're fine."

One little girl looked up at Jocelyn. She held a unicorn in her hands.

Jocelyn knelt beside her. "My name's Jocelyn. What's your name?"

The little girl didn't answer, only stared through a tangle of unkempt hair.

"She don't talk much," the woman said for the girl.

"That's okay. I didn't like to talk much when I was a kid either. I loved unicorns though. Do you love unicorns?"

The girl nodded.

"I thought as much. Looks like we have a lot in common."

The girl's eyes brightened, and she held up her unicorn.

"Really?" Jocelyn tried to act surprised. "You're going to let me hold him?"

The girl nodded.

Jocelyn pushed the tray onto the table and took the animal, whose white fur had turned gray and was speckled with stains, the smell musty and unclean. All the other children at the table watched her as she held the toy.

"Her name Rainbow," the girl said in a voice fit for a mouse, small and quiet.

"Rainbow? Well, that's the perfect name for such a special friend. Thank you for sharing it with me." Jocelyn passed the unicorn back to her.

The girl smiled at her mother and then back at Jocelyn. Moving on to the next table, Jocelyn unloaded a second helping of pancakes, sausage, and eggs to a seemingly mute pair of men. Neither of them looked up or replied to her questions about their meal before she moved on. For the next several minutes, she replenished plates until her tray was empty. Turning toward the kitchen, she bumped into Vic, his posse crowding around him and blocking her path.

Vic grinned, stained enamel sandwiched between his dry, cracked lips. He held his breakfast plate and cup. "Looks like you can't stay away from me," he said.

She gasped and stepped back.

He matched her paces, maintaining his proximity to her.

Miss Annie appeared out of nowhere and wedged her way between them, planting her fists on her hips. "Now, I warned you."

"I didn't do nuthin'." Vic ticked his head toward Jocelyn. "She ran into me."

"The proper response to a lady would be *excuse me* or *pardon me*."

"She ain't no lady."

Rubber scraped against the tile floor, and out of the corner of her eye Jocelyn saw movement, but she didn't dare take her eyes off Vic.

Miss Annie stood her ground, acting unfazed. "Apologize. Or leave."

Vic snickered, throwing a glance over his shoulder at his followers and raised his cup and plate. "Fine," he said, dropping them on the floor. His followers did the same. The clattering of silverware and plastic plates disrupted the quiet air before the men turned to leave. Their disrespectful cackling followed them out the door.

"Isaiah," Annie called. "Bring me the mop."

"I'm so sorry." Jocelyn squatted, using the rag she'd hung from her apron strings to sop up the juice puddling on the floor.

"It's not your fault," Miss Annie muttered. "He's an angry young man who's seen very little kindness in this world."

"But still, if it wasn't—"

"Hush now. Don't give him another thought."

Isaiah pushed the mop bucket next to Miss Annie. "Finish delivering seconds. We'll take care of this."

"Are you sure?"

"Yes."

Jocelyn returned to the kitchen and brought out the last of the food, making her rounds again. Eric made eye contact with her, and she twined her way through the tables to the back, where he shared a table with Sarge.

"Can I get you guys anything else?" she asked, looking down at the solitary pancake and scraps of eggs she had left.

"No thank you," Eric said. "Are you okay? After Vic…"

She nodded, but her hands shook as she eased the tray onto the table.

"Why don't you sit down?" Eric moved over to the next seat, and Jocelyn took his place across from Sarge.

"Thanks for helping me earlier." She directed her appreciation at both of them but was unsure if Sarge heard. His gaze never moved from the coffee in his mug.

Eric looked over his shoulder. "I'm just sorry Vic was a problem at all. Hopefully he won't be coming back."

Sarge remained still and quiet in his seat, his hands cupped around his mug.

"Thank you also, Sarge." She put a hand on the sleeve of his faded green jacket.

Sarge flinched, his hand knocking into his coffee cup and making it splatter.

"I'm so sorry." Jocelyn pulled her hand back as if she'd been scorched by a fire. "Let me get that." She used a stray napkin to wipe the table, careful not to touch Sarge this time. "I'm sorry," she said again.

"Are you okay, Sarge?" Eric asked.

The man nodded.

"He prefers to keep his distance from others. Don't you, Sarge?"

The other man grunted an affirmative.

"I'm sorry." Jocelyn didn't know if she could ever apologize enough. "It won't happen again, I promise."

Sarge looked up briefly. Gray whiskers covered a weather-worn face, and he nodded, finally flooding Jocelyn with a sense that she'd been forgiven.

Just then, the little girl with the unicorn came running over. She looked uneasily at Eric and Sarge before focusing on Jocelyn.

"I'm Teya," she said just above a whisper.

"Nice to meet you, Teya," Jocelyn said just as quietly, and with that, the little girl turned and rushed back to the table she had come from.

"Looks like you just made a new friend," Eric said.

"I guess so."

"Wish I could stick around." He stood and slipped his backpack straps over his shoulders. "But, I've got to get to work."

"Oh," Jocelyn said before she could cover up the surprise in her voice.

"You sound shocked."

"Yeah. No. I just thought…"

"You thought because I ate the food, it meant I didn't have any means to pay for it."

"Well, something like that, I guess." Jocelyn's voice softened. "Sorry."

"It's okay. And I'd probably think the same thing. Truth is, even with my job, I still have a hard time making ends meet with three kids at home and both my wife and I in school. Taking my meals here means there's more at home for my children. I help out in the kitchen when I can, but it hasn't been easy for my family the last few years. Lots of the folks here are trying to make ends meet by taking Miss Annie up on her generosity to feed all."

"I didn't realize." She stood and picked up her tray.

"That's okay. Not many people do." Eric pointed. "Take Lisette over there."

Jocelyn noticed a plump woman captivating her table with animated gestures.

"She's a cashier at the convenience store. Single mom of two boys. Her mother is on disability right now and stays home with the kids most of the time, but those checks are about to stop coming, and she's not sure how she's going to keep paying the rent."

"What about them?" Jocelyn gestured toward Teya's table.

"Not sure. Today's the first day I've seen them."

They stood in silence for a moment.

"And there's Jimbo and Sally. She was in a terrible car accident two years ago. When the insurance ran out, they had to sell their house. Jimbo was laid off from his job shortly after all that. Sally couldn't return to work, and the medical bills were too much. He works from home now doing telemarketing or something like that, but it's just enough to keep them afloat, especially with four kids in college."

"Wow." Jocelyn scanned the faces in the room. "So many stories."

"That's for sure." Eric picked up his plate and stashed his utensils in his empty cup. "I'll see you later, Sarge. Stay out of trouble, okay?"

Sarge nodded.

Jocelyn followed Eric back to the kitchen, where he handed his plate to Miss Annie. "Breakfast was wonderful as usual. Wish I could stay and wash the dishes, but I've got to pull a double shift at the hospital today."

"Don't you worry about it," Annie said, pulling him into a hug. "You go on and get to work, and don't forget to say hello to that beautiful wife of yours for me."

"I will. And Jocelyn, it was nice meeting you today too. Hope you come back."

"Oh, I think I will."

Jocelyn stuck around to help clear the tables and put many of them away in a storage closet before she cabbed it across town to the park where the youth cleanup was taking place. She crossed the park and found the director, Frank, in a red jacket and matching hat.

"Hi, I'm here to help," Jocelyn said.

"I think you've done enough already," he said with equal parts spite and disgust.

Thrown by the odd greeting, Jocelyn looked around. The teens she'd met with for the interview held garbage bags and glared at her from beneath the brims of their red caps. "I'm sorry, did I do something wrong?" she asked.

"Yeah, how about that real nice article you promised us, huh?" His voice was impatient. "Instead, you go and write it up so the kids sound like no-good thugs—like this was a prison cleanup—pretty much seems to have kept everyone away. Including the families that are usually out enjoying the playground on Saturday afternoons. Not to mention how destroyed the kids are for being portrayed in the exact light they've been trying to overcome."

"I didn't write anything of the sort."

The director pulled a copy of *The Daily Report* from a stack on the bench and thrust it at her. "Here. I got a copy for all the kids today, but none of them want to take it home now, so help yourself."

Jocelyn flipped through the pages and found her headline: *Youth Cleanup at the Park*

The first lines were hers, and she kept reading. It wasn't until she was two-thirds of the way through the article when she found the additions.

…242 counts of aggravated assault, 155 drug-related charges, and 14 gun charges have been brought against the teens in this organization. These troubled teenagers will be coming together on Saturday to clean the parks in your family neighborhoods…

She couldn't read anymore. She tucked the paper under her arm and took off down the sidewalk. It was the fastest, most borderline run she'd ever put herself through, and when she got to the doors of *The Daily Report*, she was huffing and puffing. Boy did she need to start working out.

No one was behind the front desk, and as Jocelyn hoofed it up the stairs, she secretly prayed no one crossed her path before she reached Robert's office, because if they did, she could honestly say she wouldn't be able to guarantee their safety against her wrath.

She burst through his closed door. His scrappy face went pale in an instant.

Jocelyn rattled the paper in his face. "Who did this?"

"Did what?"

"Changed my work."

"I did. The story—"

"Where do you get off re-writing my story?" she fired off before he could get another word out.

Robert laced his fingers behind his head and leaned back, like he was totally at ease. "I give final approval on everything we put out."

"That doesn't give you the right to pad my story with insignificant stats."

Robert pitched forward, his hands falling to his desktop. "It does when I feel those statistics *are* significant to the story."

"But they weren't. I mentioned that the kids had records but that they're trying to pay for their mistakes. They are attempting to escape the labels you just slapped back on them."

"The people of those neighborhoods deserve to know what kind of kids will be in their parks. Dolling them up to sound like a group of Pollyannas doesn't serve anyone." He leaned back again, looking smug. "Sorry you didn't get it right the first time."

"Oh, I got it right the first time." She pressed her thighs against the edge of his desk. "From now on, if you're going to change my features before they hit the printer, the least you can do is have the guts to put your name on it like you did with Pearson, because otherwise, you're just a coward that doesn't deserve the title of senior editor."

Jocelyn spun on her heel and walked out the door before her supervisor's jaw could clamp back into place. She was sure she'd be getting a call to pack her bags before the end of the weekend based on that bold performance. But at the moment, she didn't care.

Ten

The smell of fresh cut grass clung to the warm spring air as Luke entered the corporate tent at the Pacific Players' Championship golf tournament. He rarely attended these events, leaving it to the partners to schmooze with clients, but Lottie had requested he meet her here, rather than at the office, to further discuss what it was she needed from him. Emphasis on the word *need*.

Marcus was there, a beer in his hand, as he talked with Tippy and a couple of clients.

"You're late," his brother mouthed.

Luke looked at his wrist like he was wearing a watch and made a show of shaking his head. Right on time, but of course, anything less than fifteen minutes early was late by Marcus's standards.

Lottie Jones sat smack in the center of the tent. Her bright pink and heavily polka dotted pants helping her to stand out more than ever. Coincidently, she was in conversation with Poindexter. The leveled glare Marcus shot toward the executive partner meant the man was under close observation, and Luke was sure Xavier was very aware of it.

Luke didn't hesitate as he approached his client and took up her hand, kissing her fingers like the good friends she'd predicted they would become.

Poindexter did his best to try to cover his irritation with a fake smile and happy greeting. "Aaaah, so nice of you to show up. I was just entertaining your client for you while she waited." Poindexter gritted his teeth.

"Well, I'm here now," Luke said. "So please don't let us keep you from…"

Lottie stood up and looped her arm through Luke's. "Xavier here was just telling me about his time as an amateur player. And the heritage of the sport. And I was telling him how I was thinking about branching my fashion line into the golf sector." She turned to Luke. "What do you think? Couldn't this sport use a little splash of Lot-Ti-Dots?"

"That sounds like an excellent venture. Shall we discuss it more over here?" Luke steered Lottie to a corner table and ordered them both a drink.

"Oh, he's such an old-school thing, isn't he?" Lottie swatted the air.

"Yes, Poindexter has been with the firm a long time. He's an excellent attorney, if not a little traditional."

"That's exactly why I wanted to work with you," Lottie said. "You get me. You get my style. And you won't try to bully me into doing things your way."

"Is that so?" Luke leaned back. So she was looking for a push-over, was she? "And what makes you say that?"

"When I asked you earlier this week to find me the most rundown, dilapidated, and undesirable properties in the city, you just did it. And very well, I might add." She crossed one leg over the other and took a sip of water. "Some of those places were downright condemnable."

Luke had to agree. Stacy had shrieked in his ear over the phone when he gave her the new list of criteria they were looking for. It seemed Lottie Jones wasn't going to do anything the conventional way. She'd explained to Luke that she wanted to make a big impression on her hometown. Her return needed to be big and bold. That's why she didn't want a turnkey location that she could quietly slip into and set up shop. It would be a much bigger production than that.

"You ask, I deliver." Luke spread his lips wide, knowing she loved every ounce of attention he showered upon her.

"And that's exactly why we make an incredible team."

"You said you'd tell me more about why you want to relocate to Portland."

"I did, didn't I?" Lottie took another drink. "Well, as you know, the story that broke out about my overseas factories hurt my company. Finding out about the conditions the factory workers under my label were suffering in foreign countries was horrible. I had no idea. And I know no one believes me when I say that, but I didn't. It was my own fault. I'd grown too big, too fast, and left important things like that to my legal team who, if they'd known me at all, would have known that overworked and underpaid employees were not in line with who I am nor in keeping with my vision of the company. It almost did me in professionally." Lottie sighed and shook her head.

Luke waited, giving her a moment before she continued.

"I wanted to give the whole thing up, but then I remembered all the good things that have come from my business, and when I refocused on that, I realized I needed to come back home. To start again with the vision I originally created. I need this step to be big. I need to be a hero again, not a villain. I want this city to throw a parade in my honor. To name statues and parks after me because of the contribution I'll bring to their economy. That's why I want to take the property no else wants and turn it into something to be proud of. Into the sort of place that people line up to work at."

"That's quite a vision you have," Luke said. "But why me?"

"Because we're much the same." Lottie leaned toward him. "It seems as though we both have a reputation to overcome."

"And just how would you have come by that information?"

"Oh, I have my ways," Lottie said, a tease to her tone.

"So, it's not my former reputation that piqued your interest in my services."

"Quite the contrary." Lottie laughed. "You are a delicious young thing, but I have no intention of making our relationship anything but professional." Lottie laughed again, this time laying a hand on his chest and leaning into his ear. "But there's no reason we can't have a little fun along the way, riling up the stuffy old men around here. I do like to have fun with my work. Don't you?"

From the corner of his eye, Luke saw Xavier's posture stiffen and his eyes narrow in Luke's direction.

"I do." Luke kissed Lottie's hand before pushing it away. "So, now that that's out of the way, should we discuss the properties I sent you?"

"Oh yes. I've selected a short list of the ones I like. My assistant will email them to you this afternoon."

"All right. I'll let you know when you can tour them personally."

"No." Lottie checked her watch. "I've got to be in New York tonight. I'm leaving this decision completely in your hands. Go see the properties yourself and get a feel for them. I trust you'll know which one is right for me."

"And how exactly do you think I'll know?"

"Just go inside and say to yourself, 'what would Lottie think?' and you'll know."

"I'll know, huh?"

"You'll know." She stood and put a hand on his shoulder when he tried to stand too. "I'll be in touch," she whispered in his ear. "And get it done yesterday. I'm not a patient woman."

* * *

Monday morning, Luke and Stacy pulled up in front of a large brick building in the part of town that had once been called "Skid Road." The architecture on this block was unique to the city. All the cast-iron facades spoke to an era long forgotten. A number of actions had been taken over the years to save the buildings near the waterfront. Their historical significance as the birthplace of the port city was one thing, but the financial resources to modernize and maintain the neighborhood ran thin.

This particular building, with its arched entryway and boarded-up windows, was the largest property Luke and Stacy had seen today.

"It smells like a toilet," Stacy said as they climbed the stairs.

Luke had to agree. This part of the city was known for its homeless population, and he had to imagine these steps had served multiple purposes over the years. Beneath the covered walkway that extended from the doors was one such man. A faded green jacket and worn duffel bag sat next to him as he used a knife to scrape away at a piece of wood. He didn't seem to take notice of either Luke or Stacy.

Working with tentative fingers, Stacy retrieved the key and opened the front door. From Luke's research, he knew that over the years, the structure had served many purposes—a warehouse, a steel mill, and an activity center—until it closed down ten years ago because of lack of funding. As of today, only a small section of the building was being utilized by a non-profit organization.

Inside the large entrance, Luke turned around and gazed up. Wouldn't Lottie love that? He imagined the flood of natural light that would illuminate the tiled entry when the boards were removed from the windows above. If the walls were redone and a crystal chandelier hung from the ceiling, it would shine like a palace.

"Eeeew, eeeew, eeeew. This place is so gross." Stacy tiptoed over the tiles in her shiny black heels. "Are you sure this is what she's looking for?"

"Yeah." Luke took a moment to just feel the space and imagine what Lottie would say. "Yeah, I think it is."

They quickly covered the rest of the building. The upper open floor would serve Lot-Ti-Dots well as a production space. The third and fourth floors would provide plenty of space for offices and conference rooms, while the second floor had larger rooms and could house the daycare, gym, and possibly a few more offices. That left the entire first floor open, and the possibilities there were endless. It was big enough for a theater, an auditorium, a ballroom, or even a museum dedicated to the inspiring life of Lottie Jones. Lottie would love it.

"Let's get a contractor over here right away and see what the extent of the renovations will be. But I'd say whatever the cost, it doesn't matter, because this is exactly what Lottie will want."

By the end of the next day, Luke had a proposal all written up, the cost estimates from the contractor, and the okay from Lottie herself to make an offer on the big abandoned building. He was so pleased with how quickly everything had fallen into place that he whistled out of the office. He whistled while he shopped for the supplies for Brayden's sleepover. And he whistled on the elevator, only stopping when he got off and found a woman on the floor, peering under a chair, her backside in the air.

Eleven

Jocelyn didn't take her eyes off the cat under the chair—not a chair, but a settee or small sofa, judging by the size of the thing. Honestly, it didn't matter what it was, only that it harbored a runaway Bodhi.

W-ho on God's green earth thought it was a good idea to put this ridiculous chair in the hallway? Like anyone was just going to suddenly decide this was a good place to sit and have a rest. Seriously? This was a hallway—a corridor—a place for passing through, not to unwind after a hard day's work. Thanks to someone's numskull design sense, she was on her hands and knees, cheek pressed to the disgusting brown carpet trying to coax Bodhi from beneath it. Who knew the old cat could move some fast?

"Come here kitty, kitty, kitty." She kept her voice so syrupy sweet. Why wouldn't the stupid cat come to her? She kept her head down, reaching through the small opening between the chair and floor. Why couldn't the decorator have opted for a wooden legged chair instead of this plush modern monstrosity that was so low to the ground? Her fingers brushed fur, but it was no use—no way could she get Bodhi out without moving the chair, and if she did that, she risked him escaping again.

She was now officially the world's worst roommate, and she'd secure that title for life if she actually lost the cat. No, that wasn't going to happen. She had to win this standoff and put Bodhi back where he belonged.

Behind her, a man cleared his throat. "Do you need some help?"

Oh, no. It was her neighbor. Luke—wasn't that the name she'd heard the woman moan from behind his door the other night? And here she was in the most unglamorous, idiotic position ever.

"Nope. Got this just fine." She kept her head at the opening, feeling the petals of embarrassment bloom on her face.

Meow.

"Is there a cat under there?" Luke knelt beside her. The spicy scent of a man blew in from his direction.

"Yes, it's my roommate's cat," Jocelyn said, trying not to let him distract her.

Next thing she knew, he was peering at her and Bodhi from the adjacent side of the chair. What a pair they made, half lying on the floor trying to capture a cat.

"Hello kitty," he said. "Aren't you a pretty cat?"

"I don't think he responds to sweet talk, if that's what you're trying."

"No, just trying to size up the opposition. What's his name?"

"Bodhi."

"Well, Bodhi you look like a very sweet boy."

"Looks can be deceiving," Jocelyn said, her patience running thin.

The moment she'd walked into the apartment, the sharp smell of urine overtook the otherwise lavendery scent. Puddles were scattered throughout—on the welcome mat, on the bathroom rug, and on an old T-shirt Jocelyn had left on the floor. And now chasing the cat was about the last straw. Especially after the day she'd had with Robert passing her more obituaries to proofread and press releases to shuffle through. Plus the fact that everyone at the paper avoided her like she carried the plague. She didn't know what rumors Robert had spread to the masses, but she was feeling no love from her colleagues, least of all Robert himself. All she had wanted to do was cuddle in her Zen apartment and forget the past few days, not lay with her cheek to the filthy floor trying to call out an obstinate cat.

Luke sat up, a plastic bag rustled next to him, and then he was down again, lying with his back on the floor. "Well, lucky for us, we can outsmart him."

Jocelyn caught the wink he shot her way.

"When I say go, tip the chair forward, and I'll grab him. I'll have to be fast so he doesn't sneak under that table. Are you ready?"

Jocelyn sat back and put her hands on the arms of the chair. "Ready."

"Then, go."

She tipped the chair, and Luke, in his gray suit with his body pressed to the floor, squirmed toward the cat.

"Got him."

Jocelyn set the chair back as Luke sat upright and petted the cat. He stood, cradling Bodhi in one arm, and picked up his gigantic shopping bag. What did he have in there?

"Thank you." Jocelyn patted down her non-pocketed sweatpants and realized she didn't have her keys. "Oh, no."

"What?"

"I must've dropped my keys somewhere." She retraced her steps to the apartment. No abandoned keys in her trail.

"It's okay." Luke hoisted the cat. "Go downstairs and ask Chester for a key. He'll act grumpy about it. He acts grumpy about everything, but everyone gets one free pass. You only get fined on subsequent offenses."

Jocelyn looked down at her oversized t-shirt, sweats, and bunny slippers. Oh yeah, she'd forgotten she'd been wearing those too. What a fashion failure she looked like right now, nothing like that toned, petite woman he'd been with last weekend. No wonder he was more interested in the cat than her right now.

He must have noticed her assessing her outfit. "You look fine. Really cute."

Cute? That was the equivalent of having a good personality, wasn't it? Not very flattering at all.

"Go on," he encouraged. "I'll take Bodhi over to my place while you're gone, because Chester won't be happy if he finds him out of the apartment off leash—he's a real stickler for the rules—and once you're back in, you can come get him."

"You don't have to do that," Jocelyn said.

"It's all right. I don't mind." He scratched Bodhi under the chin, and Bodhi arched his head back, showing how much he enjoyed the attention. "We'll have a little male bonding time."

"Okay, but be careful. He gets scared easily and doesn't always make it to the litter box in time. I would hate to—"

"It's no problem. I'll keep a close eye on him, and you'll be back in before we know it."

She watched Luke turn down the hall to his apartment before she took off for the elevator. Chester without uttering so much as a word, let her into the apartment. And there were her keys on the floor next to the garbage bag she'd been trying to carry out. As soon as Chester was gone, she picked up the bag and dumped it down the garbage chute before knocking on Luke's door.

"There she is," Luke said to Bodhi, as if the feline were an actual human being. "I told you she'd be right back."

"I hope he wasn't any trouble." She took Bodhi from him.

"None at all, and you'll be pleased to know he kept all his bodily functions to himself."

"I'm so proud of him," she said flatly.

"Did Chester give you any problems?"

"No, he didn't say a word, actually."

"Then that means he likes you."

"I don't know why he would."

Luke leaned against his door jamb, crossing his arms over his chest. "It's probably because you're a lot the same. The quiet, keep-to-yourself kind of people."

Jocelyn scowled. "What's wrong with being the quiet type?"

"Nothing wrong with it." Luke put his hands up. "It sometimes just gives people the impression you're too good for them. Or that you don't want to be bothered. Like how your window is the only one that's never open during the day. Kinda screams back off."

"Maybe I like my windows closed up, so I don't have neighbors peering in at me."

"Sure, that makes sense if you're strutting around over there in nothing but those bunny slippers." His eyes slowly drew down her body to the fuzzy slippers, and she didn't know what it made her feel. But she certainly wasn't going to call it excitement.

"Are you picturing me in nothing but my slippers right now?"

"I hadn't been." His lips pulled apart, and she tried to force her eyes away. "But now that you mention it…"

Her mouth went dry, and she fumbled for the right words. "I…my…" But when nothing appropriate came out, she spun around and walked away.

Back in the apartment, she leaned against the door.

Of all the juvenile, pretentious things for him to say. And do.

Bodhi squirmed in her arms, and she rushed him off to the litter box, not wanting him to get distracted along the way if all this excitement had gotten his overactive bladder worked up again. The curtains in the living room were closed, like always, the faint light from the evening sky sneaking around the corners. Her peeping neighbor could keep his fantasies to himself. She wasn't going to give him any chance to see what she was doing in the privacy of her four walls.

It just went to show how powerful her instincts were. Sure, Luke had been nice enough to help her retrieve Bodhi. Not that she couldn't have done it all on her own if she'd just thought it through a little more. But instead, she'd had to endure an ogling from her playboy neighbor.

What a week this was turning out to be. She picked up her phone and dialed her sister, hoping she'd pick up this time. Since their last conversation, Sophie hadn't returned one of Jocelyn's calls. And the last time she'd checked the GPS tracking app, there had been no new information. Sophie most definitely had disabled her location settings, not that Jocelyn blamed her, but it was one more reminder of how disconnected she'd become from her family in such a short time.

The call went through to voicemail. She left a message.

"Hi, Soph," she said, trying to sound cheery, but failing miserably. "I could really use a sister moment if you can find it in your heart to spare me one. I know you're still mad at me, but I've honestly had the world's worst week with the world's worst boss, and just now, I had to suffer through my neighbor picturing me naked." She flopped on the couch, a deep sigh releasing into the phone. "Anyway, I'd love to hear about what's going on back home. Call me. Please."

Bodhi sauntered out of the bathroom, sat back on his haunches, and licked his front paw. He stretched the paw clear over his head and scrubbed behind his ear.

"Yeah, I'd be scrubbing off that man's scent too, if I were you." The faint reminder of the spicy smell she caught as he knelt on the floor gave her stomach that warm sensation again.

"A good cologne does not equal a good man," she said to the cat, even though it was a reminder to herself. Paulo had worn something similar. Fresh and spicy. It took her right back to that time when she'd completely let go of her senses and trusted that a man would and could love her, quiet and brainy as she was. But it wasn't love, and she'd been afraid ever since then of mistaking the power of lust for true love if it ever came her way again.

Bodhi jumped up next to her and rubbed his head against her arm, breaking her out of those thoughts.

"I bet you're hungry." She scratched him under the chin. "It's going to be a full dose of meds for you tonight. I don't want to wake up to a little surprise from you in the morning."

She pushed off the couch, Bodhi trotting along behind her to his food dish where she loaded him up with kibble and meds. Her own stomach gave a low rumble, reminding her it was time to eat.

In the kitchen, she pulled open the refrigerator, nothing but bare shelves. Her unsteady future at the paper weighed so heavily on her mind that everything else had slid down the priority list.

She was about to slip into a moment of despair when she remembered how much she had to be thankful for. This job wasn't forever, and when her time was done here, she'd return home to the job and the people she loved.

Her thoughts turned over to the soup kitchen and the people there tonight who were blessed to have Miss Annie looking out for them. That's exactly what she needed, she thought as she reached for a pint of mint chocolate chip ice cream. She'd volunteer tomorrow and forget about her petty woes.

Digging her spoon into the ice cream, she noticed the big waxy-leafed tree leaning to the left. That hadn't been like that before, had it? The smaller flowering plant next to it was doing the same thing, leaning left. She walked closer and noticed a distinct tint of yellow to the wilted leaves. She just watered them yesterday, she was sure of it. So what was going on? She didn't want to add plant-killer to her list of roommate infractions. Fiona would have no choice but to kick her out as soon as she returned.

The plants along the other wall were doing the same thing, only leaning to the right. All at once it hit her. *The window*. The plants were starving for sunlight. She pulled open the curtains, letting the last of the sun's rays filter inside.

How could she have been so thoughtless—more worried about saving herself from a peek at her neighbor than nurturing the plants in her care?

Turning back to the plants, she said, "A full day of sunshine tomorrow, I promise."

Hopefully, Mother Nature would cooperate with her and keep the clouds away. She turned to the window again, the sun glinting around the edge of the clouds now, illuminating their silver lining. What a beautiful view it was with the lush courtyard garden, the brick building, and iron-gated balconies set against the gorgeous clouds above. It was exactly the kind of scene her mother would have painted. Clouds with a silver lining were one of her favorite subjects.

Lifting her spoon, loaded with chocolate speckled green ice cream, she tried not to let her eyes travel to the apartment across the way.

But it was no use. They moved against her will and guzzled up the sight of Luke, shirtless and sweaty as he performed the most perfect set of chin ups Jocelyn had ever seen. The muscles of his back and shoulders tightening with the movement. It was almost tantalizing.

He released his grasp and turned, waving when he caught Jocelyn in her window. She stood frozen as drops of cold ice cream dripped onto her shirt.

* * *

Jocelyn heaped a pile of green beans onto a plate. Miss Annie had moved her into the role of server this evening.

This was good. This was exactly what she'd needed to get her mind off Robert and his demeaning attitude. Today was another day of proofing obits and cataloging press releases. Every interesting lead she'd come across was passed off to someone else, and Robert sent her back to her cubicle to dig up more interesting stories for the others to cover.

"It's beef stroganoff, your favorite," Miss Annie said from beside Jocelyn as she scooped out a spoonful of the meat and sauce for Sarge.

He stepped forward, and Jocelyn served him the green beans. "Enjoy," she said, noticing the thick gauze bandages encasing his hands.

His eyes briefly met hers before he hobbled off to the far back corner.

Eric had slowed the line, pausing in front of Miss Annie. Their whispered conversation loud enough for Jocelyn to overhear.

"How's he doing?" Miss Annie asked.

"All right, I guess. I'll change the bandages before I leave tonight. But if there's any sign of infection, he'll have to go to the hospital."

"Let's hope it doesn't come to that."

Eric nodded and moved on.

"Hey." Eric smiled. "So glad you finally decided to come back."

"My work has had me miserably pre-occupied." Jocelyn performed a half eye-roll and held back her questions about Sarge. It wasn't any of her business, but that didn't mean she wasn't itching to uncover what had happened.

"I'm on dish duty tonight. Are you going to stick around till the end of dinner?"

"Can't think of anywhere else I have to be," she said.

"Great. I'll see you later."

When service ended, Jocelyn carried her empty pan to the dishwashing area.

"We just served a hundred and fourteen people," Miss Annie announced.

"That's more than last night," Isaiah said.

"I know." A worried crease edged its way between Miss Annie's eyes.

"Is that bad?" Jocelyn asked.

Miss Annie shook her head. "Could just mean more people are finding out about our good cooking." The woman tried to brave a smile. "Or…"

"Or what?"

"Or that we're cycling back to a time of heavy need for folks."

Miss Annie's shoulders sagged as she returned to the serving area and brought back more empty pans. "Looks like there won't be any seconds tonight," she said before passing a pitcher of water to Jocelyn. "Here. See if anyone needs a refill."

As Jocelyn rounded the tables, topping off water glasses, she scanned the faces in the crowded room for Teya. She hadn't seen her come through the line and wondered if she'd missed her. But she didn't see the little girl and her unicorn anywhere.

By the time she reached Eric and Sarge's table in the back, her pitcher was empty. She should return to the kitchen for a refill, but Miss Annie had joined the two men, and Jocelyn caught a snippet of their conversation.

"Sarge says a whole host of suits have been hanging around the building this week," Eric said.

Miss Annie's eyes narrowed. "And you think there's a connection between them and last night?"

Sarge's gray-haired head nodded.

"What happened last night?" Jocelyn asked, setting her pitcher on the table. She couldn't keep the question bottled inside. Something was going on, and she was determined to know what it was.

Eric and Miss Annie looked up, surprise registering on their faces.

"I'm sorry. I just overheard you talking." She turned to Sarge. "Does this have something to do with how you hurt your hands?"

He didn't answer.

"A fire was set in the back alley, and a couple of windows were broken out of the basement. We think whoever started the fire was going to make sure it got inside, but Sarge put it out before any real damage was done."

"So his hands are burned?"

Sarge nodded, his dirt stained fingers peeking out of the bandages.

"Did you call the police?" she asked Miss Annie.

"I did. They said they'd send someone out, but nobody's been by, have they Sarge?"

He shook his head.

"They said it was probably just someone trying to stay warm last night, and they'd be sure to send out an extra patrol car tonight to drive by the place."

Jocelyn pulled a chair to the table. "That's good, isn't it?"

"Maybe." Miss Annie shrugged. "They've never taken much interest in us before and probably won't until this place is actually burned to the ground."

"So, who do you think the people in the suits were?"

"Oh, could've been anybody really. The city. The historical society. New buyers." Annie rubbed her palms together. "It's hard to say."

"But you think there's a connection between their presence and the fire that was started last night."

"I don't know. Sarge here is the one who thinks it's a possibility. You know," Miss Annie said, furrowing her brow at Jocelyn. "You sure do ask a lot of questions."

"Sorry, it's an occupational hazard. I'm a reporter for *The Daily Report*. In fact, I'd like to do a feature on you, Miss Annie. Your work and the building. Maybe I can bring a little attention to your cause and help the police as well as other organizations become aware of the important work you do under this roof."

Miss Annie gave her a sunshiney smile. "Well, that sounds like a nice idea."

Jocelyn turned to Sarge, wishing she hadn't left her tablet in her bag in the kitchen. She didn't want to miss a detail. "I'd like to know why you think one of the people you saw in the building earlier this week might have been involved in the fire. Did you see something? Or someone?"

Sarge shook his head. "Heard it."

"What'd you hear?" Annie leaned forward in her chair. Eric too seemed surprised by this new information.

Sarge pulled out a small cell phone.

"Where did that come from?" Jocelyn asked.

"I gave it to him," Miss Annie said. "I leave a window open for Sarge. So he can have somewhere private to get out of the rain. And he keeps an eye on things around here for me. Don't you, Sarge? Haven't had a single broken window since Sarge moved in…until last night." Miss Annie's face dropped. "You're not going to write about that though, are you? Nobody knows. The city wouldn't approve and would probably toss me and Sarge out if they found out."

"I won't tell a soul," Jocelyn promised before turning back to Sarge. "Now, what did you hear?"

The man's large fingers worked to press the tiny buttons. A video came on the screen, a star speckled sky in the frame. Then Sarge's voice low and scratchy. "A million stars shine on me tonight. A million souls…" His beautifully pained words were cut off by hurried steps on pavement. Through the echoey speaker came a new voice. "It's all set," a man rushed the words out. "The boys'll make it look like an accident. Just like you wanted. Your man said he'd meet me on the steps of the courthouse in the morning with my payment…Yes…Yes. All taken care of." The voice was rushed. All four of them stared down at the phone as footsteps gave way to soft raindrops.

"Can I take this?" Jocelyn asked. "I think I know someone who could help us. And once I print this story, you'll be a difficult cause to ignore, Miss Annie."

Now if only Jocelyn could get Robert to guarantee he'd print it without changing up the heart of her story.

* * *

The next morning, as luck would have it, Jocelyn met Jerry at the bottom of the steps, and they climbed to the second story together.

"Are you feeling settled in yet?" Jerry asked her.

"Yes. I am. Definitely getting a feel for the city."

"Good. Good." Jerry paused at the top. "I'm really looking forward to seeing some of your work on the pages."

"About that." Jocelyn twisted the cup of tea in her hands. "I'd like to work on a series of features about the working class poor in the city. See

I've started volunteering at a soup kitchen. There are so many untold stories there—"

"I think that's a fantastic idea." Jerry face split into a grin.

"What's so fantastic?" Robert asked, joining them.

Jocelyn forced a pleasant smile. "I was just telling Jerry about an idea I had for a feature on the working class poor in a soup kitchen where I volunteer."

"Is that so?" Robert said.

"Yes, and I think it's exactly what the paper needs. Don't you?"

"It sounds inspiring," Robert said with mock-enthusiasm.

"Can't wait to see it in print, my dear," Jerry said before heading to his office.

Robert stepped intimidatingly close to her, but she didn't shrink away. "Don't think you can go behind my back and get away with it," Robert growled before stalking off.

"Wouldn't dream of it," Jocelyn breathed. She headed to her cubicle and finalized the article she'd written last night when all the details of the kitchen and possible arson attempt were still fresh in her mind.

Twelve

Luke was going to get this right today. He'd offended his neighbor the other night, and he wanted to fix it. The not-so-subtle snub she gave him in the lobby yesterday morning made it perfectly clear. He wanted to change that. This morning, he decided to forgo his run and showered and dressed for work, eager to catch her.

He pumped two cups full of coffee. *Sugar?* Would she want sugar? He figured he'd doctor one up with cream and sugar and leave the other black. Whichever one his neighbor chose, he'd have the other.

He'd felt bad about the way things had ended when she came to pick up her roommate's cat. His joking manner hadn't been received well and had him thinking of the thirteen women who'd suffered sexual harassment at the hand of the CEO at Prestige Bank. The thought of his neighbor perceiving him that way was unthinkable, and he would see to it that she understood he meant no disrespect.

She wasn't going to get by him this morning until he had a chance to apologize. He positioned himself, leaning up against the wall next to the table with the coffee fixings. Crossing one leg over the other, he tried to appear relaxed. A moment passed before he decided it looked too staged, too much like he was waiting for her, and that might throw her off.

He turned around, his back to the elevator, and read from the notices tacked to the bulletin board. This was casual, wasn't it? But once he'd read about the guitar lessons at the music store, the soup kitchen, and the futon that was free to a good home, his eyes just stared. This no longer felt natural.

Luke sauntered toward the front desk. "Good morning, Chester."

The doorman looked up but didn't say anything in return.

Luke wasn't deterred. "How'd the Blazers do last night?"

Thanks to Marcus and his family obligation, Luke had a spare ticket to the game tonight and wondered if his neighbor was a basketball fan. The tickets were tucked in his breast pocket, and if this morning went as he hoped, he'd be giving her one before he left for the office.

Chester passed the sports section of the paper to Luke as the elevator dinged and out stepped his neighbor in black heels and a short black skirt.

"Good morning," he said, stepping away from the desk. "Would you care for a cup of coffee?"

Her eyes grew big as she studied the two cups in his hands. "No, thank you," she finally said as she brushed by him.

She was out the door before he could recover. "Wait!"

Chester cleared his throat, and Luke stopped.

"Next time, try tea. Earl Gray. No milk. No sugar." The doorman briefly looked up from the paper before returning to it.

"Thanks." Luke hustled out the door, pouring the coffees in the dirt of a planter box and dumping the cups in the trash. He rushed to catch up with his neighbor, but she was already across the street, and the light had turned red. Giving up, he trudged the rest of the way to the office. Why was this girl so hard to impress? And why did he care so much?

The first drops of rain began to fall as he stepped into the office building, noticing that it was much more crowded at this hour of the morning than when he usually arrived. Pressed into the back corner of the elevator, he rode to the eighteenth floor. The rocky start to his morning made him unusually abrupt with his fellow passengers as he pushed his way out.

The first face he saw as he entered the law office was his brother's, and the grim veil he wore told Luke his day was about to get worse.

"Have you seen this?" Marcus followed him to his office and tossed the newspaper down on Luke's desk.

"Good morning to you too," he said, wishing he hadn't ditched the coffee cups, because he could really use the drink right about now.

Marcus's frown was unflagging. Luke glanced away, not in the mood to try to charm a smile out of his brother. Picking up the paper, he read the front-page headline, *Miss Annie's Soup Kitchen Threatened*.

"Who's Miss Annie?" Luke asked.

"Apparently the woman you're about to put out on the streets with Lottie's acquisition of the Hitchcock Building."

"What? This isn't public knowledge yet."

"It seems someone knows more than you do."

Luke scanned the article of all out praise for a woman named Miss Annie that served at a soup kitchen in the building Lottie was trying to acquire. "When news breaks that Lottie is the one buying the building, they'll hate her. It makes it sound like she's going to leave this woman homeless or something. And what's this about an arson attempt?" He smacked the paper with the back of his hand. "This is a ridiculous accusation."

Marcus stood up straight and tall, folding his arms over his chest. "So what are you going to do about it?"

Luke shook his head. This morning was snowballing. What was it going to be next? He wanted to close his eyes and make this whole thing go away, to laugh it off and pretend it was no big deal, but that wouldn't work in this case. He was handling a high-profile deal, and he needed to think like a high-profile lawyer. What would Marcus do?

Luke sighed as he folded the paper. "Looks like I'm going pay J.J. Banks at *The Portland Daily Report* a visit."

Marcus nodded his approval. "Do you want me go with you?"

"No, I can handle this." Luke gathered the paper and his bag.

In the hall, Tippy hurried toward him, holding up the front page.

"Did you see this? Did you…"

"I saw it," Luke reassured him. "And I'm on my way to take care of it. Don't worry. I have this under control."

Tippy looked worried and unconvinced, but Luke didn't waste any more time trying to reassure him. He would straighten out this whole situation.

A few blocks away, he entered the newspaper office. It was larger and more modern than he'd imagined, considering how downsized newspapers had become. A woman behind a large desk seemed to sense his approach.

"How can I help you?" she asked, eyes remaining glued to her computer screen.

"I'd like to speak with J.J. Banks about the article in today's paper," he said abruptly. The tone bore an alarming similarity to his brother's.

She punched a button on her desk phone and finally turned her eyes on him, holding him hostage with her glare as she rang for J.J.

"Someone's here to see you about the soup kitchen piece," the woman said before hanging up the phone. "It'll be just a moment."

Released from the glare, Luke sat in the chair she'd pointed out and waited. It wasn't long until the clacking of high heels came out to meet him. He looked up into the frozen expression of his neighbor.

"Are you J.J. Banks?" he asked slowly.

She nodded.

He rose to his feet, delighted by the way all the curt and vengeful feelings he'd had racing through him simply slipped away at the sight of his neighbor. "At least now I have a name to go with that pretty face."

Pink flooded her cheeks, and the woman behind the desk snapped her head up. He'd done it again. Made her feel uncomfortable, and he sobered, tempering his flirtatious side.

She raised her chin. "Are you the one here to talk to me about the article?"

"I am. Is there someplace private we can talk?"

She nodded, and he followed her up a set of stairs. Inside a heavily windowed room, she walked around a large table and finally turned to face him, her beautiful thin lips set in a straight line. Those blue-gray eyes he'd glimpsed up close outside his apartment the other night were just as appealing today. He wanted to step closer and stare into them, but her hostile posture suggested now was not the time.

He invited himself to sit down, taking his time to get comfortable, and pulled out the paper. "So J.J.—"

"My name is Jocelyn. Not J.J."

He looked up at her, confused.

"It's my editor's way of undermining me."

If he didn't know any better, he'd say the one person in the world she disliked more than him at the moment was this editor of hers.

He didn't press the issue, even though he wanted a full rundown of every offense this person had committed against her. First, he had to fix things with her.

"Jocelyn then," he said, liking the sound of it. Her name was soft and sophisticated, just like her. "I would like to start by apologizing for the other night."

"Apologizing for what exactly?"

"For making you feel uncomfortable. Not everyone gets my sense of humor."

"You thought picturing me naked was funny."

He held up a hand. "Let's be clear that you were the one to bring that up in the first place. And in my defense, I thought you were flirting with me." Her eyes widened, and he amended his statement. "I mean, I thought *we* were flirting with each other, or at least I'd hoped we were. But, I can see I was wrong. And I'm sorry. Please, accept my apology."

She hesitated for a moment before her shoulders relaxed, and she nodded. "Apology accepted."

He closed the distance between them and held out his hand. "Friends?"

She didn't return the gesture, but her lips twitched in the slightest way that could have possibly been construed as the beginning of a smile. "Not so fast."

"Probably a good idea." He dropped his hand. "Because it would be much harder for me to sue a friend on the grounds of character defamation than it would be a bunny-slipper-wearing neighbor of mine."

"Sue me?" Horror struck her blue-gray eyes.

"Sorry. My sense of humor thing, it's getting away from me again."

"You need to work on that. Because threatening a lawsuit isn't funny."

"I can see that." Luke took his seat again, hoping the distance would help him stay focused on the reason he was here. "I'm interested in knowing how you claim to know so much about my client's plans."

"Your client?"

"I happen to be one of the suits you mention in your article. I've been in the building, assisting my client in the acquisition process. Her offer was only just accepted, and we're still undergoing negotiations. The future plans for the non-profit haven't been discussed thus far. I'm sorry to inform you that this article is very…misleading."

"I never stated the non-profit was in jeopardy. I only told the story of the people who could be affected by its shut down. I simply raised the question about its future. Feel free to read it anyway you want."

"Sneaky, aren't you?"

She shrugged. "If that's the way you see it." Jocelyn's eyebrows suddenly arched, then scrunched down. "Did you say you've been in the building?"

"Yes. It's in pretty rough shape, but I'm confidant my client will do what it takes to bring it back to its former glory."

She took three slow steps toward him, her arms never uncrossing. "I need to know where you were two nights ago at approximately ten p.m.?"

"I believe you know exactly where I was."

Her expression changed as she remembered.

"After assisting in the rescue of an escaped cat, I was in my apartment. I didn't go out again and probably have a number of neighbors that could testify to that. Or even Chester could tell you. Why?"

Jocelyn twitched her lips. "I have a recording of a man at the scene telling someone that everything was set. And that it would look like an accident. Twenty minutes later, a fire broke out in the back alley."

"Where did this recording come from?"

"A very reliable source."

"You wouldn't happen to have it on hand, would you?"

"Of course not. It's someplace safe. But if it wasn't you making the call, then who was it?"

"First of all," Luke said, hoping his sense of humor wasn't about to get him in trouble again. "I'm going to ignore the fact that you even considered it a possibility that I'm behind this arson attempt at all. I guess it just goes to show that we need to get to know each other better. But as for the true culprit, I think that's something I'd like to know as much as you."

Jocelyn didn't seem to miss a beat. "Would your client be working with someone else? An arsonist? To get the building condemned or to create a spectacle for publicity sake or something?"

"My client is seeking publicity, but not that kind. I'll look into it, but I'm almost certain I can assure you my client is in no way involved in something illegal."

Jocelyn paced. "Something's not adding up. I'll have to do more digging tonight."

"Tonight?"

"Yes, when I'm at the kitchen again. Maybe the police have been by or another witness was located." She bit her lower lip in concentration.

Just then, a short, thin man poked his head inside the room.

"Hey," he barked at Jocelyn. "Pearson doesn't want to cover the little league awards tonight, so you'll have to do it."

It didn't take a genius to realize this was someone Jocelyn didn't like. Her posture turned defensive again, and the humiliated look in her eyes when they fell to Luke confirmed his suspicion.

The little man brushed a lock of dark hair from his eyes as he realized Jocelyn wasn't alone and shot questioning eyes at Luke.

"Luke Lewis," he said, standing. "Senior associate at Lewis and Sons Law Firm. Maybe you've heard of my family's firm?"

The way the little man postured, puffing out his chest, assured Luke the firm's reputation had made its way to him.

"Robert Kaminsky, senior editor."

"Pleasure to make your acquaintance, Mr. Kaminsky." Luke shook the man's clammy hand.

"Mr. Lewis is here about the soup kitchen article." Jocelyn's voice came from behind him.

"Is that so?" Mr. Kaminsky folded his arms over his bony chest and widened his stance.

"I'm one of the suits mentioned in Jocelyn's article and was just following up with her."

Mr. Kaminsky's face paled. "Is there a problem with the article? If there's any kind of—"

"No, there's no problem. In fact, Jocelyn and I were just talking about joining forces to get even more out of the story. I'll have lots of inside details in the coming weeks that I'm prepared to offer to her exclusively." He walked back to where Jocelyn stood and threw an arm around her waist. A sweet flowery smell enveloped him. "And that's why she won't be able to cover the little league awards tonight. We have plans." Forget the basketball game. He'd pass the tickets off to Dennis or one of the other associates. This opportunity would serve his interests much better, both personally and professionally. "What time did you say again?"

Jocelyn swallowed but didn't look at him. "Six o'clock."

"Six o'clock it is. See you tonight." Without thinking, he gently placed a kiss on her cheek. It was soft and warm. The sweet scent of her clouded his brain for a moment, and he nearly forgot to pick up his bag.

"Use the side door," Jocelyn said as he pulled the strap over his head, a nervous lilt to her voice.

"Will do." He couldn't suppress the grin spreading across his face. And he left, looking forward to six o'clock.

He finally had a name for the woman who'd been occupying his thoughts, and she smelled sweeter than a rose.

Luke wasn't back in his chair but five minutes before Marcus came bursting through his door. "Well, did you fix it?"

"Sort of," Luke said, logging into his computer.

"What do you mean, 'sort of?'" Poindexter marched into his office next with a timid looking Tippy right behind him. "Has Lottie seen this yet?"

"Not that I'm aware of," Luke said. "Besides, it doesn't mention her by name. And once I confirm her lack of involvement in the vandalism, her name won't be printed until I say so. But it sounds like there's more to this story. Someone is up to something involving this building."

"Who?" Marcus demanded.

"I'm not sure yet." Luke typed on his keyboard, ignoring the stares from the three other men.

"Do you think there's someone else going after the building? Are there multiple offers on the table?" Poindexter asked.

"Not that I'm aware of, but I'll be looking into it." Luke drew his eyes away from the screen. "Jocelyn has a recording that suggests someone wants this property to burn."

"Who's Jocelyn?" Marcus asked.

"The reporter from *The Daily Report*. And a friend."

Poindexter put his hands on his hips. "A recording? Every reporter says they've got a recording."

"I believe her." Luke challenged Poindexter's scowl.

"Did you hear it?" Tippy asked, his voice shaky. "Because if it was recorded without consent, it may not be admissible as evidence."

"Good point." He looked up. Leave it to Tippy to go straight to the law books on something like this. "If you'll excuse me," he said, dismissing the men from his office. "I need to inform my client of this recent turn of events."

* * *

Lottie had been as shocked as Luke to learn about the possible arson attempt on the building. And as for the future of the soup kitchen, she'd told Luke she trusted him to figure it out. A sizable donation, assistance in relocation, she'd do whatever she needed to look like a hero in the eyes of the community. The soup kitchen would benefit, she'd reassured Luke before hanging up.

He'd spent the rest of the day drafting, and re-drafting, the historical tax credit documents he'd need to file.

When he approached his building at a quarter past five—he didn't want to be late meeting up with Jocelyn—he was surprised to find Tippy outside, reaching for the front door.

"Evening, Tippy," Luke said as Chester opened the door.

"Luke! Hello." Tippy walked inside with him.

Chester greeted them with a stiff nod.

"I didn't know you lived here." Tippy said as they approached the elevators.

"I sure do. Fifth floor. You know someone in the building?"

The elevator arrived, and they stepped on.

"My niece."

"Your niece lives here?" Luke punched the button for the fifth floor. "What floor?"

"What? No, she doesn't live here. She's…she's thinking about it. That's why I'm here, to look at an available unit with her. But, as usual, I'm running late, and she's already up there."

"I know how that goes." Luke pressed the button for his floor. "So what floor are you going to?"

Tippy retrieved his handkerchief and dabbed at his forehead while glancing around the elevator cabin.

"Which floor are you meeting your niece on?"

"My what?" Tippy looked at him bewildered. "Oh yes, my niece." He glanced at the buttons. "Seven…seventh floor, please." The doors closed. "How's the acquisition going? For Ms. Jones?"

"Slow." Luke checked his watch. "You know how these things are. A lot of red tape to get through, but it's going all right."

"Good. Good." Tippy rocked back on his heels. "Too bad it's not a condemned building. You could get it for cheap and avoid all the lengthy procedures."

"That's true, but unless Mother Nature is going to send earth, wind, or fire in to help us out, it looks like we're going about this the old-fashioned way." The elevator arrived at the fifth floor, and Luke stepped off but turned back and held the door. "I hope your niece likes it here. What's her name again?"

"Oh, it's…" Tippy worked to put the handkerchief away. "It's Matilda. Lovely girl."

"I'm sure she is. Well, tell Matilda to look me up if she decides to move in."

"I'll do that. Thank you." Tippy grasped his briefcase with both hands and nodded as the doors slid closed.

"Wait." Luke stopped the doors and pushed them open. "I forgot I had these." He pulled the white envelope with the tickets out of his pocket. "Maybe you and Matilda could catch the game later."

"Oh." Tippy's eyebrows went up as he took the envelope. "Maybe we will. Thank you."

Luke rushed to his apartment, tossing the keys on the counter. He couldn't resist a quick look across the courtyard at Jocelyn's window, hoping that maybe she'd stopped off at home before going to the soup kitchen too. But it didn't appear that anyone was home.

A few minutes later, Luke came out of his room feeling much more comfortable now that he'd shed his work attire. He crossed the apartment and threw one more glance at Jocelyn's curtained window before he hustled out the door and headed for the soup kitchen.

Thirteen

Jocelyn couldn't help turning around every time the soup kitchen door opened. It wasn't six o'clock yet, but as the minutes ticked closer to the hour, she wondered if Luke would show up.

She'd been distracted by the thought of him all day. The heat of his touch. The burn of his lips on her skin. She was blushing again, and it had nothing to do with the broiler she stood over, or the garlic toast sizzling inside as it browned.

It was Paulo all over again, she told herself every time a flutter of butterflies released on the inside, that lustful feeling crowding out all other thoughts. The whole show he put on of slipping an arm around her and planting a kiss on her cheek. It wasn't until her snively boss showed up that Luke had made a move to touch her. Not even that night at his apartment, when they'd been alone, and he'd assumed they were flirting with each other, had he been so bold.

It was a testosterone-induced move, one man to another, showing dominance. And the worst part was, she'd let him do it—use her as an object to play against Robert. There was no denying her own pleasure in seeing Robert's reaction, but that was no reason to let her fantasies run wild. Luke was not the sort of catch that would be good for her.

The door opened, and Jocelyn whirled around. Isaiah came inside, removing his coat. "Sorry I'm late," he said, donning his grease stained apron. "Traffic was crazy on the bridge."

"Just glad you made it here safe and sound," Miss Annie said as she sniffed the air. "Something's burning."

Jocelyn jumped to attention and checked the broiler. The edges of the toast were starting to blacken. She pulled them out before they became inedible and moved them to the basket. As she refilled the tray with slices of bread and coated them with garlic butter, a knock sounded on the door.

Isaiah opened it as Jocelyn set the tray on a rack. Anticipation drummed in her heart.

"Can I help you?" Isaiah asked.

Without turning around, she knew Luke had come.

"I'm Luke. Jocelyn invited me to help out tonight."

She closed the oven door, leaving it open a crack, and walked over to where he stood framed in the doorway with the gray evening clouds as his backdrop. He no longer wore his suit but jeans and a t-shirt that his upper body filled out nicely, thanks to those daily workouts she had the pleasure of observing. She was blushing again, thinking about what was beneath the shirt that gave the fabric across his chest a gentle pull and left a small gap between his bicep and the cuff of his short sleeves.

"Hi," he said, all smiles—oh, what a smile.

"Hi," she replied as he stepped inside, and all the kitchen activity around her stalled. She knew what they were thinking. *How could she score a man like that?* The answer was, she couldn't. He was here to look after his own interests, which didn't include her.

"Everyone, this is Luke," she said, closing the door behind him.

"Hi," everyone said before resuming their duties.

"Welcome to my kitchen," Miss Annie said. "What's your specialty? Roasting chicken, sautéing green beans, or burning toast like little Miss Distracted here?"

Jocelyn rushed back to her oven at Miss Annie's reminder and pulled out her barely burned bread.

"I'll admit I don't have much experience in the kitchen," Luke said almost shyly.

"Then what good are you to me?" Miss Annie teased as she handed him an apron.

"He's good at pouring coffee." Jocelyn shot over her shoulder.

"But not everybody likes to drink my well-poured coffee." Luke looped the apron over his head.

"Uh-huh." Miss Annie shifted her gaze from Luke to Jocelyn and back again. "Coffee it is. Right this way."

As Miss Annie led Luke to the beverage table, he passed behind Jocelyn and leaned in to whisper, "Tomorrow I'll be perfecting a cup of Earl Gray tea, if you'd like to join me."

Earl Gray? How had he figured that out?

He moved on before she had a chance to answer, his shoulder brushing against hers.

Was that intentional? Quit trying to read his every move, she chided herself as she turned back to her work.

But she couldn't keep her eyes off him, no matter how hard she tried, discreetly looking his way every chance she got. When Luke finished listening to Miss Annie's instructions, he threw Jocelyn a dashing smile that sent a thrilling shock up her spine.

Stop it. Don't be fooled.

"Toast," Miss Annie whispered as she walked by.

Jocelyn reacted and rescued another tray from the heat before it turned black.

* * *

After serving over one hundred dinners, Miss Annie exclaimed they were done with service. Jocelyn's bread had been exhausted, leaving nothing left to offer for seconds. She went over to Luke and held up a pitcher of water and a pot of coffee.

"Which would you like?" she asked.

"I'll take the coffee, since you have such a dislike for it."

She handed it to him and turned around. "Come on," she said over her shoulder. "I'll introduce you to the people here."

"Right behind you."

She tossed a coquettish grin at him. *Stop flirting right now.* No reason to give him the wrong idea.

During dinner service, she'd noticed Teya was back with her family. It was the first table she stopped at.

"Hello, again." She refilled the water glasses.

No one answered, but Teya looked up. Her mother's eyes remained downcast. Jocelyn knelt and stroked the stuffed unicorn's fur. "How's Rainbow doing today?"

Teya didn't answer but glanced at her mother who could no longer hide her face from Jocelyn. Black and blue tinged the skin around her eyes, and her nose was swollen. Jocelyn met her eyes before standing up, neither one mentioning the injuries.

Jocelyn exchanged a glance with Luke that told her he'd seen the bruises too.

"Can I get you anything besides coffee?" he asked as he refilled her cup.

"No, this is fine. Thank you." The woman's voice was soft.

"If you need anything else, just ask," Jocelyn said, feeling helpless as they moved on to the next table.

"Does she show up here like that often?" Luke asked quietly.

"I've only seen them here once before." Jocelyn poured water for the next table while Luke refilled two coffee cups. As they walked away, she continued. "She wasn't bruised the last time they came in."

"Do you know her name?"

Jocelyn shook her head.

They were both quiet as they finished visiting the other tables. When they reached the back table, Jocelyn introduced Luke to Sarge and Eric.

"Please, join us," Eric said, moving to the other side of the table. He wore blue scrubs under a light jacket. Jocelyn sat down, but Luke hesitated, his gaze traveling back to the table with the bruised woman.

"Excuse me." He set the coffee pot down. "I'll be right back."

"He seems nice," Eric said. "You two been dating long?"

"What? Dating? No not us. He's…he's just…uh…my neighbor." She watched Luke kneel beside the woman, her head barely turning to look at him. "He came to my office today after reading the article. Turns out he's a lawyer, and it's his client that's interested in buying the building. He's as interested as we are to know more about the arson attempt." She pulled her eyes off him and looked at Sarge. "Did the police ever show up here?"

Sarge nodded.

"This afternoon," Eric said. "An Officer Reyes stopped by and walked around."

"Did you talk to him?" Jocelyn asked Sarge, her gaze focused on Luke and the woman. The woman shook her head, and Luke handed her something.

Sarge said nothing.

"No," Eric answered for him. "Sarge doesn't make it a habit of talking to the police."

Luke headed back toward the table. Jocelyn kept her attention on him as he approached and eased into the chair next to her.

"Did you ask her about what happened?" She hoped he might have the answers to some of her questions.

"She didn't say much." Luke watched the woman and her children head for the door. Teya, with the unicorn tucked under one arm, turned back to wave at Jocelyn. Her arm stretched out of the sleeve of a coat that was too small for her.

Jocelyn waved back, hoping she'd see them again tomorrow. "What were you telling her?"

"That if she needed to file a restraining order, I could help her." He shook his head, looking defeated. "I don't think she wanted my help."

"At least you tried." Jocelyn put a hand on his shoulder, and he covered it with his. A gesture that was shockingly intimate and natural all at the same time.

"Thanks." Without letting go of her fingers he pulled her hand to his lap, sandwiching it between his. His skin was smooth and soft over hers, minus the tiny callous that brushed her knuckles. It instantly reminded her of the chin-up bar in his apartment.

"What's going on with her?" Eric asked.

Jocelyn crossed her legs. "Her face was badly bruised."

Sarge's eyes shot toward the door, but the family was gone.

"Oh, no." Eric's shoulders sagged. "We better make sure to tell Miss Annie. She'll want to keep an eye out for them."

"Tell me what?" Miss Annie walked up to the table, her cheeks rosy and bright.

"About that family that just left," Jocelyn said. "The woman looked like she'd been beat up."

"I saw it when she came through the line. Did she say anything to you?" Miss Annie asked Luke.

"No. I was just offering to help her with a restraining order if she wanted one," Luke replied.

"I didn't realize you were that kind of lawyer," Miss Annie said. "I figured you were just into the big money clients, like the one trying to buy this building from the city."

Luke smiled. "I've spent time representing many different clients, but yes, I do specialize in corporate law with big money clients."

"Uh-huh." Miss Annie eyed Jocelyn's hand in his. "And I suppose this big fancy pants client of yours wants us outta here."

"My client is aware of your presence in the building, and just so you know, these acquisitions take a good deal of time to close, so nothing is going to change in the near future. But, I think once my client does take ownership, you'll find her to be very amicable when it comes to assisting you in relocating."

"Relocating?" Annie's voice rang off the walls. "I can't relocate. The people here count on me being *here*. Not somewhere else. You tell your highfalutin client she ain't heard the last of Miss Annie and her kitchen. Isn't that right, Jocelyn?" Miss Annie dropped something on the table before she walked away. "This is for you, Sarge. It's programmed just like the last one."

Sarge picked up the new cell phone, cradling the device in his bandaged hands before dropping it in a pocket.

"Are you the one who stopped the fire?" Luke asked.

Sarge remained mute and stood up from the table.

"Uh…looks like we're going," Eric said, following Sarge's lead. "I need to get Sarge's bandages changed before I head to the hospital. It was nice meeting you, Luke."

"You too," Luke said, shaking Eric's hand.

Jocelyn pulled back, their contact having been severed. Luke turned to her, his knee brushing hers. "It doesn't seem like too many of your friends liked my being here."

"Oh no," Jocelyn said, but the smile he cracked told her it hadn't broken his heart. Right, his sense of humor thing again.

"Did you like my being here?" He picked up her hand again.

Her brain scrambled as she tried to come up with another way to answer his question other than with the truth, but she couldn't think straight. "Yes."

"Then that's all that matters."

Her heart raced, and she waited for her mind to catch up and figure out what to say next. "I should go help Miss Annie. I'm sorry she got upset with you. She's usually very kind."

"She wasn't upset with me. It's my client and the situation I represent that have her rattled. I'm pretty sure she likes me."

His confident air brought a giggle to Jocelyn's lips. "Now why would you think that?"

"Because she told me when she showed me how to pour juice."

Jocelyn looked away, wishing the way they were sitting so close together and bantering didn't feel so natural, like something she wanted to do for the rest of her life. She pulled her hand away and crossed her arms over her chest. That felt safer.

"What were you talking about when you came to see me this afternoon? You mentioned an exclusive story for me? Or was that just for show?"

Luke folded his hands together. "My client has suffered from bad publicity in the past. She has some pretty intriguing life-changing goals for her operation here in the city, and she'd like to get some positive press on the whole thing when the time is right."

"Did she deserve the bad press?"

"Her company did, yes. But as you know, there's often more to a story than what's printed. It just so happens, the press hounds latched onto only one aspect of her operation. She's worked hard to make her company successful. She's made mistakes, but I believe she's learned from them."

"I bet she pays you a lot of money to believe her."

Luke sat back in his chair, bringing one hand to his chin. "I would even if she didn't pay me a lot of money." His eyes didn't leave hers. "When I read your article today, I was pretty upset about how the press had used its power of influence to tell a story. But, then you said you were just telling the people's story. And I see that now." He motioned around the room that was thinning out. "The people here do have a story, and it's about to collide with another one. Let's just say my client could have her pick of any building in the city, but there's a reason she wanted the most rundown, piece of junk place I could find."

Jocelyn was intrigued, but she waited to hear the catch. There was always a catch. "Why me?"

He looked at her, drilling her with those clear blue eyes that spelled danger for her heart. "Because I trust you. I've always been a pretty good judge of people. Your boss, for instance, strikes me as the type that would turn this story on its head and make my client out to be a villain."

Jocelyn agreed. He was right about Robert, but that still wasn't a full explanation. "If your client is so big a name, doesn't she have a PR department or something that should be taking care of this?"

"She did, but she fired most of them in light of the last fiasco. She's slowly rebuilding and is looking for people she trusts to work with."

"You mean people she can pay off."

"Perhaps." Luke turned his hands upward. "But I'd be willing to put you in touch with her, seeing as how you're already knee-deep in the action around here. You'd have to sign a non-disclosure agreement, but then you could decide for yourself if this is a story you believe in or not."

She considered his offer. "What makes you think this is the kind of story I can get my editor to let me print?"

"I believe you can. If you want to."

She could sit here forever and get lost in those eyes and his sweet seductive tone. What was going on with her?

The snap of table legs as Isaiah cleared the first table from the room, broke her from the hold of his gaze.

"Fine," she said, letting her arms fall to her lap. "I'll talk with your client. And now I should go help with the dishes."

"I'd like to help too."

"No, that's all right. You've been very helpful. There's no need to for you stick around."

A flicker of hurt crossed Luke's face, and she stood, trying to get away before she lost her resolve.

"But I'd like to stay and help," he said.

"Do what you want," she said as she turned for the kitchen, carrying the pitcher of water and coffee pot.

Jocelyn made a conscious effort to keep her focus glued to the sink full of dishes in front of her, but her wayward eyes kept catching glimpses of Luke helping Isaiah with the tables.

She called for a taxi before hanging up her apron and saying goodnight to Miss Annie. Outside, the cool evening air greeted her as it teased the tendrils of hair that had fallen out of her bun. A yellow cab pulled into the back alley as the door opened and closed behind her.

"Mind if we share a cab?" Luke asked.

Darkness had fallen, and his features were shadowed. She desperately wished she didn't want to sit in the backseat with him all snuggled up.

"Well…" she said with hesitation, even though it made sense, since they were going to the same location. But she certainly didn't want to send the wrong signal. She wasn't interested in the heartbreak this guy was certain to deliver. "I guess…"

The cab came to a stop, and he opened the door. "That's okay," he smiled. "I see you're not exactly ready to take this relationship to the intimate level of cab sharing just yet." He winked at her. "So, how about I race you home instead?"

He peered into the cab and addressed the driver, "What do you say? Give me a five second head start."

The driver shrugged.

"All right. Then it's on." Luke gestured for Jocelyn to get inside.

"You're going to race the cab back to the building?"

"Why not? I haven't had time for a run today, and it's a beautiful cloudless night." He gazed up at the stars overhead. When his eyes came down to meet hers again, they were serious. "I hope you're not accustomed to winning."

"I hope you're accustomed to losing," she said, matching his tone as she slid into the backseat. "Because there'll be no head start for you."

"Fine with me." He stepped back to close the door before pulling it open again. "Loser pays the fare."

And he was off. Jocelyn turned to watch him out the back window as he left the alley, taking off at a jogger's pace, his arms and legs moving with athletic grace. She quickly rattled off the address, and the driver slowly pulled onto the backstreet and circled the block back to the main road. Luke would surely beat her at this rate. She could see him two blocks ahead. But then they passed him as the cab hit a series of green lights. She waved as they drove by. The next light turned red, and the cab stopped. She turned in her seat but didn't see him along the sidewalks.

"He probably turned on Stark," the driver said. "We'll catch up again soon. Is he your boyfriend?"

"No, my neighbor." Jocelyn whipped her head in both directions. "Why didn't we take Stark?"

"Because it's a one-way," the cab driver said as they started to move again. "Well, you and your neighbor make a nice couple."

Couple? No, no, no. They were not a couple. They turned down another street, and Jocelyn scanned the pedestrians, looking for Luke, but she didn't see him. Her building was a block away, and still there was no sign of him. Looked like she would win.

The cab pulled up in front of her building, and she got out. Luke was nowhere in sight. She glanced around, suddenly worried something had happened to him, when he came walking down the sidewalk.

"So you beat me," he said, not one bit out of breath. "Guess I'd better pay up." He pulled out his wallet and paid the cab driver while Jocelyn stood by.

When the cab pulled away, she looked him in the eye. "Why do I get the sense you were just standing at the corner waiting for me to pull up?"

"Because you have very good instincts." He came close and reached for her hand, his assessment having frozen her in place. "Come on, let's go inside."

Chester held the door open.

The elevator brought them to their floor, and Jocelyn felt their time together coming to a close. Unless she wanted to extend their evening by inviting him in, which she certainly was not going to do, because that was probably what he intended. And she wasn't about to let some man think she was that kind of a girl.

She needed to set her boundaries now. Make things crystal clear. She hadn't come to the city to fool around and return home all broken hearted.

They passed the hall to his apartment, and when he stopped at her door with her, she knew he was expecting an invitation.

"Please don't kiss me again," she said. It was the first thing that popped into her head. And why was she staring at his lips when she said it?

"Are you just talking about tonight or ever again?"

She looked down at the floor. "Why did you kiss me in front of my boss? And hold my hand?"

His face went serious. "Would you believe me," he took her hand in his, "if I said it was because it felt as natural to me as breathing?"

That's exactly how it'd felt to her too. And foolishly, she wanted to swoon. But that was probably his plan—that's how these smooth-talking guys worked. He wanted her to forget all of her good senses and let him into the apartment, and it wouldn't end there. She grabbed her keys, ready to escape his eyes and the pull he had on her.

"Thank you for inviting me to spend time with you tonight," he said, brushing away the hair that tickled her cheek.

Her knees went weak, and she leaned against the door, only to have it fall open against her weight.

Fourteen

Luke reacted quickly and pulled Jocelyn to her feet. "Are you okay?"

She rubbed her head. "Yeah. What just happened?"

Luke stepped around her, found a light switch, and flipped it on.

Meow.

The hollow and frightened call of the cat came from somewhere in the back of the apartment. As he ventured inside, Jocelyn clutching the back of his shirt, he picked up a broom that lay in his path. He gripped the handle with both hands, ready to swing it like a baseball bat if he needed to. The kitchen was to his left, every cupboard open, broken glasses and plates scattered across the floor. He advanced further into the apartment. In the living room, couch cushions were tossed like a salad, and a lamp and potted plants were overturned. Shelves had been wiped clean, their contents sprawled on the floor. Another lamp was knocked over, this one laying in pieces. He flipped on another light switch.

Meow.

Following the sound, he found the door the cat was locked behind. Slowly, he turned the knob. The door cracked open, and the cat bolted.

He eased the door the rest of the way open, tightening his hold on the broom handle, and peered inside—a bedroom.

Jocelyn gasped in his ear. "Fiona's room."

It was trashed, clothes pulled from every drawer.

Scratching sounded from the other room, and they both jumped. Jocelyn pulled in closer to him before relaxing.

"It's just Bodhi, using his litter box." Jocelyn went to close the bathroom door, keeping the cat inside. "Someone's been all through the bathroom too," she said, resuming her position behind him.

"What's over there?" He pointed to another door, slightly ajar.

"That's my room." Her voice choked on the last word.

Cautiously putting one foot in front of the other, he approached the door and pushed it open. A mattress had been flipped over on the floor, blankets pinned underneath. Books from a shelf lay like scattered leaves on the floor.

"Who would do this?" Jocelyn's voice shook.

Luke turned, putting a hand on her shoulder, and tried to get her terrified eyes to focus on him. "We need to call the police."

She nodded, and he dialed the phone.

* * *

The police were still dusting Jocelyn's apartment for fingerprints. One officer—a Sergeant Swanson—had come to Luke's apartment and was questioning her.

"Answer me, Miss Banks."

Jocelyn stared straight ahead, stroking Bodhi's back. His eyes were droopy, probably compliments of the little pill Jocelyn gave him before leaving the apartment.

Luke stood, his anger swelling. Where did the sergeant get off talking to her like that? Didn't he see what she'd just been through? Where was the man's compassion?

"I'm sorry, what did you say?" Jocelyn asked, Sergeant Swanson's briskness seeming to bead off her.

"I asked what you might have of value that someone would be seeking."

"You think she was targeted?" Luke asked. "Couldn't this have been a random break in?"

"With the way the apartment looks, it seems someone was after something specific." Sergeant Swanson faced Jocelyn. "Did you have something hidden in there?"

"Hidden?" Luke pushed his fingers through his hair. He didn't like how the Sergeant seemed to be turning this on Jocelyn, like she'd done something wrong. Like she was the criminal they were tracking.

"No, nothing I can think of. I moved here a couple of weeks ago. I'm only staying for a while and didn't bring many things with me. Certainly nothing valuable, except my laptop and tablet, but I keep those with me."

Sergeant Swanson wrote something down. "What about your roommate?"

"What about her?" Jocelyn asked.

"Have you noticed any suspicious behavior? Strangers hanging around the place?"

"No. Fiona left the day after I got here."

The sergeant looked up. "And where is she now?"

"Bali," Jocelyn replied. "On a yoga retreat."

The sergeant gave Luke a skeptical glance before he wrote something down. "We'll look into it. In the meantime, if you think of anything else, let us know."

"Wait." Luke slid onto the couch next to Jocelyn. "What about your boss? Robert? I didn't get a good vibe from him when I was at your office."

Jocelyn scratched Bodhi behind the ear, the purring steady and calm. "What motivation would he have?"

"To intimidate you."

Jocelyn shrugged. "Maybe?"

"What is this man's name?" Sergeant Swanson asked.

"Robert Kaminsky. He works with me at *The Portland Daily Report*."

The officer wrote the information down. "We'll check him out. Anyone else come to mind?"

"What about your source? The one who gave you the recording. Any chance he turned on you?"

Jocelyn shook her head. "I can't imagine that he would. I'd trust that man with my life. He has a vested interest in getting to the bottom of this as much as we do."

"What recording are you talking about?" Sergeant Swanson interrupted.

"I have friends at Miss Annie's soup kitchen. A couple of nights ago, someone lit a fire near the building. We have reason to believe it was meant to do a lot more damage than it did. One of the patrons there was making a video recording when it captured another voice, leading us to suspect this was an arson attempt. I turned the recording in at the police station. I left it with Officer Reyes."

"Reyes." Sergeant Swanson jotted that down. "Who else has knowledge of this recording?"

Jocelyn listed off the people at the soup kitchen that were aware of the recording in addition to the police and her editor. Luke added that three of the partners at his firm were also told of the recording.

"We'll look into all of them," the officer said, putting away his notepad. "I'll go see if they've uncovered any fingerprints at your apartment."

When Sergeant Swanson was gone, Luke wandered to the window. The shades were still drawn on Jocelyn's apartment. He could have sworn they'd been open when he came home, but he really couldn't be sure.

He returned to the couch and rubbed the top of Bodhi's head. "If only this little guy could talk, I bet he'd tell us exactly what happened."

"It must have been terrifying for him."

"I don't know." Luke sized up the sedated cat. "I think he's a lot tougher than he looks."

Jocelyn didn't reply, her eyes having gone vacant.

Luke cleared his throat. "Can I get you anything? Water? Dinner? Are you hungry?"

She shook her head, coming out of the deep stare. "No, thank you. I'm not hungry."

"That's okay," Luke said, going to the kitchen. "I'm not either. But once the food gets here, you might feel differently."

"No," Jocelyn said over her shoulder. "You don't have to do that. I'm sure the police will be done soon, and I can go home."

"First of all," Luke dialed his phone and pressed it to his ear, "I want to order you dinner. And second of all, you're not going home tonight. Not while there's a criminal on the loose that wants something from you. And definitely not before you get more reinforcing locks."

Her mouth dropped open as the line was answered, and Luke cut her off by ordering two supreme burritos from the takeout place across the street. He'd gotten to know the manager there, Tracie—a sweet woman with two kids and a husband who worked for the bus department. She was more than happy to arrange to have the meal delivered after hearing about the break in at his neighbor's.

By the time he'd gotten off the phone, Jocelyn had moved to the window. He joined her there.

"Why would someone do this?" Her voice trembled.

"I wish I knew." Without a second thought, he drew an arm around her shoulder. Bodhi purred peacefully in her arms. To his surprise, she didn't pull away or go rigid and apprehensive. Instead, she softened, laying her head against his chest.

"It kind of makes you lose your faith in humanity, doesn't it?"

A gentle laugh rocked his shoulders. "My faith in humanity, huh? I guess I hadn't really thought about it like that."

They stood there, him holding her in his arms, for a while. Luke lost track of time, only aware of the sweet flowery scent from her skin and the way he wanted to keep her safe, to take away the fear he'd seen in her eyes.

There was a knock at the door, and the way she jumped at the sound had him internally cursing the person who'd done this. Reluctantly, he moved away from her and answered the door. Sergeant Swanson stood there.

"You're free to return to your apartment," he said, looking past Luke's shoulders. "We weren't able to obtain any prints. The apartment looks clean. If you notice anything missing later, give us a call. In the meantime, we'll review the security tapes from the building and let you know if we come up with anything."

"Thank you," Luke said as the officer retreated.

Before he could close the door, the delivery person arrived with their dinner. Luke paid and shut the door, turning back to Jocelyn, who still stared out the window.

He set the bag of warm food down in the kitchen and walked to her side, gently extracting the limp cat from her hold. In the corner, they'd set up Bodhi's bed and litter box. He set the cat on the plush cushion.

Jocelyn meandered back to the couch, and Luke detoured into the kitchen, bringing dinner with him.

"Here you go," he said, pulling out a foil-wrapped burrito for her.

She didn't take it. He set it on the coffee table in front of her before pulling out one for himself. Sitting on the floor, he quietly started in on his dinner.

"Have you tried this place before?" He bit into the tortilla shell.

"No." She slid to her knees on the floor and sat across the table from him.

"They're pretty good. Nice and fresh if you like that."

She nodded and pulled back the foil. "Is this how you dine with all your dates?"

He paused mid-bite. "Is this supposed to be a date?"

Shock pierced her blue-gray eyes. "No, I was—"

"Then, it's not a date. And to answer your earlier question, no. I have never dined on the floor with a date or a non-date. You're my first."

She batted her eyes away bashfully.

"So, where are you from?" he asked between bites.

She lifted her eyes to look at him. "That's a very first-date kind of question, don't you think?"

"It would be if we were on a date, but we're not, so it's just conversation."

She smoothed out the foil on the table. "River's Edge," she answered. "Ever heard of it?"

"No, I haven't. What's it like there?"

"Much smaller than here. The population barely breaks ten thousand. It's right in the heart of Oregon's wine country."

"Wine country? It must be beautiful there."

"It is. At least outside of town where all the vineyards are."

"So, are you a grape farmer?"

She giggled, soft and light. "No, I live in town with my father."

"I see." Luke wiped his hands again. "So, what brought you here to the city?"

"You're awfully full of questions." She grinned as she bit into her burrito.

Good, she was eating. He'd hoped to distract her enough to get her mind off the break in. "Just curious about my elusive neighbor who lives with someone else's cat."

Jocelyn snickered. "You make it sound strange."

"That's okay. I like strange. So what brought you here?"

"A job, I guess. I've been working for my uncle at his newspaper back home since before I graduated college. He insisted it was time I got some big city experience before…"

"Before what?" he prompted.

Jocelyn tipped her head. "I'm not sure exactly, but I get the feeling he's thinking about retiring soon and wants to pass the paper to me."

"Is that what you want?"

"I guess so." Jocelyn shrugged and tried to bite daintily into the generous burrito.

"Yeah, I know how that goes."

She looked at him curiously. "How what goes?"

"Doing what you think your family wants you to do."

"Oh no," Jocelyn amended. "I want to go back to River's Edge. My father's there, and he needs me."

"Why's that?"

Silence lingered in the air as she seemed to consider her next words. Jocelyn sat back, putting her hands in her lap. "My mother died during my senior year of college."

He froze. "I'm sorry to hear that. How did she die?"

She pushed back tears and stalled by picking at a bean with a plastic fork. "Cancer. She was diagnosed with stage-four breast cancer during fall term. I came home right away and finished my classes over the internet while interning with my uncle. Once she was gone, I couldn't leave my dad."

"Oh wow. I can't imagine."

"It was tough." She picked at another bean.

"Was the plan always to go back home?"

"No, not at all. I had big dreams of becoming an investigative reporter in a big city."

"So you're finally living your dream." He cracked a smile.

"I guess. But it won't be for long. This job is temporary. More like a favor to my uncle, and when the time is right, I'll head back home."

"Any chance you'd stick around if the job turned permanent?"

Jocelyn looked at him like she was considering his question but her answer came quickly. "No, not a chance."

A beat of silence passed between them.

"What about you?" she asked. "Has it always been your dream to work in the family firm?"

"Nope, never."

Jocelyn looked shocked. "Then what are you doing there?"

Luke rolled his lips together, trying to think of the best way to explain what his life was like. "I never had a dream job, because I wasn't allowed to dream."

"You weren't allowed to?"

He shook his head. "When you grow up with your name already printed on a door, it's just a given. It says Lewis and Sons. Well I'm a son, and therefore, this is my job."

"This is America, you know. The land of freedom and choice."

"It might be America where you live, but my life has always been a dictatorship."

"So, if you were able to overthrow this government of yours, what would you do?"

Luke dusted his hands clean and crumpled the foil wrapper into a ball. "I've never been able to figure that out. Maybe own a surf shop on a beach somewhere."

"You surf?"

"No, but doesn't that sound like an ideal job?"

"I don't know. I think the ideal job is something that brings meaning and purpose to your life. Something that you feel good about doing day after day."

"Like being a lawyer."

"It doesn't seem like such a bad career choice."

"It's not. And there are parts I enjoy. The law is actually very interesting. It's just a shame when it's used in the wrong fashion."

"What do you mean?"

"Like how the government continues to pass laws saving the wealthy from additional taxes when having them pay a fraction more of what they already do could aid so many more less fortunate."

"Some would say that's their privilege."

"I guess, but isn't it our duty as a society to help as many as we can? Like your friends at the soup kitchen. How many of them could benefit from fifty or a hundred dollars more a month?"

"You sound very civic-minded."

"I try to be. But I find myself wondering more and more if what I'm doing matters. If it's what I'm really meant to do. You, on the other hand, seem certain about what you want."

"I wouldn't say I'm completely certain about what I want, but I do know that I love reporting, digging into stories. But, I *am* rethinking this big city gig. It's a little too cut throat…too many *if it bleeds it leads* stories for my taste. I kind of miss the feel-good stories from my little town. All this fascination with death and destruction can get a little morbid."

"Uninspiring."

"Exactly."

"Like finding tax cuts for the wealthy day in and day out." He held her gaze, feeling like she knew exactly what he was talking about, and she was seeing him in a whole new light. He didn't want to let that feeling go.

"I'll take your word for it," Jocelyn said as she pushed her half-eaten burrito back in the bag and wiped her hands down her legs. "So, what about you?" she asked. "Have you always lived in Portland?"

"No, I'm actually pretty new to the area too. I've been at the founding office in Seattle, where I was raised, for a couple of years and needed a change. Not so much from the office but my personal life. I had a woman catch me with another. I guess she thought we were something more than I had intended. And let's just say, when she tried to knock me out with a porcelain vase, it made me take stock of what kind of life I was living."

"I see." She wiped her hands again. "And you like it here?"

He gathered up their garbage, wondering if it was a good thing she'd skipped over his past or not. "Most of the time, sure. Working for my brother has actually been more bearable than I thought it would be."

"Are you close? You and your brother?"

He carried the garbage to the kitchen. "I guess. It's been better the last couple years. He went through some pretty tough stuff with his ex-wife, but he's got his life on track now, and it's great to see him so happy again." Luke thought about how untouchable Marcus had been when he left Seattle for the Portland office. All the drama he'd tried to overcome on his own. Keeping himself at a distance from everyone.

"What about you and your sister?" Luke asked, returning to the living room with two bottles of water. He handed one to Jocelyn. "Are you close?"

"Not really." She toyed with the label. "After our mom died, she got pretty lost. Really flighty, never finishing what she started. She changed majors three times in college. She ended up with a degree in humanities, whatever that's good for, and still flits from idea to idea. I doubt she'll ever get her head on straight and figure out what she wants to do."

"That's not really your concern, is it? I mean, you're her sister, not her mother. Maybe she's happy with the way her life is. And you should be happy for her."

"How can I be happy for her? She has no money in the bank. She lives in a tiny apartment above the town's dance and psychic studio, and teaches three hours of yoga a week."

"A dance and psychic studio? Now this sounds like an interesting place."

Jocelyn waved a hand at him. "Don't get me started on Madame Christine. She's nice enough and has taught dance classes in River's Edge since I was a girl. About ten years ago, though, after her husband passed away, she started talking about how she could commune with the dead."

"Do you believe her?"

"No, of course not, but Sophie sits down with her every couple of weeks for one of her séances or whatever and says she talks to Mom while she's there."

"What does she say?"

"Who?"

"Your mom?"

"Last time, Sophie said she said this move was good for me and to be careful."

"Sounds like motherly advice."

"Which Madame Christine could have easily made up and convinced Sophie it came from my mother's mouth." Jocelyn stifled a yawn.

"Would you like to lie down?"

Jocelyn looked at him out of the corner of her eye. "Do you use that line often?"

Luke, who usually downplayed those types of remarks, didn't know how to answer. He didn't want Jocelyn to think any less of him. "If you're tired, you can have my room."

"That's all right, I should probably be going now."

"You're not going anywhere until a new lock with a chain or something is put on that door."

"I'll be fine." She stood.

He got to his feet as well. "If you're insisting on going back to your place, then I'll go with you. We can sleep there."

She let out a tin-sounding laugh. "That's not what I was suggesting."

"I know, but it's what I'm insisting on. You stay here. Or I stay there. And seeing as how Bodhi is all tuckered out over there, I suggest you stay here."

Jocelyn set her jaw, determination in her eye. "Okay, but I'm *not* sleeping with you."

"Who said anything about sleeping together? See, there you go again, putting ideas into my head that weren't there to begin with."

"Ha ha. Your innocent act doesn't fool me at all. I know your type. I've fallen for it once before, and I won't do it again."

He moved closer to her, the vulnerability in her eyes pulling him in. "I have no intention of fooling you about anything. Now, please stay because I'm offering you a safe place to be."

After another electric moment passed between them, she nodded and sat on the couch. He fluffed the pillow next to her. "Lie back, and try to relax," he said.

She let the bun out of her hair, the tresses falling around her face. After she lay back, he reached down to slip her feet out of her high heels. Red marks showed where her skin had been pinched. He pulled her feet into his lap and gently rubbed them.

"Now, are you going to tell me about the time you were fooled by love, or do I get to use my imagination?"

"That's a deeply guarded secret, that I have no intention of sharing with anyone."

"Then off to the land of imagination it is."

"Oh, come on. Don't do that. Isn't there a secret you've kept private?"

"Actually, there is." He moved his hands up her legs, rubbing her calves. "It happened when I was twelve."

"Twelve?"

Luke nodded slowly, the image of the scrawny boy he'd been coming back to him. "I went to a very elite private school in Seattle. All the kids' parents were doctors, lawyers, stockbrokers, famous people—television stars and athletes."

"Must have been nice."

Luke shrugged. "I think all schools are pretty much the same."

"Says the boy who didn't go to kindergarten in a broom closet."

"Broom closet?"

She nodded and yawned at the same time. "Small school. There were only six of us in the class, but still, it was a tiny room that the janitor used to use."

Jocelyn looked beautiful laying there, her hair fanned out against the pillow. He realized she was the only woman he'd had in the apartment—aside from Stacy. But Stacy hadn't fit. Her fancy made-up face and uncomfortably tight clothes made her stand out against the comfortable space, but not Jocelyn. She fit.

He cleared his throat. "What I mean is that all schools have their same groups. The smart kids who go to science camp in the summer and make studying into an early profession. Then there are the sports stars and the slackers who get by on their good looks and ability to bribe others to get them through their classes."

"Which group were you in?"

"None really. My brother, however..." Luke smiled, remembering Marcus always walking around with his nose in a book, until he discovered basketball. Then his book time became shared with the court. "He was smart and super athletic. The all-American boy. And I, well, I was just his little brother, who was nowhere near as smart or talented."

Jocelyn yawned.

"Am I boring you?"

"Not at all. Please continue."

"Anyway, I was small for my age, and by the time I was twelve, all the girls were taller than me, and most of the boys were at least starting to show signs of puberty, but not me."

"You were a late bloomer."

"It sounds sweet when you say it, but for a twelve year old boy, it's torture. And it didn't take long for the kids to nickname me Lulu."

Jocelyn's hand covered her mouth. "Lulu?"

"Yeah. Apparently, my parents didn't think the whole Luke Lewis thing through before they named me. It easily lends itself to shortening. It's funny now, but back then it killed me. I remember asking my mom one time if I could legally change my name. She asked why I'd want to do a silly thing like that. I told her I was afraid kids might call me Lulu. She laughed and said that was ridiculous because we were Lewises, and the Lewis-family name was highly respected."

"But, kids don't care about prestige do they?"

"No." He loved how she understood without him having to explain it. He'd never told anyone this story, afraid they'd laugh at him like his mother had, telling him it was a silly schoolboy story, and not validate the true hurt he'd felt that year, even if it was a long time ago. He propped his elbow on the arm of the couch as a yawn crept up. "The worst part was that the instigator was a girl."

"A girl?"

"Yeah, the biggest, tallest, strongest, meanest girl in the class. Everyone was afraid of her. Nobody picked on her because she could inflict bodily harm if she chose to. I think her dad was a professional wrestler or boxer or something like that."

"What was her name?"

It came to him surprisingly fast. He would have thought it buried deeper than that in his memory. "Molly. Molly Johnson." Her round face, her mouth filled with shiny silver braces, and those knee socks that could never stay up on her meaty calves all rushed in as if it had been yesterday. "Huh?" he said, shaking his head. "I haven't thought about her in years."

"When did she stop teasing you?"

"I don't remember exactly. But it was springtime, and she'd finally progressed to the point where she was threatening to pound my face in, and I was supposed to meet her at the soccer field after school one day."

"Charming girl."

"Yeah."

"So what did you do?"

"I wrote her a poem."

"A poem?" Jocelyn sounded surprised. "Do you remember it?"

Luke closed his eyes, trying to remember the words, but they didn't come easily. "It was something about how her hair shined and her smile glimmered—you know, because she had all these braces in her mouth."

Jocelyn's laugh mixed with his, and he liked the sound of it.

"I don't remember any more, but I thought for sure I'd get a double pounding for it. When I was done reading, I looked up, and she was crying. Real tears, crying. And she walked up and kissed me."

"Kissed you?"

"Oh yeah. Full-on lip-to-lip contact." Luke laughed at the memory. How surprised he'd been. He rubbed his hand across his forehead. "That's when I realized no one had probably ever said those sorts of things to her before."

"Kindness trumps all."

"Something like that." A revelation hit him. That's why he did it—okay, not the only reason—but, he'd liked making women feel good about themselves because it made him feel good about himself—temporarily, but still. All this time, he'd thought it was simply to get the attention of his parents. The more inappropriate the woman, the more flack he'd catch, until his parents gave up and went back to ignoring him. *Huh?* Wonder what Dr. Pike would make of this little epiphany?

"What is it?" Jocelyn asked.

"Nothing." Luke shook his head. "I was just remembering how from then on, girls would stop by my locker all the time. Now, I think it's because they were looking for someone to be nice to them. Back then, I thought it was something different."

"I bet you were a sweet kid." Jocelyn's eyes looked heavy.

"I guess that all depends on who you ask." He studied her stretched across his couch, her eyes drifting closed. "How did you just do that?"

"Do what?" Her voice was lazy.

"Get me to tell you my deepest secret? No one, and I mean no one, knows about Lulu."

"You wouldn't have told me if it wasn't a story you wanted to tell."

He'd never wanted to tell it. Until now. But why? Why her? "What about you?" he asked. "Don't you want to tell me about your secret lover?"

"No." Her eyes were closed.

"Then at least tell me if he was good in bed." He was joking, of course, but he couldn't deny that he was curious.

"I wouldn't know." She yawned. "I've never had anyone to compare him to."

Fifteen

Jocelyn slung her bag over her shoulder and scratched Bodhi between the ears. She hoped the disarray of the apartment wouldn't upset him, but she didn't have time to do any more cleaning this morning.

"Be tough today, okay big guy?" she said before closing the door behind her. Thanks to the on-call locksmith she'd enlisted this morning, two new locks—make that three, if you count the replacement for the door handle lock that had been picked—were installed. She turned her key in the deadbolt and hurried for the elevator. It wasn't until her feet hit the sidewalk that she finally slowed down, safe from a run in with Luke.

Waking in his apartment this morning with her feet stretched in his lap had been oddly intimate and left her feeling vulnerable. It had taken a great deal of stealth to slip out of there with Bodhi and not wake him. Although, that funny slouched position she'd left him in didn't look very comfortable, and she'd wanted to move him.

Her cell phone rang, and she wondered if it was Fiona. She'd left a message on her phone this morning, and even though she'd said she wouldn't have access to her phone while in Bali, Jocelyn still hoped for an opportunity to explain to her roommate. But it was Sophie. Jocelyn prayed her sister had forgiven her by now, because she didn't need to add a sister-fight to the beginning of this day.

"Hello."

"You answered," Sophie said, sounding surprised. "I didn't expect you to answer. I thought you'd be at work already. Why aren't you at work?"

"I'm on my way there now." Jocelyn stopped at the food trailer on the corner. No way was she going to make it through this day without a little help from caffeine.

"Okay, well, I was just going to leave you a message."

"A message about what?" It was Jocelyn's turn to order, and she tipped the phone away from her mouth. "A medium coffee. Black, please."

"Wait. You're ordering coffee? You never order coffee."

"Well, today I do." She paid and grabbed the steaming cup. "Now what did you want to tell me?"

"Sounds like somebody got up on the wrong side of the bed this morning."

Jocelyn wasn't in the mood for her sister's patronizing tone. "I'm almost to the office. Is there something you needed to say or not?"

"Yeah. Last night when I was at dinner with Dad and Madame Christine—"

"You didn't bring Dad to one of your voodoo chats, did you?" Jocelyn stopped in the middle of the sidewalk, oncoming pedestrians veering around her.

"No. It was dinner. We all just had dinner. Sheesh. Get a grip, will you?"

"Sorry." Jocelyn continued walking. "You were saying?"

"Anyway, I told them I was staying with you this weekend because I'm heading to Albany again. I'll be at the same building all weekend long, so no need to send out a search party or anything, and I'll call when I'm home again on Sunday. Okay?"

"Yeah, fine." Jocelyn sipped her coffee, the bitter brew puckering her face. How did people stand to drink this stuff?

"What? That's it? Just yeah and fine. No interrogation? What's gotten into you?"

She thought about what Luke had said last night. How maybe Sophie was happy with what she was doing. "Does it make you happy?"

"Does what make me happy?"

"Whatever you're doing that you won't tell me about."

"Yeah, I guess." Sophie sounded confused.

"Then I wish you the best, as long as it's nothing illegal."

"You do? Since when? This isn't like you."

"I'm trying, Soph. I'm trying to let you live your life the way that works for you." She stopped along the sidewalk and leaned against the stone wall of her office building. "Just leave me a description of what you're wearing so I can report it to the police if you go missing."

Sophie laughed, the wall of tension between them crumbling down. "Now that sounds more like the sister I know and love."

"It's good to hear your voice this morning. Thanks for calling."

"Yeah. I got your message about your boss and your neighbor. How are things going now?"

"Better, I guess." A well of tears surfaced in her eyes, her vision going blurry as she remembered how scared she'd felt last night, coming home to a ravaged apartment. She didn't know what she'd have done, who she would have called if Luke hadn't been there. The last thing she wanted to do was worry her family, but she needed to tell someone. "Can you keep a secret? Promise me you won't tell Dad, or Uncle Larry, or even Madame Christine."

"Oh wow. This is new. Me keeping a secret for you. Of course you can trust me."

Jocelyn took a deep breath. "My apartment was broken into last night."

"You're kidding. Are you all right? Why didn't you say something?"

"Because this call was supposed to be all about you, right?" Jocelyn tried to make it sound like a joke.

"That's not funny. This is serious. Tell me what happened."

"It happened before I got home—"

"Thank goodness for that."

"And basically everything in the apartment was trashed."

"You mean nothing was stolen?"

"Not that I can see. But a lot of things were broken. Fiona's going to kill me."

"I don't think so. She'll be more glad that you're okay. It could have happened to anyone."

"No, it was someone targeting me."

"Really? Why?"

"I think it has something to do with a story I've been working on."

Sophie gasped. "Mom said to be careful. Remember, I told you she said that."

"I remember."

"No wonder you're so grumpy this morning. You probably didn't sleep a wink in that apartment after that happened."

"Actually, my neighbor let me stay over at his place."

Another gasp. "The one who was picturing you naked?"

Jocelyn blushed. "I may have over exaggerated. Look, I'm already late getting to work, so I should go. But have a good time this weekend, and be safe."

"You too. And call if you need anything."

"Thanks, Soph."

Feeling remotely better than she had before, Jocelyn dropped the cell phone in her pocket and took a sip of coffee. *Oh, that's disgusting.*

She walked into the office and slunk to her desk, wishing the day was already over.

* * *

Twenty minutes later, Robert made an appearance at Jocelyn's cubicle. She tried to hide the effort she was making to keep her eyes peeled open. The coffee—straight up black and bold—hadn't even remotely kicked in.

Her fingers had yet to touch the keyboard and type a single word. She wished she could say it was the break-in clouding her thoughts, but that would be a lie. Luke had her mind swimming. All the reasons he was wrong for her and all the reasons she couldn't get him out of her mind, like the way he rubbed her feet. The way he told her the story about being picked on. How he'd so openly told her about being with other women.

She'd assumed as much, but she'd never imagined he'd be so forthcoming about it. Paulo certainly never was.

"What's with you, Banks?" Robert stepped into her cubicle.

Jocelyn blinked. "Nothing."

"Your boyfriend keep you out too late last night? Because that's not an acceptable excuse for being late."

"No," she said, ignoring the wishful rush that hit her belly at the thought of Luke again. She put a hand to her forehead, hoping that might clear the fog. "I sent you a text this morning. I was having the locks replaced on my apartment after it was broken into last night."

Pulling out his cell phone, Robert opened his tiny jaw, apparently ready to bark at her about not receiving the message. But he put it away with a shrug.

"Last night you said? While you were home?"

She wished she wasn't so tired—that she could rely on her instincts to read Robert right now, because she couldn't register whether that question actually came from a place of concern for her or for himself.

"No, while I was out. I'm trying to get caught up now."

"Well, shake it off. You've got work to do. I need your next cutesy little humanitarian piece before five o'clock."

He moved on before she could respond, which was probably a good thing. She tried to refocus on her computer screen and the story she was sharing about Sally and Jimbo finding themselves relying on the kindness of strangers.

Before her next breath, the desk phone rang.

"Jocelyn Banks," she said into the mouthpiece.

"Hi. It's Annie. I'm just leaving the hospital and thought you'd want to know Sarge was brought in. There was another fire attempt at the building. He's burned but also beaten up. It's pretty bad."

"I'm on my way." Jocelyn's blood ran cold at the thought of Sarge being hurt.

"I'll tell Eric to keep an eye out for you."

Jocelyn shut down her laptop.

"Where do you think you're going?" Robert snapped as she stepped from her cubicle with her bag packed.

She didn't want to deal with him right now. "Another fire was set last night. A man was injured, and I'm going to get an exclusive on it."

Robert couldn't shy away from an exclusive, so he stepped aside and let her pass.

"Don't forget. Five o'clock, or your stories are done being printed," he called after her.

She didn't bother answering. He'd have his story.

The cab dropped her in front of the hospital, and Eric met her at the front doors. He wore blue-green scrubs and his white sneakers squeaked as he crossed the linoleum floor.

"Hey there," he said. "I heard about what happened at your place last night. You okay?"

"I'm fine." Jocelyn brushed away his concern. "How's Sarge?"

"He's hanging in there. Come on. I'll take you to him."

As they passed through the lobby, Jocelyn peppered Eric with questions.

"What time did the fire start?"

"Around eleven p.m. Officer Reyes and his partner had shown up to question Sarge about what happened at your place. They found three guys wailing on him and a fire blazing inside the building."

"How much damage was there?"

"Enough," Eric said when the elevator doors opened. He paused in the corridor, facing Jocelyn. "They broke out a window in the kitchen and threw flaming rags inside. The fire department got there as soon as they could, but the damage was extensive."

"Oh no." Jocelyn's knees went weak. "How's Miss Annie taking it?"

"All right, I guess." He nodded sorrowfully. "When she left here, she said she was on her way to see the building. Knowing her, she's probably mopping it up as we speak."

They continued walking until they reached a set of double doors where Eric punched a code into a keypad. The doors clicked and swished open.

"What is this place?" Jocelyn asked, not used to the added security of the hospital. When her mother had been admitted, they'd been able to walk into the halls without pass codes and escorts.

"This is the Inpatient Behavioral Health Unit."

"What's that code for?"

Eric's shoulders slumped. "It's the psych ward."

"What's Sarge doing in here?" The words rushed out in a harsh whisper.

"He seems to suffer from PTSD. A result of his three tours in Afghanistan, I'm guessing. Don't know any more than that. But as you've probably noticed, he prefers to keep to himself and will occasionally fade in and out of his role from the war. I think he was some kind of commanding officer. We all call him Sarge, but no one knows for sure if that was his real ranking. When he's provoked, or senses a hostile situation, his war-mindset seems to take over. That's why he'd never survive in a shelter. Too many of those guys get possessive and confrontational. Sarge was brought in once before after an altercation. He doesn't do well here. Confronted and confined. That's why Miss Annie leaves the window open for him in the basement. That way he can stay somewhere solitary and quiet."

"That's awful. Does he have any family?"

"Not sure. He doesn't carry ID, and none of us know his real name. He's been Sarge for as long as I've known him. When Officer Reyes left, he said he'd let me know as soon as they came up with any leads."

Jocelyn rubbed the ache in her neck right between her shoulders.

"You don't look so good. Are you sure you're all right? You had a rough night too."

"I'm fine. I just think sleeping over at my neighbor's left me with a giant pain in my neck."

"Oh, I get it. So, the two of you didn't do much sleeping last night."

"Yeah," Jocelyn said before noting the tease in his voice. She swatted his arm. "Don't be like that."

"Like what?"

"A man with only one thing on his mind."

"Oh, that. Fine, but you still have that look in your eye."

"What look? The tired, puffy-eyed look?"

"Something like that." He danced his eyebrows up and down.

"Quit teasing me."

"Okay." Eric led her to a door and peered through the window. "Go on in. You and Miss Annie will likely be the only visitors he gets. He's heavily medicated right now and may not know you. Also, he's restrained in case he should come to and have an episode." He looked back at Jocelyn, deep lines drawn across his forehead. "It's for your protection as well as his. I'll check back in a while to see if you need anything. Stay as long as you'd like."

"Thanks." She pushed through the door.

Sarge lay clothed in a white gown and tucked beneath a sheet. His worn and wrinkled skin was puffed and bruised, one eye completely swollen shut. Jocelyn reached for his hands but pulled back when she noticed the new bandages that completely encased his fingers and wrapped to his elbow, as well as cloth restraints tied to the bed. A security camera was perched in the corner of the ceiling. Only his chest moved up and down.

Jocelyn pulled a chair across the linoleum, wanting to sit at his bedside. She paused when the wooden leg made a loud scraping sound, but it didn't seem to alert Sarge.

Settling into the chair with machines and monitors all around her, Jocelyn was reminded of sitting with her mother after her double mastectomy. It wasn't a common procedure in that stage of cancer, but the doctor had been a hot-shot—in Jocelyn's opinion—and said the removal would lessen the number of malignant tumors ravaging her body. Best case, he'd said, it would gain her six more months of life. But it didn't. Two weeks later, the cancer had won its war.

Jocelyn rested her elbow on the arm of the chair and let her head fall into her hand. She didn't know how long she sat there like that, remembering her mother's last days cooped in a hospital. The rustling of sheets pulled her out of her reverie.

Sarge's less swollen eye lazily pulled open, then closed. He tried again, keeping it ajar and focusing on Jocelyn.

"Hey, Sarge." She stepped to the edge of the bed, careful not to touch him. "You're doing great. Keep resting, and you'll be out of here in no time."

His lips parted, and he made an effort to speak, but nothing came out. He tried again, "Sigh...sigh..."

Jocelyn picked up the plastic cup on his bedside table. "Do you want a drink?"

He nodded, and she held the straw to his mouth as he drew in two long pulls.

She set the cup down as he tried to speak again.

"Side," he said, rolling his head away from her. "Side…er."

Jocelyn didn't know what to make of his moment of consciousness. Side? Did he mean the side door? Or was he simply mumbling?

Eric came back in. "How's he doing?"

"He woke up. Sort of. He was saying something about side. The side of the building or the side door, or something? I'm going to go down to the kitchen, see if Miss Annie is still there. Maybe she'll know what he's talking about."

"Be careful," Eric said.

"I will."

* * *

After poking around the building for the better part of an hour, Jocelyn headed home. There was nothing there that she could see. Miss Annie wasn't there either. Long streams of yellow tape covered every possible entrance into the place. Completely discouraged, she headed for home, calling Officer Reyes on the way. She got the details on what happened and reported what Sarge had told her. He kindly reminded her that the borderline conscious ramblings of a patient in a psych ward were hardly solid pieces of evidence but that he'd keep it in mind as the investigation continued.

"But I'm glad you called," Officer Reyes said. "We've had a chance to look over the security footage from your building."

"And…" Jocelyn didn't know if she wanted more information.

"Three persons of interest entered your building through the parking garage entrance at five-thirty p.m. They look identical to the perpetrators my partner and I saw fleeing the scene last night. We've notified your doorman, but their faces were never caught on camera, and we still haven't been able to make a positive identification."

"Any luck with the voice on the video yet?"

"No, not yet. But we're still working on it."

After she arrived home and sat down with Officer Reyes's information, she didn't know if she felt better or worse. Having actual visual evidence of the people that had been in her home made the whole violation even more real. She looked around at the plants she'd repotted and the shelves she'd straightened. What were they looking for? If it was the recording, then who from the very short list of people that knew about it, was behind the forced entry to retrieve it?

By five o'clock, Jocelyn had her next story submitted to Robert—a full report on the confirmed arson attack on the Hitchcock Building, in lieu of her humanitarian piece on Sally and Jimbo. As she pushed send, there was a heavy knock at her door.

Through the peep hole, she was pleased to see Luke on the other side.

"Hey, there," she said after releasing the series of locks that now protected her.

"Hi. You look tired." He let his thumb draw down her cheek, the sensation soothing.

"I am."

"Why don't you rest?"

"I can't."

"Why not?"

"Just can't." She didn't want to tell him that when she thought about closing her eyes, the fear of not just one, but three criminals, who trashed apartments, set fire to buildings, and attacked a man like Sarge, came rushing to the surface. At any moment, they could break through her door. So, she went with something a little safer and said, "Sarge was hurt last night, and I'm worried about him."

Luke pulled her to his chest. His fingers slipped through her hair, and she closed her eyes. Everything inside her felt protected and safe.

He walked her inside, securing the new deadbolts and sat with her on the couch.

"Why don't you close your eyes?" He wrapped an arm around her shoulder, nestling her head on his chest.

"I couldn't…"

He rubbed his hand up and down her arm.

The knotted tension of her muscles relaxed.

"Yes, you can," he said, and it was the last thing Jocelyn remembered hearing.

Sixteen

Luke pulled the stack of papers off the copy machine and put them in the file folder. This was work that he could have passed off to a paralegal or one of the newer associates, but they were all pinch-hitting for Poindexter, who'd left suddenly last week on a family emergency. Luke didn't mind so much, though. He liked the excuse to get up and mingle with the other side of the office. He wasn't one of those lawyers who was content to dwell behind the desk all day. He'd already killed an hour visiting with Dennis and answering questions for Blair about the housing discrimination case she'd inherited from him. It was almost noon, and normally he'd slip out for a bite to eat, but today he had a client meeting with Lottie. She was getting some local television time based on the sudden media release of her interest in the Hitchcock Building.

Jocelyn did a stellar job depicting Lottie as a heroine—the exact perception she'd been trying to achieve. And the best part was that Lottie really was the genuine article. Lottie was sincere about her mission to create a soulful business, and that message rang through in the feature story.

Luke walked into the hall and stopped at Tippy's slightly ajar door. He knocked before pushing it all the way open. It had been days since they'd talked.

"Oh, Luke!" A haphazard mess of papers covered the man's desk, and he made an attempt to throw pages back into file folders.

"I can see you're busy." Luke said from the doorway. "But I just wanted to see if Matilda liked the building?"

"The building?"

It had almost been a week, and there was a chance Tippy had forgotten all about seeing Luke at his apartment building, considering the lapses that sometimes crept up in the man's short-term memory. "Yes, the apartment in the same building as mine. Will your niece and I soon be neighbors?"

"Oh, yes, yes. The apartment." Tippy dropped his hands over the files on his desk. "No, she didn't take that place. Too far from her work or some silly nonsense like that. You know how particular women can be."

"Sure. Well, it's a big city. I'm sure she'll find what she's looking for. Where does she work anyway?"

Tippy's gaze had wandered out the window. "Does what?"

"Work. Where does she work?"

"Oh, oh. Down by the waterfront. A little shop...a flower shop."

"Is it the Harbor Street Flower Shop? I run by it sometimes."

Tippy drummed his fingers. "Yeah, yeah. That's the one." Tippy's eyes went distant. "Maude loves flowers. I should send her some. Don't you think?"

The pain in his eyes pulled at Luke's heart. The poor man so obviously missed his wife. "I'm sure she'd love it."

"Yes, yes. I think you're right." Tippy picked up the phone, and Luke quietly slipped out of his office.

Coming through the reception area, Luke intercepted Lottie. A bright blue and white polka dot scarf tied in her hair matched the pants she wore with an understated blue jacket, a polka dot ribbon at the cuffs. A simple silver chain hung around her neck and hoop earrings sparkled from under her hair.

He escorted her to his office and adjusted his tie as he took a seat.

"You look lovely as always," he said.

Lottie crossed her legs. "What else would you expect? I'm about to be on television. Thanks to your friend's article."

"Jocelyn does pen a good story. But she had a very fine subject."

Lottie fanned her lashes up and down. "Yes well, we're not quite to parade-throwing status yet though, are we?"

"No." Luke leaned forward. "But we are well on our way. That's why I asked you here today. I have something for you to consider that just might thrust you into sainthood."

Lottie sat up straighter. "Don't keep me in suspense."

Luke passed her today's copy of *The Daily Report*. Jocelyn's latest humanitarian piece was on the front page. She'd featured a couple named Jimbo and Sally. Their story was both parts heartbreaking and uplifting—a testament to the resiliency of the human spirit.

Lottie quickly scanned the article. "This is quite a story," she said. "But what does it have to do with my comeback?"

"Jimbo and Sally are regulars at the soup kitchen that has previously been housed in the Hitchcock Building." He pulled a whole stack of papers onto his desk. "Jocelyn's been doing a series of reports on the people the kitchen serves."

Understanding registered in her eyes. "And if I throw them out, then I'm the Big Bad Wolf."

"Possibly. But I think you can do more than just offer Miss Annie the use of the kitchen to continue her work."

"More how?" Lottie raised her eyebrows.

"I've been there. I've met these people. I met a woman who'd been beaten badly and wouldn't take the help I offered. I met a man who served in the war yet suffers from his time there and can't find his place back in society. I met another man who's trying to support his wife and three kids while he's working and going to college, trying to make a better life for all of them."

"So what do you want me to do?"

"I think you should open the Lottie Jones Foundation. A non-profit organization that offers affordable housing. I took the liberty of looking into the building next door, which needs extensive work, but could be turned into condos no problem. In the lower level, you could offer a legal clinic for those who can't afford legal representation and institute a business program that teaches skills to those that wouldn't have the opportunity to learn elsewhere, possibly in exchange for some work experience in the La-Ti-Dots Empire. Who better to teach people to rise above their circumstances than a local hero such as yourself?"

Lottie uncrossed her legs but took a long moment to actually respond. "But I already have charitable organizations I donate to. I send proceeds to Africa for clean drinking water in their villages."

"That's good, and it looks great on paper, but I'm talking about doing more. Something big in your own backyard, and you'll have loyal fans for life."

"You've been thinking about this for a while now."

"Yes."

"And does your girlfriend have anything to do with this?"

"My girlfriend?"

"This reporter." Lottie pointed a boney finger at the stack of papers.

"We're just friends."

Lottie shot up an eyebrow. "You mean you got the girl to write that kind of article without sleeping with her? I was even impressed with myself."

"Because you're an amazing woman with an amazing story. Jocelyn has a gift for seeing the heart of a story and putting it into print. And I've already told you, I don't play like that anymore."

She laughed. "You may think you're still a young pup, but trust me, it's hard for an old dog to learn new tricks." Lottie shook a finger at him. "We all fall down sometimes." Lottie walked to the window and gazed out over the river. "I guess I would need an attorney to oversee the new foundation."

"That would be my advice."

She crossed her arms and looked back at him. "Very well. You would be my first and only choice."

"I'm not..." he began.

Lottie returned to the chair and picked up her bag. "Don't draw up the papers unless you're in charge. Once you're on board, make it happen."

She headed for the door and called over her shoulder, "Don't take too long to decide. I'm not a patient woman, you know?"

In the hallway, Lottie exchanged hellos with Marcus and Dennis, their voices carrying into Luke's office.

Marcus stepped into Luke's doorway, his back to him. "Get the revisions on my desk, and we'll talk." Dennis passed by before Marcus came fully in Luke's office. "What was that about?"

Luke shook his head as he cleared the newspapers from his desk. "I'm still trying to figure that out myself, but I think I was just offered a job."

Marcus sat down. "By Ms. Jones?"

"I proposed for her to expand her presence in the neighborhood, to start a foundation to help build up the community."

"That sounds like a good move for her—tax-wise and for her image."

"Exactly what I thought." Luke rubbed at his chin. "But she's only on board if I run it for her."

Marcus sat back in his chair. "Does that interest you?"

"I haven't had time to think about it."

"Looks like now is the perfect time then."

"Really? You're not going to tell me all the reasons not to do it?"

"I want you to do what's best for you. And if working for La-Ti-Dots instead of me is a better opportunity for you, I'd never stand in the way."

Luke nodded. Marcus would support him no matter what decision he made, unlike his parents. Looked like he had a lot to think about.

"Speaking of your happiness. How's your friend? Jocelyn—was that her name?"

"Yes." Luke couldn't suppress the smile spreading across his face.

"You interested in her?"

"Does the fact that she never leaves my mind mean something?"

"Likely." Marcus smiled. "She's really gotten to you, hasn't she?"

"I guess so."

"And you two aren't..."

"No, we're not."

"I hate to break it to you little brother, but I think you're finally falling in love."

"I think you're right."

"And how does she feel about you?"

"Good question."

"I wouldn't wait too long to find out if I were you. The right girl only comes around once, you know." Marcus scooted to the edge of his seat. "Sorry to change the subject, but the real reason I'm here is to talk to you about Brayden."

"What is it?"

"I don't want him to hear about the fires in the Hitchcock Building. Especially with Emma and me leaving town."

After many difficult years, time in therapy, and the consistent support of Marcus and Emma, Brayden was healing the emotional wounds he'd suffered from surviving a house fire when he was young.

Luke nodded. "I promise he won't hear it from me."

* * *

Luke left the office early on Friday. Marcus and Emma were catching the red eye flight to Orlando tonight, and they'd be bringing Brayden by before they left. Lottie's offer still weighed heavily on his mind, and he wished he had someone to talk to about it. Okay, he wished he could talk to Jocelyn about it. Every night this week, he'd waited for the lights in her window to glow, but they never came on until late.

Yesterday, the one morning he'd caught up with her in the lobby, she said she'd been helping Miss Annie pass out brown bag dinners from the back of Isaiah's van and spending time with Sarge whenever she could.

He knew she was also spending more time at work. The articles she was putting out about the Historic Old Town district were receiving rave responses. When he asked how her boss was liking the results, she gave a lukewarm shrug, meaning the guy was still being a jerk. That was all the conversation he'd had with her in over a week, and he wanted more.

He wondered now what it would be like to go home to her. She said she'd been fooled by a man before, but he couldn't imagine what had happened to keep her so reserved. And why was he so enamored?

Her distant resolve to keep him from getting too close was a challenge he'd never had to overcome before. But he'd also never wanted anyone like Jocelyn before. Serious and focused, more his brother's type than his own. It was downright scary to consider he was morphing into his brother's way of thinking. Perfect Marcus with the perfect family. Could he ever dream of having that too? Did he even want it?

The way he couldn't stop imagining Jocelyn in his life had him thinking he did. He wanted to protect her and comfort her, just like that night in her apartment.

He tried to play it cool yesterday morning when he'd seen her, hiding his overwhelming desire to hold her close and never let her go. He wasn't accustomed to being patient, and that's exactly what Dr. Pike had recommended he do.

After his last realization, he'd broken down and called the good doctor. *Time will tell if this is a relationship worth pursuing.* Time? Luke knew exactly how he wanted to spend his time right now. With Jocelyn, who never seemed to be home anymore.

From the window, he glanced in the direction of Jocelyn's apartment. The curtains were open, but the lights were off. Through the iron rails of the balcony, he saw Bodhi languidly licking his paws, the sunlight glinting off his golden fur.

Luke forced himself to walk away and change out of his suit. Opting for a pair of shorts and a t-shirt since the spring sunshine had warmed his home while he was away. He went to the closet where he'd been storing all the supplies he'd picked up for Brayden's stay. The first thing he pulled from the bags was the pop-up tent. The A-frame dwelling that would be for his nephew fit nicely in the corner. It covered up the laundry closet doors, but that didn't matter since Luke used a laundry service—life with live-in help had made him a dependent man, and he wasn't ashamed to admit it. The corner of the tent overlapped the bathroom door a little, so he'd have to be careful walking out of there in the mornings. But he figured it was a good spot—little kids always had to go to the bathroom in the night, right?

It didn't take long for him to have everything set up. The self-inflating sleeping mat covered the floor of the tent. The Star Wars sleeping bag, which Luke would likely steal if he were two feet shorter, lay atop the mat. The wilderness posters he'd found at the bookstore down the street with pictures of raccoons and snakes and deer were tacked to the inside walls. He hoped Brayden wouldn't be too bummed, knowing his nephew had always had a fascination with dinosaurs, but Luke had thought the forest animals created a better scene to fall asleep under than a giant toothed T-Rex ripping into the carcass of a Triceratops.

He checked the batteries in the lantern that illuminated stars on the ceiling of the tent—or at least they would when it was dark, because right now he could barely make out their geometric forms with all the daylight flooding the apartment.

Emma, Marcus, and Brayden arrived as Luke crawled out of the tent.

"Is this for me?" The moment Brayden was through the door, he ran straight for it.

"Sure is," Luke said.

Emma's jaw dropped open. "Oh, Luke, that's perfect. Where did you get that idea?"

"It just came to me." He winked at his sister-in-law, who looked ravishing in her dark jeans and red maternity sweater.

Emma carried Brayden's bags to the tent and crawled inside with him. As they commented to each other about the set up, Marcus pulled Luke into the kitchen.

"Poindexter came into my office today," Marcus said.

"He's back? Where was he all this time?"

"Apparently his family emergency was in Seattle." Marcus gritted his teeth and checked to make sure Brayden and Emma were still out of earshot. "And while he was there, attending his ailing father, he met up with Dad. Seems he'll be making an office transfer at the end of the month."

"What? Why's he doing that?"

"The official statement is so he can be closer to his family."

"And unofficially?"

"It's because he no longer has faith in the way I run the office. Sounds like he wove some pretty interesting tales to Dad while he was there."

"Is everything okay? You didn't lose your perfect-son status did you?" This wasn't something to joke about, but Luke couldn't resist. Their father had always sung Marcus's praises while virtually ignoring everything Luke did.

"I got an I'm-watching-you speech, but it's nothing I can't handle." Marcus clasped his hand on Luke's shoulder. "Looks like there'll be two partner offices opening up soon if you decide to stick around."

Luke rolled his eyes. "Don't start with that again."

"Start with what?" Emma asked, sliding an arm around Marcus's waist.

"It's nothing." Marcus kissed the top of her head. "Just office talk. Are you ready to go?"

"I guess so." She threw a look toward Brayden, sitting in the tent. "I'm having a hard time thinking about not getting to kiss him goodnight."

"Then don't think about it." Luke guided them to the door. "Think about us ordering pizza every night and watching TV."

Emma's brows drew down into a frown. "Pizza every night?"

"With a salad on the side, of course."

"And not too much TV," she added. "He has to do his homework first. Remember that."

"Homework, then family-friendly TV, I promise."

Emma wrapped her arms around Luke's neck. "Thank you," she said, tears in her voice.

Marcus gently peeled his wife away. "It'll be good for him."

"It'll be good for both of us," Luke added, hoping his company would be a good distraction from the woman occupying his mind. "Brayden, come on over here and say goodbye to your parents so they'll leave and we can start having some fun."

Brayden ran over, his hair tossing side to side. "Bye, Dad." He jumped into Marcus's arms. "Bye, Mom." He leaned over to kiss Emma's cheek before sliding out of Marcus's arms. "Have a great time in Florida."

With a tearful wave, Emma finally walked away, and Luke tried to remember a time when his mother had ever looked so sad leaving him behind.

"What kind of pizza do you want for dinner tonight, Bray?" Luke asked as soon as the door closed.

"I like pepperoni."

"Me too." Luke dialed, wishing he had a good excuse to order a bigger size, but another look out his window told him Jocelyn still wasn't home.

After dinner, Brayden came out of the tent with a deck of cards, begging to play Go Fish. As the first game was dealt, the light came on across the way.

By the time they were into their third game, Luke's mind was completely somewhere else.

"I'm whooping you, Uncle Luke."

"You and your dad. Born to win, I guess." Luke sighed.

"Well, maybe if you quit looking out the window all the time, you'd know I just asked for a six."

"Sorry, little buddy. You're right. Whose turn is it again?"

"Mine."

"Right."

"So, is it that girl you keep looking at?"

"What girl?"

"Over there. Are you looking at that girl?" As if to prove his point, Brayden put down his cards and went to the window. Luke was right behind him.

Jocelyn sat on her balcony, the cat in her lap, and turned the page of a magazine.

"That girl." Brayden pointed.

Jocelyn looked up, and Luke darted out of the way. "Did she see me?"

Brayden waved. "I don't know."

"Don't wave."

"I have to. She's waving at me."

Luke's head fell back, hitting the wall. *There goes my cool guy image.*

Brayden dropped his hand and walked back to the table. "She seems nice. Have you taken her on a date?"

"No." Luke sat in his chair again and picked up his hand.

"Why not?"

Luke thought about it. "I guess I don't know if she'd say yes."

"Do you want me to vet her for you?" Brayden moved his cards around, like he was sorting them.

Luke lowered his cards. "Vet her for me? Do you even know what that means?"

"Of course I do." Brayden looked at him. "I can see your cards," he said before returning to his card sorting. "I'm the son of a corporate lawyer *and* a teacher. Mom makes sure I know what all of Dad's big words mean. To vet someone means to investigate them. Look into what they're thinking."

"Don't you think that'd be too obvious?"

"Nah. Not if we do it right."

"And how would we do it right?" Luke asked, weary of taking relationship advice from someone who hadn't even hit puberty.

"Here's what I'm thinking…"

* * *

Luke was pretty sure Emma would revoke his babysitting license if she knew he was using Brayden to get to a girl. But it was the kid's idea. Not that that would hold up in the court of Emma Lewis. He'd just have to hope she never found out about it. Marcus, on the other hand, would probably approve—proud of his son's strategic thinking. Or so Luke hoped.

He knocked on Jocelyn's door before he put anymore thought into the plan. It would be five minutes. Ten, tops.

Jocelyn opened the door in her baggy gray t-shirt. She looked down at Brayden. "Hello."

"Hi." Brayden waved.

"This is Brayden," Luke said.

She didn't reply, her brow wrinkling as she stared down at his nephew.

"Can you watch him for a little while?" Luke rushed.

Jocelyn's brows shot up in surprise.

Talking faster than he could think, he blurted out, "I've got to do…um…do something for work. I won't be long, but I just can't take him with me."

"So, you want me to watch him?"

"If you don't mind. Like I said it won't be long."

"I'm very well-behaved," Brayden said, and Luke had no doubt his nephew was trying to charm her with his smile. Looks like the apple didn't fall too far from the uncle tree.

"I'm sure you are." Jocelyn looked down at Brayden before meeting Luke's eyes again. "If it's just for a little while, then…"

"Great." Luke didn't let her finish. "I'll be back soon. And he loves mint chocolate chip ice cream. If you have any left." Her eyes grew wide as he made like he was heading for the elevator, but as soon as he heard Jocelyn's door close, he retraced his steps to his apartment, hoping he wasn't going to regret this plan hatched by a second grader.

Seventeen

So, Luke Lewis had a son he'd never thought to mention. Brayden was the spitting image of the overgrown man-child. Who did he think he was, knocking on her door, asking her to play babysitter while he took care of whatever just came up? She knew exactly what had suddenly come up. Probably something petite, perky, and…

Oh, it didn't matter now. He'd fooled her with his I'm-a-changed-man routine, and now she was paying for it. How could she have ever entertained the notion that Luke was any different than Paulo?

"So, Brayden." She leaned against the closed door. "Do you have any idea how long your dad will be gone?"

Brayden scrunched his brows down. "My dad? He's going to be gone for ten days."

Ten days! Sucker punched, she fell against the door and searched for the handle.

"I get to stay with Uncle Luke the whole time he and my mom are gone."

Uncle? "Luke is your uncle?"

"Uh-huh." Brayden looked around the apartment. "This is a lovely home you have."

"Thank you." She'd spent every spare moment she'd had since the break-in reorganizing the shelves and furniture, using her memory to set things straight. And it looked like all the plants that had been uprooted would survive thanks to her careful attention. She'd refilled their pots with soil, babied them with little sips of water, and played calm music while she was gone. It supposedly worked, according to the Internet.

Brayden strode across the living room, straight to the patio door. "Mind if we sit outside? It's such a nice evening."

"Sure." She stepped away from the door. "Would you like some ice cream?"

"Yes, thank you," he said as he stepped outside.

Such a polite boy. She scooped ice cream into a beige-colored bowl—part of the replacement set she'd bought after all of Fiona's had been shattered. Insurance would take care of the rest for her when she returned from her retreat. But for now the least Jocelyn felt like she could do was replace a few plates since she was the one responsible for the raid on the apartment. She hoped when Fiona came home next week, she'd approve of the stoneware. They were the closest thing she could find to what had been in the cupboards before.

Brayden was in the chair she'd come to refer to as Fiona's—the one that faced Luke's apartment. Jocelyn had just been sitting there, but that's because the light at this time of day was better on that side. Not because of the view.

Jocelyn set the bowl of ice cream next to him.

"Wow." Brayden craned his neck. "You can see right into my uncle's apartment from here."

Busted. She turned to match her line of sight to his. "Oh yeah. Look at that."

"You can see my tent too." Brayden stood and pointed.

"Your tent?" Jocelyn got out of her chair and leaned on the railing. Sure enough, there was a small brown tent fixed in the corner beyond the bedroom door where she'd seen Luke pull off his amazing strength building workouts. "That's pretty cool."

"It's going to be like I'm camping, but not really." He sat back in his chair, his feet dangling close to the ground and took a bite of ice cream. "Do you like to go camping?"

"I've never been."

"Me neither." Brayden picked up his deck of cards. "Hey do you like to play Go Fish?"

"Sure I do." Jocelyn turned her chair to face him.

Brayden shuffled the deck and dealt the cards, his eyes constantly flitting beyond her shoulder. He must be wishing his uncle was back already.

"Don't worry," she said, trying to console him. "I'm sure your uncle will be back soon."

"Oh, I'm not worried." He picked up his hand and, if she wasn't mistaken, flashed a thumbs up.

He must have a good hand.

Jocelyn picked up her cards. All singles. Go figure.

"Would you like to go first?" he asked. "Since I dealt."

"That's okay. You can start."

"All right. Do you have any twos?"

"No," she replied, and he reached for a card from the pile.

"So, what do you think about my uncle?" Brayden asked, pulling the card into his hand.

"What do I think about your uncle? Hmm." She pondered the question. "He's a good neighbor, and it seems like he works hard."

Brayden's eyes lit up. "Yeah, but not as hard as my dad. He's always talking about how Uncle Luke is the last one in at the office and the first one out."

"Oh?" Jocelyn remembered Luke talking about his perfect brother.

"My mom says he still works hard. It's just different from how my dad does."

"Your mom sounds like a nice lady."

"She is. She used to be my teacher, but now she's my mom. I don't remember my real mom. She died."

Jocelyn's heart clenched. The way he said it so matter-of-factly, whereas she needed to hold back a tsunami of tears every time she contemplated saying the words. Like right now. She swallowed. "My mom died too."

Brayden's eyes shot to hers. "She did?"

Jocelyn nodded. "I was much older than you are when it happened. I was already in college when she got sick."

"I'm sorry," the boy said with a surprising amount of genuine sounding empathy. "Do you have a stepmom now?"

"No." Jocelyn suppressed a chuckle. The idea of her dad remarrying didn't seem possible. How could he ever replace the love of his life?

"Your turn."

"Do you have any tens?" she asked.

He handed one over to her. "So do you think you might want to marry Uncle Luke?"

Jocelyn startled. Had she heard him right? *Marry Luke?*

Brayden continued when she didn't respond. "Because if you're thinking about it, then it might be a good idea to go on a date. That's what my mom and dad did before they got married."

Somehow she found her voice. "It *is* a good idea to date before you get married."

"So, if he asked you, would you say yes?"

"To getting married?"

"No. To going on a date." Brayden scooped up a spoonful of ice cream.

"Oh, well…I don't know." It had suddenly gotten warm outside—a burst of sunshine or something. That had to be it. She fanned her face with her cards.

"So maybe?"

"Yes, definitely maybe." She looked at Brayden sideways.

Brayden set his fist on the table, his thumb in the air. "Do you have any eights?"

Jocelyn passed him the eight of hearts and debated if she should ask the question trolling through her mind right now.

"Your uncle has had a lot of girlfriends, hasn't he? Been on a lot of dates, I mean." She cringed ever so slightly. What was she doing, pumping a little boy for information?

"I don't think so. I mean, I've never seen him with anyone. Sometimes at parties he brings a girl, but I don't think they're girlfriends. I heard my mom call them one-night stands once."

Bingo. That's what she'd been afraid of. He hadn't changed his ways.

"But I don't get it," Brayden said after another bite of ice cream.

"Get what?"

"Why you'd want to stand around with someone all night. It sounds boring."

Jocelyn held her breath, making it seem like she was considering his point while doing everything humanly possible to keep from laughing. She slowly exhaled. "You're right. That does sound pretty superficial."

Brayden furrowed his brow at her. "What does superficial mean?"

"Well, I guess it means pointless."

"As in why would somebody do that?"

"Exactly."

"Because it would be boring." Brayden bobbed his head emphatically with every word.

"Likely. Yes."

"Your turn." Brayden scraped the bottom of his bowl.

"Any aces?"

"No. Go fish." Brayden studied his cards. "My mom says she hopes he finds someone special soon, though."

"Really, why is that?"

"Because ever since he moved to Portland, he spends the weekends at our house and plays basketball with my dad on Sundays. I think she wishes he had more friends here."

Jocelyn could think of one friend she'd seen him with since she'd moved in, but then again, she hadn't seen that woman again. Guess that one night of standing around hadn't been so inspiring after all. Or maybe he really was changing his ways.

"Do you like fettucine?" Brayden asked, his body bouncing as he swung his legs beneath the chair.

"Fettuccini?" Jocelyn remembered the woman she heard behind Luke's door. *Was that another hot date she'd happened upon?*

"Yeah, he made it for me and my mom and dad a few weeks ago. My mom still can't stop talking about it. So maybe you'd like to come over tomorrow night, and he could make it for you too. It would be a date. As long as you promise not to be superficial and stand around the whole time. We'd play games and have fun, I promise. What do you say?"

Jocelyn couldn't help it. She threw her head back and laughed. A deep, down belly laugh that felt good in her soul. So he'd been having dinner with Brayden's family the night she'd come home to smell garlic in the air. The memory made her mouth water again.

When she looked back at Brayden, she found his gaze focused over her shoulder again, and he was shaking his head.

She glanced over her shoulder but didn't see anything, except Luke's open window. *Had it been cracked this whole time?* She didn't remember.

Turning back to Brayden, she dabbed at the errant tear that had leaked out during her bout of laughter. She tapped her cards on the table, regaining her serious composure. "I promise no superficial one-night standing with your uncle. Ever."

"Great." Brayden grinned from ear to ear, his thumb popping up again. "So if he asked you for tomorrow night, you'd say yes?"

"Yes."

Brayden hopped out of his chair, making a big show of stretching and yawning. "Boy, I'm pretty tired."

Jocelyn sat back as he picked up the pile of cards. "But our game—"

A loud knock came from inside the apartment.

"I bet that's my uncle now." Brayden shoved the cards in the box as she looked to the door and back at the little boy.

Why did she get the feeling she'd just been had?

Brayden put his cards in a pocket and carried his ice cream bowl to the kitchen while Jocelyn went to the door. Water ran in the sink as Brayden rinsed the bowl clean.

She opened the door and wasn't the least bit surprised to find Luke standing on the other side. As seriously as possible, Jocelyn folded her arms over her chest. "Did you send your nephew over here to ask me out?"

"What?" Luke's gorgeous lips fell open. "No…I…he." His cheeks turned an adorable shade of pink. "What did he say?"

"Nothing. He was a perfect gentleman. You on the other hand, I'm not so sure about."

Brayden wormed his way between them to get to the hall. "She said yes, Uncle Luke. Ask her to dinner at your place tomorrow night, and she'll say yes. She promised."

Brayden slipped between them and bounded down the hall.

Luke's mouth dropped open as he turned back to Jocelyn. He seemed to be at a loss for words, and it made him appear even more charming.

She tsked. "Uncle Lulu."

His face lit up with his smile. "You said yes? To dinner tomorrow night?"

"Yes." Before she could extinguish the flirtatious spark that raced through her body, she reached for him, tugging his shirt to pull him closer. Their bodies touched, her lips lingering a whisper's distance away from his ear. "But he also told me you have a habit of one-night stands."

Luke pulled back, his eyes popping with questions.

She leaned in again. "Don't worry, he doesn't really know what it means, but I do. So, if that's what you expect from me, don't bother asking."

His eyes searched hers, and she waited for the roll of laughter to tumble off his lips, but it didn't.

"Would you do me the honor of having dinner at my place with me?" He glanced down the hall where Brayden was waiting for him at the corner. "And Brayden."

She let out a trapped breath. "Yes."

Luke pulled her close. His arms slid around her back, and he pressed his lips to hers. No part of her, not even the sensible side, could resist him.

"Uncle Luke!" Brayden's voice broke them apart as he came closer. "First you have the date. Then, you kiss her." He spun around, throwing his hands in the air. "Even I know these things."

Luke took a step back, holding Jocelyn's hands. "Then I guess we'll have to do it again tomorrow night."

Mercy me. She knew she was grinning like an idiot, but she couldn't help it. "I guess we will."

Luke leaned in again, brushing his lips across her cheek. "See you tomorrow. Say seven?"

She nodded before he walked away. Back inside, she closed the door. She was about to get herself into a heap of trouble with this guy.

Eighteen

Luke opened his window. Jocelyn was sitting out on her porch in gray sweatpants and a baggy T-shirt. Bodhi lay at her bunny-slipper-covered feet. "Good morning," he called across to her.

"Good morning," she called back, her smile brightening his day.

"We're going for a walk. Want to come along?"

"Sure. Just give me a minute." She pulled the cat inside with her and disappeared.

It was only a matter of minutes before she met them in the hall, but a buzz of anticipation sat with Luke as he waited. She'd traded her sweats in for jeans and her slippers for sneakers. Underneath her jacket, he saw the same T-shirt she'd had on before. She hadn't changed out of it, nor had she wasted a ridiculous amount of time smearing her face with make-up. And she couldn't have looked more beautiful.

"Good morning, Brayden," she said.

"Good morning, Miss Jocelyn."

"Shall we?" Luke offered her his arm, delighted when she took it.

The day was perfect, the sky a robin's egg blue. Clouds stretched thin across the sky while the snowcapped mountains in the distance popped against the crisp blueness. The trees lining the sidewalk of the waterfront were an explosion of pink and white blossoms. A flock of geese pecked at the grass, and Brayden skipped along the path ahead of him and Jocelyn.

"You know," Luke said, tilting his head toward her and catching the scent of wildflowers. "You could have brought Bodhi along. On his leash, I mean."

"Yeah, I don't think so." The corner of her mouth turned up. "For one, I didn't sign on for cat walking, and second, that poodle over there would probably give the old cat a heart attack if it turned its yapping bark on him."

The poodle, anchored to something next to a couple sitting on a blanket, let loose its piercing bark as they passed, going completely unnoticed by the young couple, engrossed with one another.

Young love.

"You're right." Luke rubbed his hand across her fingers. "It's a jungle out here."

Up ahead, a flock of seagulls took to the air as Brayden skipped at full speed, encroaching on their territory. He stopped and watched the squawking birds scatter in the air. The poodle behind them barked even more fervently.

"How's Sarge doing?" Luke asked when Brayden started skipping again.

"He's doing okay." Jocelyn bit her lip. "The doctors still have him pretty heavily medicated to keep him calm."

"Any luck with finding his family yet?"

"No. He's still not very responsive. With all the medication."

Luke nodded, wondering what he could do to help. *If* he could do anything to help.

"The only word he's said is *side*."

"Side?"

"Yeah." Jocelyn kept her gaze on Brayden. "He said it to me the first time I visited him, and the staff say he's said it a couple times since."

"Does that mean anything to anyone? Maybe it's a name?"

"It's possible. Or it could just be the meds talking. I wish we knew more about him."

"That must be hard." Luke squinted against the sun. "I can't imagine what his family is going through, not knowing where he is."

"It's hard to say what happened after he came home from the war. And why he doesn't have their support."

Luke nodded. "I wonder if he'd let me help him."

"Help him, how?"

"I don't know." Luke sighed. "I've been talking to Lottie about creating a foundation in conjunction with her set up in the Hitchcock Building. I think the community could use a free legal clinic, some affordable housing, and work programs."

Jocelyn stopped walking. "Why didn't she mention it to me? It's a fantastic opportunity, and it would catapult her image into a positive spotlight."

Brayden stopped up ahead, and Luke started them walking again to catch up with his nephew. "Because she's still waiting for my answer."

"What answer?"

"She wants me to run it."

"And you don't want to?"

"It's just that I've never imagined doing something other than being a part of the law firm."

"And you don't think your family will approve?"

"Marcus does. He's given his blessing no matter what I decide. But, not my parents. I definitely don't expect them to be supportive." He was so sure about it, that he'd avoided taking his father's phone calls for the entire week, not wanting to hear how they were all waiting for him to make the family proud by joining the ranks of partner. And the question of another son would most certainly come up again. Lewis and Sons needed more sons to keep the office running, his father would say.

He looked ahead at his nephew and wondered if Brayden would get trapped into the life laid out for him by his ancestors, but he got the distinct feeling he wouldn't. Not with Marcus and Emma looking out for him. Envy coursed through him as he thought about how Brayden, despite his last name, would be free to choose his own life path.

"So what are you going to do?" Jocelyn asked.

"Keep considering it, I guess."

She didn't say anything in response, and he found himself desperate to know what she thought.

"Do you think I should take it?" he asked.

"You should do what would make you happy. It's your life—"

"Uncle Luke! Uncle Luke!" Brayden ran back to meet up with them.

"What is it, buddy?"

Brayden blew out a breath. "I'm hungry. Can we go get some lunch?"

"What did you have in mind?"

"A burger and root beer float." Brayden's eyes twinkled with hope.

"Sounds good to me." He looked at Jocelyn. "Will you join us?"

"I'd be happy to."

They made their way to a crosswalk. This was part of Luke's loop when he ran. The shops were familiar, and he stopped when Jocelyn got lost in a window display. A white, rustic window frame hung behind a white wooden chair with a watering can full of tulips set on it. He gave her a moment, and when she still didn't turn to keep walking, he put an arm around her.

"Do you have a thing for tulips? Or is it the chair you like?" he asked.

She cracked a smile. "My mom loved tulips. This just reminded me of the kind of scene she'd want to paint."

"Oh, yeah? She was a painter?"

Jocelyn nodded. "Watercolors."

Luke looked through the pane with *Harbor Street Blossoms* painted on it. "This would make a very pretty picture."

After another moment, they moved on, her arm slipping around his waist.

* * *

The diner was only half full, a benefit of Brayden's hunger striking before the rest of the city piled in for a mid-day meal. They crossed the black and white tile floor and found a red vinyl booth next to the video game corner.

"Dad and I used to come to this place." Brayden climbed in next to Jocelyn. "They have great burgers."

A waitress approached and pulled a pencil out of her bun before asking to take their order. It wasn't hard to decide, seeing as how the menu was simple—burger, cheeseburger, fries, onion rings, and drinks. As soon as the waitress was gone, Brayden asked for quarters for the video games. Luke checked his pockets, but he didn't have any.

"Let me see what I can do." Luke walked up to the counter where the waitress was punching totals into a cash register. He pulled out a credit card and flashed it in her direction. It was all he had. "Got any quarters I can buy off you?"

Her smile grew, turning bright and flirtatious. "Sorry, we don't exchange credit for quarters here."

Luke leaned closer, his forearms flush with the cool counter. "Couldn't you make an exception just this once? You see, my nephew over there would like to play a couple of games while we wait, and being the dense uncle that I am, I forgot to bring change along. I'd hate to lose my title as coolest uncle in the world. Is there any way you'd want to help me out?"

Next thing he knew, the waitress was emptying the tip jar, pulling out the quarters, and pushing them toward him. Luke put away his credit card. "You'll get this all back, I promise."

He carried the handful of coins back to the table, interrupting Brayden and Jocelyn's conversation. His nephew's eyes bulged when Luke handed over the stack of quarters.

"Knock yourself out, little buddy," Luke said as Brayden scrambled out of the booth.

Jocelyn gave him a skeptical look as he slid into the seat across from her, but he didn't get to hear what she had to say because the waitress returned, delivering their drinks—two sodas and one root beer float.

Jocelyn sipped from her straw, a smile playing on her lips like she was pondering a funny thought.

"What is it?" Luke asked.

She shook her head. "Oh, nothing."

"I don't believe you. You find something funny, and I want in on the joke. Are you laughing at me?"

"Maybe?" She shrugged coyly.

"Then laugh on, because it brings out the color in your eyes."

"Don't think your sweet talking ways will woo me. It may work on old cats and diner waitresses, but I can see right through you."

He leaned forward to lower his voice. "And what do you see?"

The merriment drained from her eyes, and he whipped around to check on Brayden, frightened she'd witnessed something behind him. But Brayden was enraptured in his car racing game, turning the wheel as he sped around the video course. He turned back, and Jocelyn seemed to have recovered, not back to the fun-loving state she'd been in before but at least away from the terrified look he'd glimpsed. She sat back in her seat, pulling away from him.

"I was just wondering how many sexual favors you had to promise that waitress for her to give you those quarters."

Ouch. That hurt. But he supposed he deserved it. She had every right to be suspicious and wary. "Exactly zero."

"Really?"

"Yes." He looked down at the bubbles in his drink. "I'm sorry guys like me have given you reason to find my actions untrustworthy."

The waitress came to drop off their burger baskets, and Luke didn't let his eyes stray from Jocelyn. She was the only woman in the universe that had captured his attention, and she was the only woman he wanted to show that to. Finally, when she realized he wasn't going to break his hold, she smiled and thanked the waitress.

"Food's here, Brayden," she said, looking over Luke's shoulder.

"Coming." A moment later, Brayden was back and slurping down his float. Oblivious to the change in Jocelyn's demeanor, Brayden chatted on about his car race and how he wanted to try the pinball machine next. Jocelyn engaged with Brayden but didn't let her eyes meet Luke's again. As soon as Brayden was done eating, he hopped from the seat again. "Can I go use the rest of my quarters?"

"Sure can," Luke said. "As soon as you're done, we'll get going, okay?"

"Okay." Brayden bolted, change jingling in his hand.

Luke pushed his empty basket away and reached for Jocelyn's hand, glad when she didn't pull back. "I want you to know I'll do everything in my power to gain your trust."

The waitress returned to clear their baskets and drop off the check. Luke went to the counter to pay, figuring the new woman in his life might need a moment to herself. He signed the credit card slip, reimbursing the waitress for the quarters she'd taken out of the tip jar and then some.

"Thank you, and have a wonderful afternoon," she said loudly, showing off her appreciation for the ample tip.

"You too," Luke replied before returning to the table.

Jocelyn's arms were crossed, and her lips twitched. "Does it ever get old?"

"Does what get old?" He slid across the vinyl seat.

"Having women fall all over you."

He looked around in every direction. "I don't see any women falling over me, which is an honest shame considering there's one in particular that I've been trying to get to fall for me, but it seems she has her feet firmly planted on the ground."

Her lips pulled into a full smile before she relaxed her arms and changed the subject. "Thank you for lunch."

"Thank you for coming." He held his hand out, palm up. "Would you like to spend the rest of the afternoon with us? I don't know what we have planned, but whatever it is, it'll be better with you along."

She closed her fingers over his and squeezed. "I wish I could, but I have some work to do and then a date to get ready for."

"I pity every man who won't be sitting across the table from you tonight, staring into your beautiful eyes." He brushed his lips across her fingers, hoping his charms would be well received.

Jocelyn squirmed in her seat. "Yes, well…" She sounded mildly uncomfortable—but in a non-offended sort of way. "I'm counting on an evening full of stimulating conversation, not mindless staring."

"Then stimulating conversation you will have." Because whatever she wanted, he was willing to give. His brother was correct. The right girl only came along once, and he didn't want to let her get away.

Nineteen

If Jocelyn wasn't sitting down, braced against the red vinyl seat, she'd be putty on the floor. How she wanted to trust Luke. His sincerity, his honesty—it all seemed real. But the moment her guard began to fall, fear left her almost paralyzed.

Life with Luke would be wonderful—never a dull moment with that sense of humor of his, which was finally growing on her. If only she could get over her fear. And she didn't know if she'd ever get used to the way other women looked at him. Like the waitress over there, watching them walk out the door. Jocelyn had noticed the glance she'd given Luke's left hand when they ordered. The way she studied him when he wouldn't take his eyes off her. And how could Jocelyn forget about Lottie Jones? During their interviews, the woman never stopped talking about what a delicious little thing Luke was, like he was a decadent dessert to savor.

Her constant ping-ponging of interested then not must be driving Luke crazy. It almost had her out of her own mind. She couldn't calm the tiny whisper that crept up in the back of her mind every time she found herself falling for Luke's act, begging her to swear off him. But in so many ways, being with him felt like the absolute right thing to do.

The afternoon was gorgeous, the temperature perfect. More and more people were being called to the sidewalks. Brayden walked between her and Luke, and after crossing the first street, he complained about how his legs were tired and hurting. Luke solved the problem by hoisting his nephew up behind him and piggybacking him down the sidewalk. He broke into a gallop more than once, which caused Brayden to laugh and giggle, drawing the attention of countless passersby.

Safely back inside her apartment, Jocelyn tried to ignore every rush of desire, every thrilling moment when Luke had touched her.

She sat at her computer, trying to focus on the slough of emails in her inbox. Talk of Lottie Jones and La-Ti-Dots moving to Portland was capturing headlines everywhere. And so was the awareness of the city's socio-economic gap. Other stories, like the ones she'd been featuring in the paper, flooded her email, and she wondered if Lottie would create the foundation Luke suggested. Another civic program in the city was a fantastic idea, and Luke would be the perfect person to run it. As long as he could handle working for a woman who wanted to gobble him up like a slice of apple pie. She wondered what it would take for him to have the courage to accept the job.

Not my concern. She shook her head, refocusing on her work. The work that was supposed to be giving her experience to meet the next expectation her uncle had for her at *The Gazette*. She didn't need to be sitting here daydreaming about a man in the city that would surely break her heart if she gave him the chance. Because what would he do when it was time for her to return to River's Edge, follow her?

Her phone chimed before another moment passed, not letting her consider the possibilities. She looked at the screen. It was a calendar reminder to pay her dad's bills. She hadn't erased it before moving, and as she went to dismiss the reminder, she was hit with the fear that her father might not have remembered that all his bills were due on Monday. How had she not remembered to ask him the last time they spoke?

With deft fingers, she dialed his number and waited impatiently as the line rang and rang, finally going through to voicemail. She left a message and hung up. Drumming her fingers on the table, she thought about logging on to his accounts, but that would only give her access to a few.

Most of his bills were still paid the old-fashioned way, with checks, and she wouldn't know for sure unless she called everyone on her laminated payment checklist, which she'd left behind for her father to use. Why hadn't she made a copy to bring with her? Anxiety ripped through her chest and, without letting another moment pass, she dialed Sophie's number.

"Hi, I'm so glad you called." Sophie sounded bright and cheerful.

"I just tried Dad, but he didn't answer. Do you know if he paid his bills this week?"

"I don't, but I'll ask." Sophie must have pulled the phone away from her ear, because her next words were dim. "Hey Dad, Jocelyn wants to know if you paid your bills."

Jocelyn didn't hear the answer, but a moment later Sophie was back on the line. "He said yes."

Jocelyn breathed a sigh of relief. "Are you at the house?"

"No. We're at my place."

"Why is Dad there? Shouldn't he be at the gallery?"

"He's helping Madame Christine with some art she purchased. Don't worry. The new girl he hired part-time is covering the place."

"He hired someone? When did this happen?"

"Yeah. I don't know. Couple weeks ago, I guess. She's just out of college, and Dad's letting her show her work for free in exchange for covering some hours for him. Madame Christine helped him set it up."

Madame Christine? What was she doing sticking her nose in Dad's business?

"Hey," Sophie rushed on. "I've got to teach class pretty soon, but I wanted to tell you that I had a reading with Madame Christine last night."

Oh boy, here we go again. "Mmmhmm."

"I have a message for you."

Jocelyn didn't reply. She'd let whatever nonsense Madame Christine fed Sophie slide in one ear and out the other.

"Madame Christine said Mom kept talking about Apollo. That they're not all Apollo. She said the message was for you, but I don't know why Mom was talking about spaceships. Figured you're a smart girl, though, and you'd work out the meaning."

"Sorry." Jocelyn rolled her eyes, trying to sound contrite. "I don't have a clue." What was Madame Christine talking about?

"Well, think on it. Something might come to you. I gotta go. Chat again soon, okay?"

"Okay, bye." Jocelyn hung up.

Apollo? They're not all Apollo. What could that possibly mean? Apollo was a Greek god, wasn't he? Did it…no, it couldn't be. It couldn't be: *They're not all a Paulo.* How would Madame Christine know about Paulo?

The answer was she wouldn't. No one did.

* * *

"Dinosaurs roamed the earth for over one hundred sixty million years." Brayden wound the fettuccini around his fork tines before popping it in his mouth.

"That is so interesting." Luke hooked his elbow over the back of his chair and raised his wineglass to Jocelyn. "Don't you think that's interesting?"

"Very," she agreed. The fettuccini had been amazing and the bread and the wine. It was all making Jocelyn feel a little light headed.

Luke turned back to Brayden after sipping from his glass. "And what does dinosaur mean again?"

"It means terrible lizard," Brayden answered.

"You're like a walking dinosaur encyclopedia," Jocelyn smiled at Brayden. "Do you want to grow up to be a paleontologist?"

"I don't know." Brayden shrugged. "They're just kind of my thing right now."

"His thing." Jocelyn gave Luke an impressed look. "You know," she said to Brayden. "Pterodactyls have always been my favorite dinosaur."

"Technically," Brayden said, mopping up the remainder of his white sauce with a chunk of bread, "Pterodactyls aren't really dinosaurs. At least, that's what some scientists believe."

"And what do you believe?" Luke lifted his chin toward his nephew.

"I call them dinosaurs, because I mean, they were around during the time of dinosaurs, and now they're extinct, so it's just confusing if they're not called dinosaurs too."

"And what about you?" Luke turned his luminous gaze on Jocelyn.

"I'd have to agree with Brayden. They're dinosaurs." She grinned. "What about you?"

"I'm not one to argue with logic. They should all be called dinosaurs. It's just simpler that way." His magnanimous smile never wavered.

Jocelyn took a sip of wine, the warm glow hitting her insides. She rested her elbow on the table, settling her chin in her hand, and returned his rapt gaze. How had he just done that? Creating a dinner conversation that wasn't dull, yet appropriate for his nephew. He appeared keenly interested in Brayden's opinions, never down-playing his thoughts. Paulo had never taken the time to ask her opinions, except for when it related to his art, and then he only seemed to hear her if it was all high-praise.

"But there's still some controversy over whether or not dinosaurs are actually extinct," Brayden said, pointing a finger like a little professor.

"What? Why would anyone debate that?" Luke stretched his legs under the table, coming into contact with hers.

"Because," Brayden went on, "Birds are likely descendants of theropods."

"But they're birds, not dinosaurs," Luke said.

"That's what I think." Brayden crossed his silverware over his plate. "Birds are birds and alive today. Dinosaurs lived millions of years ago and are extinct. Keep it simple."

"I'm with you, little man. Keep it simple."

Simple.

"Is it time for dessert yet?" Brayden asked.

"Sure is," Luke said. "Do you want to grab the box Jocelyn brought?"

Without a reply, Brayden hopped out of his seat and went to the kitchen.

"Stimulating enough conversation for you?" Luke asked.

"And then some." Jocelyn peered over her wineglass before she took another sip.

Brayden returned with the pink box she'd gone out to get this afternoon. Three delicious cupcakes were inside. The first one to finish was Brayden, and he eagerly tried to move the evening along.

"Can I set up the game now?" he asked.

"In a minute." Luke pointed to his plate. "Clear your plate, and then you may, but be patient. We don't all have the lightning quick metabolism you do."

"Okay." Brayden moved with enthusiastic energy to do his uncle's bidding.

Jocelyn helped Luke clear the table, thinking the whole time about how Paulo never would have taken the time to have a cozy meal like this with her. Even if it was takeout. It was the best takeout she'd ever experienced. She couldn't think of a single instance when Paulo treated her to something special, always claiming his art was calling him, and letting her eat frozen pizza while she sat silently and watched him work. How had she ever thought that was worth building a life on?

"How was dinner?" Luke asked.

"Excellent." She set down her wineglass.

"And the company?" Luke stepped closer, closing the space between them.

"Brayden…" She let go of her inhibition and laced her arms around Luke's neck. The feel of his smooth skin was tantalizingly soft. "Was a charming companion."

Luke playfully rolled his eyes to the ceiling, his fingers locked behind her back. "What about me? Did you find me charming?"

She sobered and lowered her voice, careful to keep their conversation private. "You're undeniably charming. And it scares me."

"Scares you?"

"Game's ready," Brayden called, and she dropped her arms.

"Wait." Luke grasped her hand and reeled her back in. "Why do I scare you?"

She let her lashes fall. "Because I pride myself on being responsible and level-headed." *Which includes not heeding psychic messages.* But he wasn't like Paulo. Her hand trailed up and down his arm, muscles responded to her touch. "But when I'm with you, I want to shuck all my good senses and fall hopelessly in love with you."

It must not have been what he expected her to say, because his eyes registered shock before softening.

"Jocelyn, you get to go first." Impatient politeness rang in Brayden's young voice.

"Coming," she said, releasing herself from Luke's powerful eye lock.

Luke stayed in the kitchen, plates clinking and water running. Jocelyn sat on her knees beside Brayden. The short knit skirt she'd decided to wear made floor-sitting a tricky endeavor. Brayden took his turn after her, rolling the dice and moving his token. Luke joined them, and she avoided meeting his eyes, knowing her confession may have changed things between them.

He lowered himself beside her, and she was elated when he took her hand as he reached for the dice.

"You've got to watch out for that one." Luke indicated Brayden. "He may be cute on the outside, but underneath, he's a ruthless mogul who has no problem bankrupting his own flesh and blood."

Jocelyn relaxed. It was all okay—the easy, natural way she'd grown accustomed to being with Luke hadn't been ruined. The happiness that settled in her heart had her believing that somehow this was going to work. She didn't know how, but maybe, just maybe, it would.

* * *

The game ended with Luke and Jocelyn bankrupt and Brayden rolling in the play money on the floor.

Luke stood. "Winner cleans up and then goes to bed. I told your Mom and Dad when they called an hour ago that you were heading to bed then. So, don't make a liar out of me."

"Aww, Uncle Luke, I want to stay up." Brayden whined.

Jocelyn stood, reluctant to have their time end, but it was getting late, and she was going to meet Miss Annie early in the morning to help serve brown bag breakfasts. She headed for the door.

"Clean up." Luke followed behind her.

"Goodbye, Brayden," she called from the door. "Thanks for taking all my money."

"You're so welcome." Brayden giggled.

Luke reached for her hand, the connection electric, and she held her breath.

"I'm going to walk Jocelyn home." Luke didn't look back at Brayden, even though he spoke to him. "Don't play with any matches or knives while I'm gone."

"Shouldn't you warn him off those magazines stashed under your mattress, too?" Jocelyn added quietly.

Luke scrunched his brows down low. "I don't have any magazines stashed under my mattress."

She leaned in. "Good. I was just checking."

He pulled her into the hall, and at her door, he took both her hands in his, lightly kissing her fingers. Teasing sensations shot down to her toes.

"You know," he said. "I don't usually get beat so quickly in that game, but I was a little distracted tonight."

"Distracted by what?"

"By thinking about doing this." His fingers went behind her neck, pulling her lips to his. And in that moment, she was a goner. This man had a hold on her, and she didn't know if she could break it…or if she'd ever want to.

Twenty

Luke tried to focus on the new proposal from the city for the Hitchcock Building, but his mind circled back to the woman who had been crowding it for the last few days. Jocelyn was falling hopelessly in love with him. The moment she'd said it, he knew that was exactly what had happened to him. He'd fallen for her. Her honesty, her wit—all of it had crept up and bit him on the back of the neck.

Focus. He studied the document again. *Estimated cost of damages…*

She'd been over every night this week, and he had to admit, the few stolen moments they'd shared as he walked her home were hardly enough to satisfy the want he had to be with her. Marcus and Emma would be back in a couple of days, and then he hoped he could sit down with this woman who'd turned his thinking upside down and find out if she was as set on loving him as he was her.

He looked down at the purchase agreement again. The new proposal seemed fair, but he'd have to discuss it with Lottie, and they were still waiting on a copy of the insurance claim.

Xavier stuck his long, pointed nose in Luke's office, pulling him off track again. "Have you seen Tippy?"

"Can't say that I have." Luke didn't look up, hoping to give the impression that he was deeply involved in his work. "Wasn't aware it was my turn to watch him."

Xavier strode into the office. "Being a smartass isn't going to cut it for you long-term."

Luke rocked back in his chair. "It seems to be working for me so far."

"One of these days, all your wheedling ways are going to get you into trouble. And your brother won't always be around to protect you."

"I've never needed him to protect me before."

Xavier cocked his head sideways, his wrinkled brow drawing tight over his dark eyes. "You don't know, do you?"

"Know what?"

"About Barney Bartholomew, the *former* CEO of Prestige Bank."

"What about him?"

"He's filed a suit against our firm."

Luke tried not to let shock register on his face. What grounds did Bartholomew have to come after the firm?

Xavier leaned over the polished wood desktop. "Anyone else in this firm would have settled this out of court, but you had to go and make a big deal out of it. Shame the man, his family, and the institution. For what? So you could play hero to a handful of women." Xavier's face wrinkled in disgust. "You're pathetic. And it's sad to see your brother putting so much faith in you. Like you'll ever become anything more than an honorary partner. Just so you don't embarrass the family name."

Luke stood and patiently pulled on his jacket, buttoning it closed. "You know, I have to wonder why it is that my brother is off at a national conference being honored as lawyer of the year while you're stuck here babysitting the likes of me." He picked up his bag, looping the strap over his shoulder. "Now, if you'll excuse me, I have an appointment to keep." At the door, he turned back. "Oh, and I hope you find Tippy. I'd hate to have to be the one to tell Marcus that partners are disappearing under your watch."

Luke didn't have an appointment, but he wasn't about to sit around and let Xavier Poindexter toy with him, using his power of intimidation.

"I'm going to lunch," he said, passing Gretta's desk.

Pushing his way through the crowded lobby, he ran into Stacy.

She waved and came running in his direction. "Oh, Luke! I haven't seen you in ages. Where are you going?"

"Lunch," he said with unusual crispness.

The tiny tapping of her toes followed him when he didn't stop. "I'll join you. It'll be fun."

"Sorry, Stace." He spun around. "I can't. Maybe another time."

"Yeah, sure." Disappointment settled across her face. Running a hand down his arm, she changed back to her playful ways. "You've got my number. Don't be afraid to use it." She stepped backward, giving him a finger wave as she moved away.

Luke walked down to the waterfront, the wind teasing his hair. He sucked in a deep breath and found an empty bench. He pulled out his cell phone as a seagull squawked from over the water.

Marcus picked up on the second ring. "Hey, Luke. Is everything okay?"

"Yeah. Everything's fine. How are you guys?"

"We're good."

"Great." A beat passed before Luke forced out his next words. "When were you going to tell me about Barney Bartholomew?"

"Probably never." The background noise changed, going quieter, and Luke wondered briefly what he was taking his brother away from. "It's not a solid case. The guy's mad. He's losing everything, and he wants someone to blame besides himself. How did you find out about it?"

"Poindexter."

"Figures. The guy is not a fan of ours. Sorry you had to hear about it from him, but honestly, I'm not worried about it. I have Tippy taking care of it. The old man might look like a teddy bear, but he knows how to play that to his advantage. Deep down, he has a killer instinct. And he's loyal, too. It'll be fine."

The words were easier to hear than to believe. Luke had researched the former CEO and knew he had some questionable connections in the city. "But what can I do?"

"Nothing. This isn't your battle. Lottie is your only concern right now. Does she still have her heart set on the same building? Or are you looking again since the arson attempt?"

"We're still waiting on the insurance documents, but we've received an estimated cost of the damages and what to expect in repairs. For whatever reason, she's still convinced she was meant to save this building from ruin."

"I'm sure it'll all work out then." The noise from before resumed. "Now go enjoy your lunch hour. At least I'm assuming that's why you're not in the office right now, unless you've started bringing seagulls into the building."

"I'm taking a walk after Xavier came in and puffed his chest up at me."

"Why don't you take a walk down to see a certain someone from *The Daily Report*. Might help you forget about Xavier."

Luke broke into a smile. "Now who exactly could you mean?"

"I hate to be the one to break this to you, but my son can't keep a secret. We've heard all about Miss Jocelyn, the hand holding, the kissing, and the use of a little boy as a date magnet."

"That was all his idea."

"Doesn't mean you had to go for it."

"But I'm his uncle. I have to let him do whatever he wants. It's what makes me cool."

"Try to curb that coolness until I get back, will ya?"

"Will do."

"All right, then I'd like to get back to sitting poolside with my wife before I have to go back into a conference room for the rest of the afternoon."

"I won't keep you any longer."

Luke pocketed his phone and rested against the bench. The sidewalk was filling up, the closer it came to the noon hour. A visit to the newspaper office sounded like a great idea, but he had one stop to make along the way.

* * *

"I'll take a dozen pink tulips." Luke pulled out his wallet. "On second thought, let's make it two dozen, please."

The dark-haired salesgirl, who obviously didn't require a personality for her job at Harbor Street Blossoms, moved to the cooler behind the counter and slowly counted out the twenty four stems. She had Luke wishing he'd stuck with his original order. Tapping his credit card on the counter, he hoped the sound would hurry the young woman along, but it was to no avail. And so he waited.

As the girl moved at a snail's pace to wrap the flowers in paper, Luke thought he was going to implode with impatience. He wondered if conversation would help him.

"You wouldn't happen to be Matilda, would you?" he asked, thinking it would be odd for this emotionless, slow moving worker to be Tippy's infamous lovely niece. He'd pictured a much more smiley and round-faced girl than this one, but he really had nothing to base his impression on.

"No."

Got to love the attitude and eye roll paired with her one-word answer. "Is she working today? I know her uncle."

She took his credit card and swiped it. "Don't know a Matilda."

Of course she didn't. Knowing the names of her coworkers probably wasn't high on the list of requirements for this job. He scrawled his name across the wireless tablet. At least he'd tried to be conversational. Couldn't say she'd done the same. He replaced the card in his wallet before slipping it into his pocket and picking up the flowers. The girl had disappeared into the backroom before he'd walked out the door. Customer service was not this place's strong suit. But the flowers more than made up for it. Jocelyn was going to love them.

His steps toward the newspaper office were fast and buoyant. Never could he remember feeling this excited to see a girl.

The receptionist didn't look up as he approached. "Welcome to…"

He didn't stick around to hear the end of her greeting, not even sure if she was aware he'd walked on by, but he wanted to surprise Jocelyn. See her face when he walked up unannounced, because with every beat of his heart, he hoped all he saw in those stunning blue-gray eyes was happiness.

With the flowers concealed behind his back, he slipped into her cubicle. "Hello, beautiful."

She spun around, her eyes not disappointing him. He'd never felt so alive in all his life.

"Luke! How did you get past Dena?"

"Like that's hard to do. She's not much of a watchdog. Now, is she?"

"No, I guess not." Jocelyn leaned back in her chair, looking up at him, a smile coming so easily to her lips. "What are you doing here?"

"I had to bring you something." He presented the flowers. The look on her face was the exact reason he'd never surprised a woman with flowers before, because it meant only one thing, and he felt it too. The pure desire to be with her for a very, very long time—as in forever.

He cleared his throat, the thought having distracted him. "I was also hoping to steal you away for lunch."

"I would love that." She swiveled back around in her chair and shut down her laptop. "I could use a break."

"Is the city news getting to you?"

"Hardly." She picked up her bag. "Now that the story around the building has died down a bit, I've been given other assignments."

"And by the way you just said '*other assignments*,' I'm guessing you're not very inspired by this new work."

"Yeah. The new outlet mall opening up south of the city is not my idea of big news, but it's what I was assigned."

Luke helped Jocelyn with her coat. She pulled her hair out of the neck, letting the tresses fall into place, and he couldn't resist the urge boiling up inside him to reach out and comb his fingers gently through the ends. With the flowers tucked in her arm Jocelyn reached for his hand, and they walked out.

"Do you mind if we go someplace close to the apartment? I'd like to stop off and put these in water before we eat."

"Sure, but I can't guarantee that if we go back there, we won't end up spending the whole lunch hour there." He chanced a glance in her direction. Bright red cheeks and the tight roll to her lips told him she completely understood.

"Yes, well. It *is* only an hour. I'm not sure there'll be time for lunch *and* that."

"Then how about just that?" he whispered close to her ear, the scent of wildflowers tickling his nose.

They reached the top of the steps, and before heading down, she leaned toward him, batting her eyes toward the floor. "That," she said, smoothing her hand down his tie, the tease kindling desire all over his body.

But she didn't get to finish. A round and robust voice interrupted their interlude.

"There you are, Miss Banks."

"Mr. Wilbur." Her face turned a deep shade of crimson, her innocence endearing.

Luke clasped his hand over hers, trying to send the message that no one knew what they'd been discussing, not even the senior editor who came lurking up the stairs at the same time.

"I'm so glad I caught you," the big man said. "I can't think of the last time my phone was ringing off the hook like this. For days now, my line's been bogged down with responses to your reports on the soup kitchen, the working class poor, the historical buildings of this great city, and the introduction of Lot-Ti-Dots Enterprises to the local scene. It's like you've been running your own full-blown paper inside of mine. And it's quite remarkable." He turned to Robert. "Isn't it remarkable?"

"Remarkable." Robert eyed their hands, fingers entwined.

"Flowers," Mr. Wilbur said, noticing the bundle in Jocelyn's hands. "Why didn't I think of that? Flowers certainly. Robert," he turned to the short man next to him. "Order some flowers in here for everyone."

Robert shook his head in bewilderment. "Me? But—"

"Yes. And you, Miss Banks, should take the rest of the day off. You more than deserve it. And I'm going to call your uncle straightaway to see what we can do about keeping you here permanently at *The Daily Report*." And with that, the man was off, heading toward a door with his arms waving. "That's right," he said to no one in particular. "I'm going to talk to Larry Banks right this minute."

"Well, well, well," Robert said, slow stepping in front of them. "Looks like someone's become teacher's pet by cheating on the test."

"Excuse me?" Jocelyn said.

Robert eyed their hands again. "It's easy to get so much content when you're pillow talking with your main source of information while the rest of us are out pounding the pavement the good old-fashioned way for real stories."

Jocelyn took a step toward Robert. "If you think—"

Luke tightened his grip and pulled Jocelyn back beside him before she had a chance to say something she may regret—no matter how much Robert deserved it. "We wouldn't want to keep you from all those flowers you need to order." Luke pointed at the ones he'd brought for Jocelyn. "Might I suggest Harbor Street Blossoms? They have a beautiful assortment of tulips available right now."

Without a fight, Jocelyn turned with him, and they descended the stairs, the change in the surrounding air clearly altered. All the way back to the apartment, she didn't say a word. Her playful and flirtatious lips had hardened into a straight and unwavering line.

Chester, who didn't show an ounce of surprise to see them arriving hand in hand, opened the door in the same unreadable manner as always. Inside Jocelyn's apartment, Luke sat, watching her move around the kitchen in a ball of fury. A cupboard door slammed after she pulled out a vase. She yanked the faucet on and thrust the vase beneath it before jamming the lever back down.

Bodhi came out of his hiding place and slowly sauntered up to Luke, rubbing against his pant leg. He petted the cat's soft fur. The animal sat back on his haunches and looked up with half-opened eyes, as if asking what all the midday commotion was about.

"I think you're starting to stress the cat out," Luke said as Jocelyn snipped the flower stems one-by-one before placing them in the vase.

She blew out a giant breath. "Sorry, I'm just a little…"

Luke went to stand behind her and slowly turned her to face him. "Ignore Robert. He's not worth getting all worked up over."

"He is when he makes accusations of…"

"Quid pro quo."

"Exactly," she said emphatically. "Presuming the only way to get information out of you was to sleep with you."

Her cheeks burned crimson again, but this time with anger.

"Hey." He pressed a hand to her cheek, letting his fingers wrap into her hair. "I know that's not true. And you know that's not true. I gave you all my goods, expecting no favors in return. Well, maybe not all my goods." He stepped closer to her, matching his hips to hers and delighting in the way she responded. "But I've been holding out just to make sure you're not using me."

She laughed. "Using you for what?"

"A really, really good time before running back to a place you call home." He brushed his lips across hers, feeling her body press against his, and he couldn't take it any longer. He charged both hands into her hair and he let his mouth cover hers.

Twenty One

Jocelyn stepped back, breathless. Her eyes searched Luke's.

Home?

"What's the matter?" Passion still burned in his eyes.

"I...I hadn't remembered what Jerry said until now."

"Kissing me reminded you of that old man?" His lips curved up on one side.

How could he do that? Be so sexy and so funny at the same time. "No. It was when you said *home*. I realized..." She put a hand to her forehead, her mind suddenly whirling. "I don't know what I realized."

Luke pulled her close. "Would you take a job if you were offered one?"

"I don't know." She considered it a moment longer. "I can't tell you how many times a day I remind myself that I don't have to work with Robert forever, just to get through. I don't know how long I'd last there if he was my permanent boss. But then..."

"But what?" Luke's eyes fell on hers.

But then, there's you.

She was speechless. For the first time in a very long time, she was considering a future somewhere other than River's Edge. Her cheek fell to his chest, her ear pressed against the *thump, thump, thump* of his heart. He tightened his hold around her, and she hoped he understood her silence.

Her thoughts were stalled by the ringing of her phone. Thankful for the save, she went to dig it out of her bag. She glanced at the number. "It's Miss Annie." She threw Luke a puzzled look. "I wonder what she wants."

"Better find out." The obvious attempt he made at keeping his voice unaffected stung.

She picked up the call. "Hello?"

"Hi, Jocelyn. I'm at your office. I was hoping you could do a huge favor for me?" Miss Annie's big voice sounded tired. "But there's a man here that says you're gone for the day."

"I'm having lunch with Luke right now, but I can come down and meet you if you need me to." She avoided looking at Luke.

"No, no you enjoy your time. I was going to drop off the keys to the building in hopes that you could get Sarge's things for me?"

"Of course I can do that, but why? What's going on?"

"The docs are ready to move him to a halfway house as we speak, and I thought it'd be good if he had his personal things with him. But I can pick them up later. I need to get to the house. Don't want him showing up there without a familiar face around."

"No, I can go. Leave the keys with Dena. Is she behind the desk?"

"No. What's your name?" Miss Annie asked another person. "This guy Robert is."

Robert? "Ask him if he'll put the keys in my desk for me?"

She heard Miss Annie ask him. "He says yes."

"All right. I'll pick them up in a little while, and then I'll get Sarge's things."

"Oh, you're an angel," Miss Annie said before giving her the address for the halfway house and profusely thanking her again.

"What was that about?" Luke's voice reminded her where she was.

"Sarge is being moved today, and Miss Annie wants me to pick up his things for him."

"Where are they?"

"Back at the building. Down in the basement. She's leaving the keys for me at my office. I'll get them later." She looked at him. "After we talk."

He came over, pulling her to him. "There's nothing we have to talk about right now. I was being presumptuous. You haven't had an offer. You have no decisions to make yet." He released her. "Come on. We'll get my car and pick up Sarge's things. But we need to have lunch first. I'm starving."

"Don't you have to get back to work?"

"Baby, I'm all yours until six o'clock." He kissed her nose. "That's when I have to pick up Brayden, and then you'll have to share me."

"Wait." She smiled. "You don't have to go to back to work. And I don't have to go back to work."

He stepped closer, taking both her hands in his. "Uh-huh."

"So, it seems to me, we have plenty of time for *that* now."

"Are you sure?" His expression was earnest.

"I'm absolutely sure."

* * *

"Are you still hungry?" Jocelyn trailed her fingertips across Luke's bare chest. Everything underneath his clothes was exactly as she'd imagined.

"Only if it comes with a side of you." He kissed her shoulder. The sensation of his lips on her skin still new enough to shock her.

"I think the only thing in the fridge is a block of expired tofu."

"That's a delicacy I've never tried." He pulled her on top of him and brushed her hair back, hooking it behind her ear.

"Neither have I, and I don't think we should start today." She folded her hands on his chest and rested her chin atop them. This felt so right, so unlike before.

After a moment she said, "His name was Paulo."

Luke's glance moved from her hair to her eyes, clearly not understanding.

"My deep dark secret," she whispered. "Now that I have something to compare him to, and he was mediocre at best."

Luke surprised her by rolling over and switching their positions. Beneath his sensuous gaze, she worried she'd revealed too much, left herself open.

"I want to give you the best of everything. Always," he said before lowering his toned body gently over hers and pulling up the sheet.

* * *

This was officially turning out to be the best day ever. Jocelyn blushed as she pulled on a sweatshirt. Luke was at his place, changing out of his work clothes.

She filled Bodhi's food dish before grabbing her purse and met Luke at the elevator. Her fingers easily entwined with his as the doors opened. They landed at the lobby instead of the parking garage level. "I thought we were taking your car," she said.

"We are. But it's at the office. I hadn't expected to get so preoccupied this afternoon."

She rolled her lips together and shook her head as they passed Chester at his desk. Along the way, they stopped at a deli and grabbed sandwiches before finding Luke's car in the concrete parking structure adjacent to the law firm. A nice silver BMW.

At the Hitchcock Building, Jocelyn slid Miss Annie's keys—which had been left in her desk drawer—into the lock. Thankfully, she'd escaped the office without running into Robert himself.

Through the kitchen, she noticed not much had changed since her last visit inside with Miss Annie. The blackened walls and curled black counter tops all remained in the same level of disrepair. A pile of rags sat on the griddle where Jocelyn had flipped pancakes her first morning here. Miss Annie must have been back at some point to clean. The evidence difficult to find though, considering the state of the room.

She and Luke walked through the dining room. A pungent odor hung in the air. It would be great when Lottie took ownership of the building and got this place in working order again. Jocelyn could only imagine the stories these walls could tell over the years.

They found the basement door, green metal. There was a noise from up above, a long scraping sound. "What was that?" Jocelyn asked, looking up.

"I don't know. A bat, maybe?"

"A bat, really?" She laughed and put the key in the lock.

"Yeah, bats live in rafters, don't they?"

"I don't know." She held the door open. "I'm not a bat expert."

She tried the light switch on the wall, but nothing came on.

"Power must be off." Luke pulled his cell phone out of his pocket, turned on a flashlight, and shined it down the stairs.

Jocelyn propped the door with a brick that must have been placed there for this particular purpose and followed Luke.

In a far corner, they found Sarge's green duffel. A bedroll lay next to it, and Luke knelt to roll it up. Jocelyn packed the stack of magazines from the floor, a razor, and a brush.

She wondered what it would be like to go back to River's Edge now, leaving Luke and the city behind. What if Mr. Wilbur didn't have a job for her? Or what if Uncle Larry was ready to retire and needed Jocelyn to run *The Gazette*? What then? Would she be able to walk away from the man that was a complete contradiction to everything she believed? Like right now. He was down on his hands and knees rolling up Sarge's bed mat that had probably never been washed. Most men from his upbringing would request a toxic waste suit and ventilation mask just to be near this type of scene, but here was Luke, right by her side.

He caught her looking at him. "What are you doing?"

"Thinking about you."

"Really?" His face beamed in the tiny glow of his cell phone light. "Do tell. What were you thinking?"

"How I may or may not have misjudged you the first time I laid eyes on you."

He squatted next to the duffel bag and tied the roll on with the green frayed straps. "So did you misjudge me?"

"You're very much as I judged you, only more tolerable than I'd assumed."

"Mmm." He nodded as he secured the last tie. "Tolerable. Not one of my usual top five attributes listed, but I guess there's always room for more."

"Tolerable is the new sexy, you know." She stood at the same time as him.

"No, I didn't." He wrapped his arms around her.

"Yes." She swayed in his arms. "I'll be writing it up in an editorial next week, and before you know it, the concept will spread like wildfire. That's how all new trends start."

A metal thud ricocheted off the barren brick walls, startling her.

"What was that?"

"I'm not sure." Luke dropped his arms and picked up Sarge's bag. "Probably just old-building noises, a pipe settling or something like that. Come on, let's get these things to Sarge."

When they reached the top of the stairs, the door was shut and didn't open when Luke pushed on it. He tried again, putting his shoulder into it. Still nothing budged.

"*Hello.*" He banged on the door. "Is someone there? Open up."

Just then, a loud pop and boom hit the air, like a fire cracker. Then another and another.

Smoke seeped under the door.

"Go down. Go down." Luke followed her, smoke chasing them.

Another boom. What was exploding?

Luke looked at the screen on his phone. "I don't have a signal, do you?"

Jocelyn pulled out her phone and shook her head. "The fire department will come. It's the middle of the day. People had to have heard those explosions."

"But who will know we're down here?"

Smoke spread around her.

Luke opened Sarge's bag. "What are you doing?" Jocelyn coughed.

"I'm looking to see if he has a screwdriver or something. The metal grids on the windows are too small for us to squeeze through if we break it. I'll have to take the whole thing off." He coughed.

A window. Jocelyn remembered Miss Annie saying she left one open for Sarge. The smoke was thick and dark, the hazy cloud making it nearly impossible to see. She was so disoriented, she couldn't tell which side of the building they were on.

A strobe of red lights came through the high glass windows. The temperature was rising. Sweat dampened her body.

Jocelyn got down on her knees, trying to get below the smoke. Where would Miss Annie have left a window open? More red lights streamed from outside. Good, the firefighters were here, but Luke was right. Only Miss Annie and Robert knew they were inside. How long would it be until one of them was alerted and made the connection?

She had to do something. Flames came down the wooden steps, burning boldly.

Luke was still rifling through Sarge's bag. Jocelyn pulled her sleeve to her mouth and nose and took a breath. *Think.* Her eyes traveled the upper edge of the tall brick wall. Nothing but dark smoke masked the walls. *Which window? Which window?* The words rolled over and over in her brain like a mantra. She was about to try the window right behind her when a dim light glowing in the far left corner caught her eye.

"This way." She pulled Luke's arm.

"No, I'm—"

"I know a way out." She pulled him again, and this time he followed. As they moved toward the light, it grew brighter. "There." She pointed to the window. "Try that one. See if it's open."

Luke looked at her like she was crazy but hoisted the duffel over his head and used it to push on the window. It gave way, flapping outward. He stretched up on his toes and sent the entire bag through. Next, he laced his fingers together, creating a step for Jocelyn. She placed her foot inside. He lifted her up against the glass, and with one giant heave, he pushed her up and out the window.

Before she was through, she started yelling, and a masked firefighter ran to pull her out.

"Help him." She scrambled to her knees on the cold pavement. "Help Luke. Please." *Cough.* "He's still down there."

Another firefighter hauled her to her feet and pulled her away as the first reached into the open window. Glass from above shattered with another explosion.

Twenty-Two

No one would let Luke leave, not the police and not the EMTs, until he'd answered all their questions and breathed into an oxygen mask for what felt like an eternity. Miss Annie had shown up and cried in Jocelyn's arms when she saw the destruction the fire had done to the building and heard they'd been trapped inside. Only a charred skeletal structure remained of the top floors. While Jocelyn soothed Miss Annie and talked to the reporter from her paper—Pearson, Luke thought he'd heard her call him—he'd called Lottie to let her know what had happened.

"We'll rebuild," she chirped without a moment's hesitation. "From the ground up. It will be spectacular."

"Whatever you want," Luke had said, his energy spent. "We'll discuss it when we know more."

The only thing he was thinking about was getting Brayden. Finally, when all the stars were making their debut in the sky, he and Jocelyn were released. Emma's sister, Audrey, had picked up Brayden from the afterschool program when Luke hadn't shown up. He hoped his nephew was holding up.

As he drove the car up the suburban road, Luke spied Audrey's house, a light beaming from every window. It created a warm inviting glow against the dark sky. Jocelyn sat next to him, her hands quietly set in her lap.

Luke parked in the driveway and made his way to the door. He knocked, and Audrey answered. A breath of jolly laughter and merriment came out from behind her.

Despite the way her hair was done up in a perfect twist, and not a stitch of makeup out of place, Audrey looked frazzled around the edges, in the way her smile wavered and her gaze lingered on Luke. Her worried eyes asked the questions for her.

"I'm okay," he said. "No one was hurt. Thank goodness."

"I'm so glad you're all right," she said in the same caring way Emma would have.

"Thanks for getting Brayden for me. How is he?"

As if on cue, Brayden pushed past Audrey, lugging his backpack.

"I'm here, Uncle Luke. I'm ready to go." Brayden's eyes got big at the sight of him, and Luke suddenly realized he had no idea what he looked like. His T-shirt was smudged with soot, and a bandage was on his cheek where glass had cut him as the firefighters pulled him through the window.

Audrey reached out for Brayden's shoulders as robust laughter came from inside the house. "You're welcome to stay here tonight if…"

Luke knelt, and Brayden launched himself into his arms, burying his face in his shoulder. "No." His voice was muffled against Luke's shirt. "I want to go with Uncle Luke."

Audrey's eyes met Luke's. "He's had a lot of questions."

Luke stood, scooping Brayden and his backpack up with him. "I bet he has." He rubbed Brayden's back. "Can you call Emma and Marcus for me to let them know we're on our way home and I'll call them as soon as I can?"

"Of course," Audrey said. "Call if you need anything. Anything at all."

"I will." Luke carried his nephew, whose feet dangled below his knees, to the car. When had Brayden gotten so big?

At the apartment building, Luke carried his sleeping nephew inside.

"Do you want to come over?" Luke asked Jocelyn as they stepped off the elevator on their floor.

"No, I think I'll go home. Check on Bodhi. And take a bath. You have someone who needs you right now." She stroked Brayden's hair. "I'll be fine."

"You're sure?" He wanted to reach for her hand, but his were full.

Seeming to sense his reluctance to let her go, she reached up and kissed his cheek. "I'm sure. And you smell pretty stinky yourself."

"I love you," he said as easily as if the words had been sitting there waiting to be said his whole life.

Her eyes danced in the hallway light, but she didn't say it back. "You did good today, Lulu. Real good." She turned down the hall.

He didn't walk away until she was inside her apartment. What should he make of that?

Brayden stirred as Luke laid him on the couch. "You hungry, buddy? Need some dinner."

"No, Aunt Audrey made baby back ribs." He rubbed his eyes. "Just like Mom makes. And mashed potatoes."

"Sounds yummy."

Brayden nodded and sat up, scooting to the edge of the couch. "Can I ask you something?"

Luke squatted so he was eye-to-eye with his nephew. "Anything."

"When you were in the fire…" Brayden looked away for a moment. "Were you scared, Uncle Luke?"

Luke pulled the little boy into a hug. "Terrified, little buddy. Absolutely terrified."

And that was the truth.

* * *

Morning came, and Luke was glad to find Brayden still fast asleep in his sleeping bag when he groggily headed for the shower. Despite his scrub from last night, he still smelled smoke on his skin. The hot shower brought him fully awake, and by the time he had toweled off, he was already contemplating what to do with his day. When he'd spoken with

Emma last night after Brayden was asleep she said she'd leave it to his judgement about whether or not to send Brayden to school.

"He might need time to process what happened," she'd told him. "Or he might need to stick with his routine. You decide."

Seeing as how it was almost time for the school bell to ring Luke was thinking he'd opt for the day off. He couldn't imagine Brayden would object. But before they did anything else, he wanted to see Jocelyn.

"Uncle Luke," Brayden called from the other side of the door. "Aunt Stacy's at the door."

"Let her in," he called back.

Brayden's voice came again. "I'm not supposed to open the door without an adult present."

"Fine," he muttered, slipping his jeans over his boxers. "I'm coming."

As soon as he stepped out, Brayden unlatched the locks and pulled the door open.

"Gee thanks, B." Stacy strode into the apartment, her traditional ponytail tamed into a bun. A pair of stiletto heels and a tight black dress with a high collar and rhinestone buttons were the outfit of choice this morning. "'Bout time you let your Aunt Stacy in."

Luke darted back into the bathroom for his T-shirt. The moment he reappeared, Stacy crossed the apartment toward him, her arms outstretched.

"Luke, honey," she wailed. "As soon as I heard what happened, I came right over. Are you okay?"

Without waiting for an answer, or for him to put his shirt on, Stacy threw her arms around his neck and planted a kiss square on his lips.

Twenty Three

Jocelyn barely slept a wink. Images of the fire, being trapped in the basement, and that distant glow all ran on a loop in her brain. She wouldn't believe it if she hadn't witnessed it herself, but that light came from nowhere and led them out when there was no other way. Jocelyn didn't want to admit that in that light she'd felt her mother's presence. But she had, the warm comfort of her mother's spirit still hummed in her heart.

"Good morning," she said to Bodhi as he came out of the bedroom. She picked up her tea cup and walked to the window, wondering if Luke had scored any more restorative winks than she had last night. The words *I love you*, rang in her ears behind every image from the night before. She loved him too, but she was too afraid to say it. Not anymore though. She realized how quickly life could wander off course, and she was ready to tell him. Whether Jerry offered her a job in the city or not no longer mattered. She was ready to be with Luke, and she was ready to find a way to make it happen.

Pulling the edge of the curtain back far enough to peek across the way, she looked into Luke's apartment.

Her knees buckled as she saw Luke standing half-dressed in the middle of his living room, a doll-sized woman draped over his naked top-half. The woman's legs were wrapped around his middle, and her arms caged his head, her mouth on his.

Jocelyn let the curtain fall back into place and took a step back.

Ree-oooow. Bodhi scrambled out from under foot, claws scratching across the floor. Jocelyn stumbled and fell, coming down hard on her backside. Tea poured onto the front of her shirt, burning her skin but saving the cup from shattering.

She buried her face in her hands and cried.

Twenty Four

Luke unwound himself from Stacy's vice grip. She stumbled back as her feet hit the ground, and he let go.

"Good God, woman! Control yourself." He wiped his mouth with the back of his hand. His eyes shot to Jocelyn's window, thankful the curtains were still drawn. "Get a grip, why don't you?"

Brayden appeared to have missed Stacy's spectacle, his back to them as he sat at the bar eating a bowl of cereal.

"What?" Stacy stared at him with practiced innocence. "When I thought of something happening to you, I couldn't let another minute pass without letting you know how I feel."

"That's not showing me how you feel." Luke kept steel in his tone. "That's…that's…It's just not going to happen."

"But if…"

"This isn't the time." Luke threw his shirt on over his head and buttoned his pants. He picked up Stacy's purse that she'd carelessly dropped on the couch before throwing herself at him.

She took it, looking more than a little miffed.

Luke put his hands on the back of Brayden's chair. "Now, as you can see, I'm fine, so you can go. I've got to get Brayden to school soon."

"Right. Of course." She straightened her dress. "We'll finish this later."

Luke followed her with his eyes to the door. "There won't be a later."

She turned back, batting her lashes. "Sure there will."

Relentless woman. "Hey," Luke said as she reached for the door handle. "How did you get in here, anyway? Chester didn't call to say I had a visitor."

"Oh, that." She swatted the air. "I cozied up to a balding man with a dog outside. Told him I lived with you, and we walked in together. Easy peasy."

Luke shook his head as she went out the door. That girl was crazy.

"Uncle Luke, do I really have to go to school today?"

He sat in the chair next to his nephew. "No, little buddy. I think we both deserve a day off."

"Really?"

"Yeah." He ruffled Brayden's hair.

Brayden beamed, kicking his feet under his chair as he served up another drippy spoonful of cereal. "Do you think Miss Jocelyn will take a day off?"

"I hope so." He looked around for his phone, trying to remember where he'd last had it. "But the first thing we should do is call your parents. I have a feeling they'll want to know what our plans are for today."

The phone rang, and Luke found it on the kitchen counter. Assuming it was his brother, he picked it up before checking the number on the screen.

"Good morning. Good morning," he said almost in song, hoping to convey the message that all was good with them, sparing himself a big brother lecture.

But Xavier's brute and pointed tone came back at him. "Get to the office now."

"If this is about Lottie Jones, I've—"

"The police are here to see you."

"But…" Hadn't he gone through everything with the police last night?

"Now." Xavier hung up.

"Slight change of plans, buddy." Luke turned to Brayden. "We've got to go into the office real quick, okay?"

"Okay." Brayden hopped out of his chair and went to the tent for his shoes.

What's going on now?

* * *

Minutes later, Luke and Brayden walked through the doors of the law firm. Gretta took one quick look at Brayden and came around to take the little boy's hand.

Worried lines creased her forehead. "I'll take him to Marcus's office. Everyone else is waiting in your office."

"Everyone?"

She nodded, her gray hair bobbing, before turning to Brayden. "Let's go find something to do while we wait for your uncle."

"No chair races up and down the hall until I'm done. Got it?" Luke called after them.

Brayden turned around, giving him a giant grin and thumbs up before turning into Marcus's office.

Luke dug his hands into his pocket. Whatever lay beyond his office door wasn't going to be good, and he instantly wished his brother was here. He always fared better with Marcus by his side.

Taking a deep breath, he sauntered to his office and plastered on a smile before cracking the door open. "Hey, sorry I'm late, but I didn't realize I was hosting a party today. What's the occasion?"

Xavier stared him down. Officer Reyes and another uniformed officer were there too, standing next to a laptop on Luke's desk.

"How are you feeling today, Mr. Lewis?" Officer Reyes asked, his thin mustache remaining flat above his lip.

"Fine. Thank you. And please, it's Luke." The seriousness swirling in the air stifled Luke's signature light and jovial mood.

Officer Reyes cleared his throat. "I'm afraid we're going to need to ask you a few more questions."

"Yeah, sure. No problem." He pushed his hands in his pockets again.

Xavier crossed his arms over his chest and nodded at the officers.

Officer Reyes continued. "In light of new evidence, uncovered this morning, we're reexamining this case from a new angle. Starting over again at the night of the break-in at Miss Banks's apartment."

"Okay."

"Now, you stated you were with Miss Banks that night."

"That's correct. At the soup kitchen."

"Yes, and we have plenty of witnesses that place you there. It's before that we'd like to talk about."

"Before?"

"Yes. You returned to your apartment building before meeting Miss Banks, knowing she wouldn't be there."

"I went home to change." He looked at Xavier and smiled. "Didn't think a stuffy old suit would be appropriate." No one cracked a smile. "I had no idea whether Jocelyn would be home or not."

Officer Reyes opened the laptop and typed a few keys. "Can you tell us about this?"

A video played on screen. It was a camera from the lobby of his building. Luke put his hands on the back of a chair and leaned closer, wondering what he should be looking for. And then he and Tippy appeared, talking as they passed through the doors together. Officer Reyes paused the footage.

"Is there anything you'd like to tell us about that?" Officer Reyes said.

Luke straightened and looked to the officer, then at Xavier. Their expectant gazes suggesting there was a right answer to this question. Luke wondered what it could be.

"I'm sorry. I don't know what you're getting at."

"Please keep in mind, Mr. Lewis," Officer Reyes said, "that I have two officers with this other man now, collecting his statement."

"His statement about what?" What did Tippy know?

"About the plan the two of you had for that evening."

"I didn't have any plan with Tippy."

"Luke." Xavier broke into their exchange. "Tell the officers what happened that night. Why were you and Tippy there together?"

"We weren't together. I came home and found Tippy outside. He said he was late meeting his niece. They were looking at an apartment. We walked in together. We rode the elevator together…"

He trailed off, thinking of what Stacy had said earlier about getting into his building. *I told the guy I live here…easy peasy.*

"And then what, Mr. Lewis?" Officer Reyes prompted him.

"And then nothing."

"Then, please explain this to us."

Another video played, showing Luke stepping off the elevator and handing an envelope to Tippy. The video paused mid-exchange.

"What was in the envelope, Mr. Lewis?" Officer Reyes asked.

"Blazer tickets."

"Anything else?"

"No."

Xavier cleared his throat. "Luke, as your legal counsel, I suggest you answer the officer's questions directly and honestly. The consequences for any wrongdoing may be minimized based on your cooperation."

"Wrongdoing? Giving Tippy tickets to enjoy a basketball game with his niece is a wrongdoing?"

Matilda. The girl at the flower shop said she didn't know a Matilda who worked there.

Xavier nodded at the officers again.

Officer Reyes leveled his gaze at Luke. "Mr. Tipton made a sizable deposit of cash into a bank account the next day. Are you sure there wasn't a payment inside that envelope?"

"Payment for what?"

Officer Reyes continued his questioning. "You knew Miss Banks wasn't home, and you knew she'd obtained a recording that could possibly incriminate the person who set fire to the Hitchcock Building."

Luke shook his head wildly. "You think I paid Tippy to ransack Jocelyn's apartment?"

"No." Reyes cut to another video. This one from the camera at the door leading to the parking garage. Tippy was leaving. "He was only in the building five minutes." As Tippy walked out, three people went in, all in black hooded sweatshirts. Reyes paused the frame. "We believe you paid him to let these three in."

"Seriously." Luke pulled his hands from his pockets and held them out to the screen. "I have no idea who these people are."

"They say otherwise." Officer Reyes placed three mug shots on the desk.

Recognition struck like a bolt of lightning. Luke sat, the facts piling on too fast to keep up with. He lifted the first photo. The legs of a spider wrapped around the man's neck in his profile. "Mickey?"

The man from the wedding who'd tried to take advantage of Stacy had broken into Jocelyn's apartment? But why?

"So you do know him?" Reyes asked.

"Yeah." Luke drilled the officer with his glare. "Because I reported him to the police after he got a friend of mine drunk at a wedding we attended, and I had the feeling he intended to commit a crime against her."

Officer Reyes pointed to another picture, the man's fair complexion familiar. "His friend here says you gave him your card and told him to call you."

The bartender. The two of them had been in cahoots that night? He should have realized that sooner. Why else did he continue to serve Stacy drinks?

"And then, we have this." Officer Reyes placed a document on the desktop.

Luke recognized it as a purchase agreement, or at least part of one. It didn't take him long to scan it. The Hitchcock Building was named, but it stated the building had been condemned—declared unsafe due to extensive damage. More documents followed, supporting the claim—but how? And Luke's name, his signature, was on every page.

Xavier's voice came over his shoulder. "Abigail found them on the copy machine this morning. Did Lottie Jones put you up to this?"

Luke said nothing. What was happening?

"I must admit, Mr. Lewis," Officer Reyes sounded proud. "Up until now, you've done a good job of covering your tracks, but in light of this…"

No. Luke leapt out of the chair, using his agility to his advantage, and made for the door. "There's only one person who can set this story straight," he called over his shoulder.

"Luke!"

Xavier and the officers were right behind him.

"Stop!"

He sprinted with all his might. Blair jumped out of the way, and he closed in on Tippy's door. He burst through. Two officers were inside, each flanking Tippy.

Tippy's face crumbled at the sight of him. "Luke, I'm so glad you're okay."

"They know it wasn't me." Luke said as thundering feet came to a halt behind him. "They know you don't have a niece. And they know I filed a report *against* Mickey. We are not, nor have we ever, worked together. So how are you connected to him?"

"We were introduced." Tippy's voice was meek.

"By who?" Luke took a step closer. "Who was paying you? Why was a fire set to the building with Jocelyn and me trapped inside?"

Tippy's face was earnest. "I didn't know you were there, I swear. Nobody was supposed to get hurt. I just needed the money. Had some debts to clear, so I could get the house back. So Maude would come back." His face wrinkled with emotion. "Don't tell her. Please don't tell her."

Luke didn't back down. "Tell me who it was? What was the plan?"

Xavier's hand was on Luke's shoulder. "He doesn't have to tell you anything."

Tippy's eyes darted from Luke's to Xavier's.

"No." Luke stayed calm. "But he wants to, because he knows what loyalty means, and this firm has taken care of him and his wife for many years."

Tippy looked at his lap and turned his hands up. "I was just supposed to make you appear incompetent. Make you lose your big client. See that it was public and humiliating for you."

Xavier's hold loosened.

Tippy continued. "But then there was a recording, and your client wouldn't give up, so I had to make sure everything pointed to you. No loose ends." Tippy looked up, tears in his eyes. "I'm sorry, Luke. I'm so sorry. You've always been kind to me."

Luke remained steadfast. "Who was it, Tippy?"

"Barney Bartholomew."

"The former CEO of Prestige Bank?" Xavier asked.

Tippy nodded shamefully.

Officer Reyes stepped up next to Luke. "Mr. Tipton, I'm going to have to ask you to come with us."

Tippy struggled to his feet. "I'm so sorry," he said again as the officers escorted him to the door.

For a long moment, Luke and Xavier stood in silence.

Finally, Xavier put his hands on his hips. "Son of a…" He shook his head. "I can't believe it. No, offense, but I really did believe you put him up to it."

Luke met the partner's eyes. "None taken, but in all honesty I was beginning to think you had put him up to it."

"Me?" Xavier sank into a chair and shook his head.

Luke followed suit, the adrenaline rush quickly subsiding. "Let's face it. You've never been a big fan of the Lewis brothers, have you?"

"Not really, but I might be changing my way of thinking now." Xavier cracked a smile as he rested his chin in his hand. "So, Tippy doesn't have a niece."

Luke blew out a tired breath and fell back in the chair. "My money's on no."

"And here I thought how nice it was that he had family around while Maude was gone."

"Me too," Luke said, feeling like a fool. "I think we all wanted to believe him."

Twenty-Five

Bus rides had never been Jocelyn's thing. And they never would be. She'd spent the ride to River's Edge making three phone calls. One to her sister, telling her she'd be arriving home on the next bus. The second to Dena, sweetly begging her to mail the family photo on her desk to her address in River's Edge and promising to reimburse her for the inconvenience. And finally, she'd called Fiona, leaving her a message that Chester had a new set of keys for her when she returned to the apartment later that day.

Fiona called her back immediately, having just landed in Portland. Despite hardly knowing one another, Jocelyn and her short-term roommate talked for most of the trip, like old friends. They discussed the story of Luke and why she was leaving, the ups and downs at her job, and all of Bodhi's quirky habits. The call ended when Jocelyn's battery chirped its final warning that it was dying. She hung up and was struck by how sad she was that she wouldn't have more time to get to know Fiona, but it was better this way. Jocelyn was back where she belonged.

Sophie and her dad were at the station to meet her, and together they carried her things the two blocks back to the house.

"This is such an unexpected surprise," her dad said when they were inside. He smiled, the gray-blue eyes she'd inherited looking concerned. "Glad you're here."

The familiar sounds and smells brought her comfort as she fell against her father's cotton shirt. A noise came from the kitchen, and she startled. If they were all in the entryway, who could be in the kitchen?

"Oh, you're here." Madame Christine popped her head out of the doorway, her white bangs brushing above her eyes. "Tea's almost ready."

"I'll help you," her father said, leaving Jocelyn alone with Sophie.

"What's she doing here?" Jocelyn whispered and jerked her thumb toward the kitchen.

Sophie shrugged and looped her arms around Jocelyn's. "They're becoming very good friends these days."

Very good friends. Jocelyn didn't like the way that sounded. When had her dad started befriending single women?

Sophie must have read her thoughts. "They've both been alone for a long time." She pulled them into the living room, and they sat on the couch. "It's only natural they'd seek companionship from each other. I think it's great."

Jocelyn heard their voices in the kitchen, mingling together like her parents' used to. Her throat tightened as the old memories came to mind.

"Now, do you want to tell me the whole story? Why are you here?"

Jocelyn had told Sophie about the fire and that she'd needed to take a break from the city. The appearance of her suitcases and boxes had likely poked a hole in that simple story.

"Did something happen with Luke?"

"No, we were never that serious anyway." The lie hurt, but it was the truth she'd been trying to accept since she witnessed his betrayal through the window.

Jocelyn stood, not wanting to let any more questions about Luke surface, when the front door burst open.

"I sold it. I just sold it." Uncle Larry went to the kitchen, waving a piece of paper.

The girls rushed in to join everyone. Jocelyn tried to ignore the way Madame Christine had a hold of her father's arm.

"What are you talking about?" Sophie asked for all of them.

"Oh, Jocelyn," Uncle Larry said when he saw her. "When did you get home? I thought Jerry was going to give you the news."

"What news?" Jocelyn's heart sank.

"The paper." Uncle Larry's eyes sparkled. "I just sold the paper to Jerry. He's going to absorb it into his operation out of Portland and print an edition twice a week."

"Twice a week?" Jocelyn asked. That would hardly yield enough for her salary. How could she afford a staff here?

"Yes! I think Jerry wanted to tell you himself, but since you're here, I'll do the honors. He wants you to be the managing editor for *The Gazette* from Portland, of course while you attend to your other duties at *The Daily Report*. But you'll still get to oversee everything going into our circular from the city. Isn't it wonderful? It worked out better than I'd hoped. Jerry doesn't want to let you go. I knew he wouldn't. You're one of the big dogs now."

All eyes were on her. Every one of them delighted. She tried to hold back the massive wave of tears she felt brewing inside, but it was no use. She broke down and cried.

* * *

They thought Jocelyn was happy. Of course they did. She *should* be happy, or would be, if any of these things were what she wanted. But she didn't. She wanted life to go back to the way it was before—when her father didn't have a girlfriend hanging on his arm, when she had a job to come home to, when her heart wasn't in pieces.

After a round of hugs, she dabbed at her eyes. They were waiting for her to say something.

"I need a moment." She headed for the stairs and ran to her room. Falling face first into her pillow, she begged for sleep to come to her. Maybe when she woke up, she'd find out these past weeks had all been a dream.

"Can I come in?" Sophie knocked on the door but didn't wait for an answer, which was good because Jocelyn didn't plan to say a word.

"You still haven't told me why you're here. What happened with Luke?"

"It's nothing." Jocelyn rolled over and stared at the familiar ceiling. "I just wanted to come back here and have everything go back to the way it was. But it's all changed."

"What's changed?"

"Dad. With a girlfriend. Are you kidding me?" Jocelyn propped up on her elbows. "Isn't that weird for you?"

Sophie pulled her fingers through Jocelyn's hair. "Not really. Because he's happy."

"Yeah, but for how long? These things don't always last." Wasn't she the expert on that?

"And sometimes they do." Sophie rocked toward her. "He's painting again."

"He is?"

"Yep. The art I told you he was helping Madame Christine hang. Those were paintings he'd done for her. They're beautiful. You should see them."

He's painting again?

"So, is now not such a good time to tell you I'm moving?"

Jocelyn fell back against the mattress. Sophie fell beside her.

"Where?"

"Remember that place in Albany?"

"Yeah."

"It's a new studio. I've been working with the owners, and they've offered me a position there, full-time. Teaching, training, advertising. It's going to be the only thing I do."

There was a smile in Sophie's voice. She was delighted—excited for her new adventure. Jocelyn grasped Sophie's hand and turned her head, meeting her sister nose-to-nose.

"I'm happy for you," she said, even though it killed her to think of all the changes happening.

"And I'm happy for you. This is the perfect job for you."

"Yeah." Jocelyn said wistfully. *It is.*

"Why don't you come take my class? It might help you clear your mind. But I have to warn you I use my soft-yelling yoga voice, since most of the students take their hearing aids out for class."

Twenty-Six

Luke knocked on Jocelyn's door again.

"Maybe she's not home," Brayden said.

"Love your perception, little man." Luke tried her phone. She didn't answer. "Maybe she went into work. Let's go see."

They hustled back down the hall. Luke had to get to her. He wanted to be the one to tell her about everything that had happened. But mostly, he just wanted to see her.

In the lobby, he skidded to a stop at Chester's desk. "Have you seen Jocelyn this morning?"

The doorman nodded.

"Did you talk to her?"

Again Chester nodded.

"Then do you know where she is? Did she go to work?"

He shook his head. For the first time, Luke suspected an emotion had crossed Chester's face. "She left."

"What? When?"

"About an hour ago. Suitcases and all." Chester broke his gaze away and went to the door.

Luke leaned into the desk. *Left? Without saying goodbye? Why?* A breeze waltzed in from the outside.

"What does that mean? Where did she go?" Brayden laid a hand on Luke's arm.

"She went home—where every broken-hearted girl goes." Jocelyn's roommate, Fiona, came through the door, trailing a gigantic bag behind her. An intricately patterned headband held her curly locks back and matched the flowing poncho draped over her shoulders.

"You've talked to her?" Luke asked.

Fiona nodded. "Can't tell you how surprised I was to learn my new roommate was headed back to River's Edge. Chased off by some guy who couldn't keep his hand out of the cookie jar." She glanced at Brayden, then back to Luke. "If you know what I mean."

"I *don't* know what you mean." Luke put his hands on his hips.

"There's a whole east-side of the building that knows what she means," Chester interjected.

Luke smacked his hand to his forehead. Leave it to Stacy to ruin the best thing that ever walked into his life.

"What is it, Uncle Luke?" Brayden's face was worried.

"Stacy."

"Ah, well at least you know her name." Fiona tossed her hair and pushed to the desk, holding out her hand to Chester. "My new keys, please."

"What did Aunt Stacy do?" Brayden pleaded.

Fiona whipped around, new keys in hand. "Oh, she's your aunt…and he's your uncle. Interesting."

"She's not really my aunt," Brayden went on to explain. "She's my mom's friend. And she's crazy. Isn't she, Uncle Luke?"

Luke nodded.

Brayden turned back to Fiona. "Like this morning. She ran through the apartment and jumped on Uncle Luke. Then she kissed him, which was crazy because he already has a girlfriend."

Looks like Stacy's actions hadn't gone unnoticed like Luke had hoped.

"He does?" Fiona asked.

Luke's chest tightened.

"Yeah. He loves Miss Jocelyn. I heard him tell her last night."

"Really?" Fiona quirked up an eyebrow.

Luke put an arm around Brayden. "But I don't think she feels the same, little man. That's why she left."

So, this is what heartbreak feels like? Luke tried to take a breath under the heavy weight of sadness bearing down on him.

Brayden tugged on Luke's shirt. "You have to go after her. Like Dad did when Mom left. Remember how miserable he was. You don't want to be miserable. You have to go find her."

"Sounds like the little guy knows what he's talking about." Fiona turned for the elevators. "You better get moving. You've got a drive ahead of you."

"Hey, Fiona," he called with a smile, and she looked back. "Welcome home."

"It's good to be home," she said.

He put a hand on Brayden's shoulder. "Come on, Bray. Looks like I'm going to break one more Uncle-In-Charge rule before our time together is over, 'cause I'm pretty sure a road trip to River's Edge wasn't on your parents' list of approved activities for this weekend." He fist-bumped his nephew. "Let *Operation Get Jocelyn Back* commence."

* * *

Luke slowly drove down Main Street, reading every sign. A bookstore, a coffee shop. Where was the art gallery?

When he reached the edge of town, he turned around, taking Main Street past all the same establishments again until he was almost to the end, and then he found it. The only art gallery in town, right next door was Madame Christine's Psychic Readings and Dance Studio. He parked and got out, Brayden right behind him.

The door to the gallery was locked. A sign that read: *Gone to lunch* hung behind the glass plate. He went next door, hoping Madame Christine might be able to help.

Behind the counter, eating from a takeout container, was a very tame-looking woman with long white hair tied back. A light sweater rested over her thin frame, and the man next to her in a cotton shirt ate from the same box. He was tall, dark-haired, and wiry.

"Can I help you?" the woman said.

"I'm looking for Jocelyn Banks."

The man spoke up. "She's in class right now. Is there something I can help you with?"

Luke studied the man. The paint on his hands, the serious line of his thin lips. And gray-blue eyes. "Are you Mr. Banks?"

The man nodded.

"I'm Luke Lewis." He offered his hand. "I've come to tell your daughter I'm in love with her, and I don't intend to let her go until she tells me she doesn't feel the same way."

"Okay." His hand was warmly received, but obvious bewilderment swam in the older man's eyes. "You're welcome to wait out here with us." He motioned toward a bench and threw a questioning look at the woman. "She'll be out soon."

Luke pulled his wallet out. "I'm sorry, but I can't wait. We'd like to join the class. How much for two?"

"Keep your money." The woman's smile never wavered as she handed over two yoga mats.

He and Brayden quietly went into the room, slipping off their shoes at the entrance. Everyone sat on their mats, legs crossed, and hands on their knees.

"And breathe," Sophie said from the front of the class, popping one eye open at their entrance. Her mouth gaped at the sight of him, and he held a finger to his lips.

Jocelyn was in the back, making it easy for Luke and Brayden to find her. They rolled out their mats behind a woman in a magenta sweat suit, and right next to Jocelyn. Assuming the cross legged position, Luke took a moment to admire Jocelyn's features. She was serenely beautiful with her neck stretched and her face relaxed. He closed his eyes, *Please let this go well.*

"Now bring your legs in," Sophie said placidly above the loud sound of ocean waves coming through the speakers in the corners of the room.

Everyone, who Luke now noticed was in an age group that equaled his and Jocelyn's put together, slowly changed positions.

Sophie walked around the class, talking about stretching spines, and breathing deeply. When she reached Jocelyn, she tapped her shoulder and pointed to Luke.

"What are you doing here?" Jocelyn hissed at the sight of him.

"Yoga," he said back in the same low tone. "Same as you."

"Hi, Miss Jocelyn." Brayden whispered and waved from the other side of him.

"Hi, Brayden." She kept her voice low but cheerful and then shot Luke a dozen daggers.

"Why are you here?" she asked loud enough for only him to hear.

Luke pressed his feet to the floor and rolled up, the same as everyone else. "To see you."

The woman in the magenta sweat suit turned around, eyeing him. He blew out his breath as Sophie had instructed, trying to appear calm and engaged.

"I don't want to see you," Jocelyn said softly between shoulder rolls. Her eyes shut.

Luke sidestepped toward her. He wanted to make sure she heard every word. "I found out who set the fires."

Muscles tightened in her jaw, but her eyes remained closed. "I don't care."

He admired her resolve, even if it was false. "Yes, you do. And in about ten seconds, you're going to want to know why."

Jocelyn followed Sophie's instructions, mimicking the one-legged position she was in, before she turned to look at him.

Ten seconds, indeed. Luke pulled his left foot to his knee. Two could play her game, and he tried to feign indifference. When he didn't answer her promptly, she flipped her attention away, snapping her ponytail.

Luke waited a beat, letting curiosity eat at her. He tipped toward her slightly, maintaining his one-legged position. "They were after me. Trying to ruin my career."

"You?" Concern flashed across Jocelyn's face.

Ah, so she does *still care.*

Magenta sweat suit lady turned around. Jocelyn recovered and sent the woman a warm smile before changing positions according to Sophie's instruction.

Luke did the same, standing with his feet apart and arms spread.

"Why?" she muttered tight-lipped.

"Long story. I'll save it for another time."

"Bend those knees and breathe." Sophie circled around to the back and dropped her voice when she came to them. "Everything okay here?"

"Yes," Luke answered, while Jocelyn seemed to ignore the question.

"Why?" Jocelyn spat in a whisper. "Does it start with you sleeping with someone's wife?"

"Okay," Sophie sing-songed and put her hands on Brayden's shoulders. "Why don't you come up front with me?"

Luke nodded, letting Brayden know it was okay, as Sophie picked up his mat and guided him away. He took another step toward Jocelyn. The cold from the floor seeped through his socks. "Do you really think I deserve that?"

"Yes," she hissed.

"Fine," he fired back out of the corner of his mouth. "Maybe I do, but you know what else I deserve?"

They tipped forward keeping their feet on the ground and placing their hands out front, creating an inverted v-formation. Jocelyn kept her head down.

Luke continued, making a concentrated effort to keep his tone hushed, but firm. "I deserve a real goodbye."

"That's your opinion. Not mine."

Blood rushed to his head. "Would you like to talk about what you saw this morning?"

She shook her head and wouldn't look at him as they came out of their inverted position.

"Why? Because you're afraid I'll say I want to sleep with other women? Or because you're afraid I'll say I never want to sleep with, be with, or think about any other woman but you for the rest of my life?"

Jocelyn froze. Everyone around them turned to the side. She must have realized they were the only ones not following Sophie's instructions, because she turned her back to him. Her shoulders raised and lowered as she took deep breaths.

He stepped onto her mat, getting close to her ear. "You're not even going to ask, are you?"

"And slowly turn to the other wall," Sophie said.

Jocelyn turned to face him and immediately looked away when she realized his proximity. For a split second, he thought she was going to walk out. He stepped back, giving her space, and finally, she brought her eyes to his.

"Ask me." he said under Sophie's reminders to breathe. "Because I want to tell you my side of the story."

"I saw you wearing another woman for a shirt. That's more than enough information for me. Thank you."

Luke smirked, and under his breath, he said, "You call yourself an investigative reporter?"

She shot him a deadly glare.

"Ask me her name."

She shook her head as she lunged toward the front of the room.

"Her name is Stacy."

Jocelyn flinched.

"Ask how we met."

"Don't care." Her voice came out soft and pointed.

"She's my sister-in-law's friend. Ask me how many times I've slept with her."

Jocelyn's face burned bright red.

He was no longer aware of anyone else. Jocelyn was all he saw. "Zero. And the answer will always be zero, because what she wants from me is meaningless. It's nothing compared to what I've experienced these past weeks with you." He reached for her hand when she brought it down. "Talking." He kissed her palm. "Walking." He kissed it again. "Laughing. That's what I want more of. What do you want?"

"Shh," came from the middle of the class.

"It's all right, Mrs. Hopper," Sophie said from the front. "Let's all feel the energy of the room. And breathe in clarity. Yes, clarity."

Jocelyn studied him for a moment, and he wished he knew what she was seeing.

"Are you going to work for Lottie Jones?" she asked. "Create her foundation for her?"

"What does that have to do with anything?"

"Just answer the question."

"Yes. If she'll still have me after all that's happened."

Jocelyn's eyes lit up. "She'll still have you."

He smiled at her reaction. "Why do you say that?"

"Because you have an uncanny way of turning women into putty in your hands."

"There's only one woman I care about still wanting me." He stepped closer, putting a hand on her cheek. "And she's strong and firm."

"Yeah, no. I'm pretty sure she's putty right now."

He cupped her face in his hands. "She's the most beautiful putty I've ever laid eyes on."

The room was still, and he realized everyone was watching them. Even Sophie had quit giving instructions, her arm draped over Brayden's shoulder. Mr. Banks and Madame Christine were in the doorway.

"Come on and just kiss the hunk already," a creaky voice called from the middle of the room.

Jocelyn smiled, her face reaching toward his, but he stopped her.

"I'm not a one-night stand kind of guy, so if that's what you're after, then you better save your kisses for someone else, because there's no going back after this."

She didn't hesitate for a moment, pulling him to her and kissing him as a round of applause broke out in the room.

Twenty-Seven

Two weeks later...

The wind whipped through Jocelyn's hair. Rain wasn't supposed to start falling until late in the evening, but the earthy smell of impending precipitation clung to the air. Jocelyn hurried for the doors of the office building as the first drops of rain fell. She was meeting Luke before they had dinner with his brother, sister-in-law, and Brayden at their home in the country.

She'd already talked to him on the phone, unable to contain her big news.

Robert quit today. He'd returned from lunch announcing he was taking a job with *The Storm*. On his way out the door, he'd mumbled something about the paper going too soft and girly for him. It certainly didn't hurt her feelings to see him go.

Jocelyn made her way to the elevators. The doors opened, and a flood of people spilled out before she could get on.

The elevator rose and at the eighteenth floor, she got off and walked through the doors marked Lewis and Sons Law Firm. What would it be like for Luke to enter these doors when he was no longer a part of the firm? He'd accepted Lottie's offer, and while the details of the transition were still vague, he'd decided to blaze his own path—a fact he hadn't shared with anyone in his family except his brother. He said he was waiting for the right time to tell everyone else. It was the only time she ever saw him fidget and seem uncomfortable.

Behind a large, counter-style reception desk, a woman with silvery hair and a sweater draped over her shoulders greeted Jocelyn.

"I'm here to see Luke. I mean, Mr. Lewis," she corrected when the woman raised a speculative eyebrow at her informal tone.

The woman smiled, softening her aged features, but before she could answer, a man came from the hallway. He was tall, dark-haired, and had sharp blue eyes.

"I'm Mr. Lewis," he said, closing the file in his hand. A flash of recognition crossed his eyes and brought out a smile. "But it's not me you're looking for, is it? You must be Jocelyn."

"And you must be Marcus." She accepted the hand he offered.

"Yes, and I'm so glad you and Luke are joining us this evening. My wife is very anxious to meet you. Come on." He motioned with his arm. "I'll take you to Luke. I can honestly say I'm surprised he's even still here this late on a Friday. You're obviously a very good influence on my little brother." Marcus paused in front of a large wood door. "He's a good guy, though, isn't he?"

"Yes, he is."

Marcus smiled and knocked. Before there was an answer, he opened the door.

Luke looked up from his computer screen, his eyes going from surprised to elated. He glanced back at the screen, clicked the mouse three times, and closed his laptop before returning his attention to Jocelyn and Marcus.

"Are you hassling my girl?" Luke got out of his chair and came around to meet them, taking Jocelyn in his arms, a teasing light in his crystal blue eyes.

"Doing my best," Marcus said. "It was nice to meet you, Jocelyn."

"You too."

"We'll see you two at seven." Marcus backed toward the door.

Luke pretended to look at his watch. "You know that means seven-thirty, right? I tend to get sidetracked in the company of a beautiful woman."

Jocelyn's cheeks flamed.

"I'm all too familiar with that fact," Marcus said. "But now that Emma is eating for two, her patience is almost non-existent, so I'd suggest if you want any of her good home cooking tonight, you be there on time."

"We'll be there," Jocelyn answered before Luke could crack another joke that would no doubt embarrass her.

Marcus nodded and smiled before leaving.

"You know you shouldn't make promises you can't keep." Luke drew her closer, pressing his lips against hers.

"But, it's a promise I *can* keep." She looked into his eyes. "Are you ready to go, or did I interrupt something you were working on?"

He pulled her with him and leaned against the edge of his desk. With a quick look back at his computer, he shook his head. "No, it can wait until later. There's only one thing on my mind right now."

She giggled. "Save it, mister. I'm not giving in to anything that'll make us late to your sister-in-law's dinner. We still have to stop for flowers, sparkling cider, and something for Brayden…a book, maybe? Or…"

Luke cut her off with a sweet and gentle kiss as the wind blew heavy drops of rain onto the window glass.

He pulled back, barely any space between their lips. "Are you trying to butter up my family with presents? Because they're going to love you with or without bribes."

His breath was warm against her skin. "No, it's just the polite thing to do."

Rain hit the window.

Luke slipped his hands under her jacket and her sweater, coming into contact with her bare skin. A shiver coursed down her spine.

"We need to go," she said, "if we're going to get everything done before we have to be at your brother's."

"I can think of one thing we can get done right now." Mischief played into his words.

She put her hands on his chest. "We're leaving, now."

"I love it when you get bossy with me." He released her and rounded the desk to gather his bag. She waited for him at the door and took his arm when he offered it.

The elevator was crowded on the way to the first floor. Luke kept a hand on her hip until they were outside, where they were met with sheets of pouring rain and wind that had the trees bowing.

"Please tell me that by some miracle you went home and got your car today."

"Nope, sorry." His face turned apologetic.

"Then do you have an umbrella?"

"Not one that would hold up in this kind of wind."

She blew out a defeated breath and pulled up her hood.

Luke grabbed her hand. "Come on. You can't be afraid of a little rain?"

He pulled her from the protection of the roofed entrance. The wind gusted as they ran down the sidewalk, her hood falling off. Rain streaked down Jocelyn's face.

The sidewalk was crowded with people hunched against the wind and rain, holding newspapers and hoods over their heads. Everyone stepped out of the way as Luke and Jocelyn made their mad dash back to the apartment building.

Luke pulled her to the door, and they stood for a moment, letting the rain drip from their clothes and puddle at their feet.

Jocelyn laughed and looked into in his eyes. She retraced the path a pearl of rain had created down his cheek. "That was fun."

"There's a lifetime of fun to be had with me." He winked as Chester opened the door. They walked inside hand in hand, leaving a trail of rainwater behind them.

A lifetime, huh? That sounded perfect.

Meg Gray uses a small world approach when crafting her contemporary romance novels, tying minor characters from one story into another—demonstrating how intertwined our human lives really are. The city streets and country roads she takes you down aren't necessarily a structured series, but the stories are connected. Within the pages, her readers will catch glimpses of some of their favorite characters again and again. This is a concept that mirrors itself in our everyday lives. Our worlds are much smaller than we realize, often times we are unaware of the way our lives intersect with those around us.

The best part is Meg's books keep readers inside the small world she has created so they can enjoy a completely different story with each read. Start with any one of them and be treated to repeat appearances from some of her colorful characters. To get a behind the scenes look at more of the links between her books join Meg's Insider Club to read exclusive bonus chapters.

To learn more visit: www.meggraybooks.com

Join Meg's Insider Club at www.meggraybooks.com to get the latest updates and bonus material including a follow-up chapter to *The Girl Next Door* featuring Jocelyn and Luke.

Other books by the author:

The Teacher

The Bridesmaid

The Road Home

Something to Remember

Made in the USA
Columbia, SC
29 August 2025